REFRESH, REFRESH

Also by Benjamin Percy

The Language of Elk

REFRESH, REFRESH

BENJAMIN PERCY

Stories

GRAYWOLF PRESS
Saint Paul, Minnesota

Publication of this volume is made possible in part by a grant provided by the Minnesota State Arts Board, through an appropriation by the Minnesota State Legislature; a grant from the Wells Fargo Foundation Minnesota; and a grant from the National Endowment for the Arts, which believes that a great nation deserves great art. Significant support has also been provided by the Bush Foundation; Target; the McKnight Foundation; and other generous contributions from foundations, corporations, and individuals. To these organizations and individuals we offer our heartfelt thanks.

Published by Graywolf Press
2402 University Avenue, Suite 203
Saint Paul, Minnesota 55114
All rights reserved.

www.graywolfpress.org

Published in the United States of America

ISBN 978-1-55597- 485-5

2 4 6 8 9 7 5 3

Library of Congress Control Number: 2007924769

Cover design: Kyle G. Hunter

Cover art: © Image Source/Corbis

Acknowledgments

Grateful thanks to the editors of the publications listed below for first publishing the following stories:

"The Caves in Oregon" : *Glimmer Train*
"The Woods" : *Amazing Stories*
"The Killing" : *Salt Hill Journal*
"The Faulty Builder" : *ReDivider*
"Somebody Is Going to Have to Pay for This" was originally published by *The Paris Review* (Issue 180, Spring 2007).
"The Whisper" : *The Cream City Review*
"Crash" : *Western Humanities Review*
"Refresh, Refresh" was originally published by *The Paris Review* (Issue 175, Fall 2005) and later anthologized by *Best American Short Stories 2006* and *The Pushcart Prize XXXI: Best of the Small Presses*.
"When the Bear Came" : *American Short Fiction*

Other names deserve to be on the cover.

My parents, Peter and Susan Percy, for starters. If I can ever afford to buy you a cabin on a mountain, as a result of a Lotto scratch ticket or a book deal, you'll get it. You made this happen by making me fall in love with words. And over the years, when I screwed up, you smacked me on the back of head, helpfully, deservedly. Thanks.

To Fiona McCrae, Katie Dublinski, Mary Matze, and the Graywolf staff, I feel very lucky to have joined the pack. Thank you for lighting the way. I hope to do you proud.

Thanks to Katherine Fausset, super agent, the smartest in the business.

Thanks—a million times over—to Philip Gourevitch, Nathaniel Rich, Radhika Jones, and the rest of *The Paris Review* crew for believing in my work and curing it of its inadequacies and sharing it with the world. Corny as it sounds, I love you guys. Really.

Thank you to Ann Patchett. I still owe you that pitcher of whiskey.

To Isaiah Sheffer and Sarah Montague at Symphony Space—to Jay Nicorvo at CLMP—to Jane Hamden at WUWM—for their very generous support of my work.

To James Ponsoldt, a hell of a talented guy, for giving "Refresh, Refresh" a new life and audience.

To Michael Williams, Pablo Peschiera, and all of my colleagues at UW-Stevens Point.

Thank you to those who helped me, in small ways and big ways, write these particular stories, through criticism, encouragement, inspiration, friendship, and beer. My sister—the current rock star in residence at Iowa and an all-around genius writer—Jennifer Percy. Dean Bakopoulos. Mark Gates. Peter Straub. Tim Machan. CJ Hribal. Larry Watson. Dan Wickett. Tyler Cabot. Tom Chiarella. Paul Yoon. Laura van den Berg. Daniel Woodrell. Tom Groneberg. Dave and Lynn Dummer in particular, but the larger Dummer and Spielman clans in general. Tim and Jana Dolan. Mark Ranum and Craig Bodoh. Dan Levine. Amant Dewan. Matt Santiago. Allison Joseph. Chad Simpson. Gillian King and Clint Cargile. Mark Vannier. Billy Giraldi. Steve Stassi. David Medaris. David Jasper. John Hennessy. Kris Babe. Dave and Cynthia Moore.

And finally, most importantly, to Lisa, blue-eyed Wisconsin girl, for everything. This one's for you. They'll all be for you.

For Lisa

Contents

REFRESH, REFRESH

Refresh, Refresh

Refresh, Refresh

When school let out the two of us went to my backyard to fight. We were trying to make each other tougher. So in the grass, in the shade of the pines and junipers, Gordon and I slung off our backpacks and laid down a pale green garden hose, tip to tip, making a ring. Then we stripped off our shirts and put on our gold-colored boxing gloves, and fought.

Every round went two minutes. If you stepped out of the ring, you lost. If you cried, you lost. If you got knocked out, or if you yelled, "Stop!" you lost. Afterwards we drank Coca-Colas and smoked Marlboros, our chests heaving, our faces all different shades of blacks and reds and yellows.

We began fighting after Seth Johnson—a no-neck linebacker with teeth like corn kernels and hands like T-bone steaks—beat Gordon until his face swelled and split open and purpled around the edges. Eventually he healed, the rough husks of scabs peeling away to reveal a different face than the one I remembered, older, squarer, fiercer, his left eyebrow separated by a gummy white scar. It was his idea, fighting each other. He wanted to be ready. He wanted to hurt back those who hurt him. And if he went down, he

3

would go down swinging, as his father would have wanted. This was what we all wanted, to please our fathers, to make them proud, even though they had left us.

This was Tumalo, Oregon, a high desert town in the foothills of the Cascade Mountains. In Tumalo, we have fifteen hundred people, a Dairy Queen, a BP gas station, a Food-4-Less, a meat-packing plant, a bright green football field irrigated by canal water, and your standard assortment of taverns and churches. Nothing distinguishes us from Bend or Redmond or La Pine or any of the other nowhere towns off Route 97, except for this: we are home to the 2nd Battalion, 34th Marines. The 50-acre base, built in the 1980s, is a collection of one-story cinder-block buildings interrupted by cheatgrass and sagebrush. Apparently conditions here in Oregon's ranch country match very closely those of the Middle East, particularly the mountainous terrain of Afghanistan and Northern Iraq, and throughout my childhood I could hear, if I cupped a hand to my ear, the lowing of bulls, the bleating of sheep, the report of assault rifles shouting from the hilltops.

Our fathers—Gordon's and mine—were like the other fathers in Tumalo. All of them, just about, had enlisted as part-time soldiers, as reservists, for drill pay: several thousand a year for a private and several thousand more for a sergeant. Beer pay, they called it, and for two weeks every year plus one weekend a month, they trained. They threw on their cammies and filled their rucksacks and kissed us good-bye, then the gates of the 2nd Battalion drew closed behind them.

Our fathers would vanish into the pine-studded hills, returning to us Sunday night with their faces reddened from weather, with their biceps trembling from fatigue and their hands smelling of rifle grease. They would use terms like ECP and PRP and MEU and WMD and they would do push-ups in the middle of the living room and they would call six o'clock *eighteen hundred hours* and they would high-five and yell "Semper Fi!" Then a few days would pass and they would go back to the way they were, to the men we knew: Coors-drinking, baseball-throwing, crotch-scratching, Aqua Velva-smelling fathers.

No longer. In January, the battalion was activated, and in March they shipped off for Iraq. Our fathers—our coaches, our teachers, our barbers, our cooks, our gas-station attendants and UPS deliverymen and deputies and firemen and mechanics—our fathers, so many of them, climbed onto the olive green school buses and pressed their palms to the windows and gave us the bravest, most hopeful smiles you can imagine, and vanished. Just like that.

Nights, I sometimes got on my Honda dirt bike and rode through the hills and canyons of Deschutes County. Beneath me the engine growled and shuddered while all around me the wind, like something alive, bullied me, tried to drag me from my bike. A dark world slipped past as I downshifted, leaning into a turn, and accelerated on a straightaway— my speed seventy, then eighty—concentrating only on the twenty yards of road glowing ahead of me. On this bike I could ride and ride and ride, away from here, up and over the Cascades, through the Willamette Valley, until I reached the ocean, where the broad black backs of whales regularly broke the surface of the water, and even farther—farther still— until I caught up with the horizon, where my father would be waiting. Inevitably, I ended up at Hole in the Ground.

Many years ago a meteor came screeching down from space and left behind a crater five thousand feet wide and three hundred feet deep. Hole in the Ground is frequented during the winter by the daredevil sledders among us, and during the summer by bearded geologists from OSU interested in the metal fragments strewn across its bottom. I dangled my feet over the edge of the crater and leaned back on my elbows and took in the sky—no moon, only stars—just a little lighter black than a crow. Every few minutes a star seemed to come unstuck, streaking through the night in a bright flash that burned into nothingness. In the near distance the grayish green glow of Tumalo dampened the sky—a reminder of how close we came, fifty years ago, to oblivion. A chunk of space ice or a solar wind at just the right moment could have jogged the meteor sideways, and rather than landing here, it could have landed there, at the intersection of Main and Farwell. No Dairy Queen, no Tumalo High, no 2nd Battalion. It didn't take much imagination to realize how something can drop out the sky and change everything.

This was October, when Gordon and I circled each other in the backyard after school. We wore our golden boxing gloves, cracked with age and letting off flakes when we pounded them together. Browned grass crunched beneath our sneakers and dust rose in little puffs like distress signals.

Gordon was thin to the point of being scrawny. His collarbone poked against his skin like a swallowed coat hanger. His head was too big for his body and his eyes were too big for his head and the football players—Seth Johnson among them—regularly tossed him into garbage cans and called him E.T. He had had a bad day. And I could tell from the look on his face—the watery eyes, the trembling lips that revealed, in quick flashes, his buckteeth—that he wanted, he *needed*, to hit me. So I let him. I raised my gloves to my face and pulled my elbows against my ribs and Gordon lunged forward, his arms snapping like rubber bands. I stood still, allowing his fists to work up and down my body, allowing him to throw the weight of his anger on me, until eventually he grew too tired to hit anymore and I opened up my stance and floored him with a right cross to the temple. He lay there, sprawled out in the grass with a small smile on his E.T. face. "Damn," he said in a dreamy voice. A drop of blood gathered along the corner of his eye and streaked down his temple into his hair.

My father wore steel-toed boots, Carhartt jeans, a T-shirt advertising some place he had traveled, maybe Yellowstone or Seattle. He looked like someone you might see shopping for motor oil at Bi-Mart. To hide his receding hairline he wore a John Deere cap that laid a shadow across his face. His brown eyes blinked above a considerable nose underlined by a gray mustache. Like me, my father was short and squat, a bulldog. His belly was a swollen bag and his shoulders were broad, good for carrying me during parades, and at fairs, when I was younger. He laughed a lot. He liked game shows. He drank too much beer and smoked too many cigarettes and spent too much time with his buddies, fishing, hunting, bullshitting, which probably had something to do with why my mother divorced him and moved to Boise with a hairdresser/triathlete named Chuck.

At first, when my father left, like all of the other fathers, he would e-mail whenever he could. He would tell me about the heat, the gallons of water he drank every day, the sand that got into everything, the baths he took with baby wipes. He would tell me how safe he was, how very safe. This was when he was stationed in Turkey. Then the 2nd Battalion shipped for Kirkuk, where insurgents and sandstorms attacked almost daily. The e-mails came less and less frequently, with weeks of silence between them.

Sometimes, on the computer, I would hit refresh, refresh, *refresh*, hoping. In October, I received an e-mail that read, "Hi Josh. I'm OK. Don't worry. Do your homework. Love, Dad." I printed it up and hung it on my door with a piece of Scotch tape.

For twenty years my father worked at Noseler, Inc.—the bullet manufacturer based out of Bend—and the Marines trained him as an ammunition technician. Gordon liked to say his father was a Gunnery Sergeant, and he was, but we all knew he was also the battalion mess manager, a cook, which was how he made his living in Tumalo, tending the grill at Hamburger Patty's. We knew their titles but we didn't know, not really, what their titles meant, what our fathers *did* over there. We imagined them doing heroic things. Rescuing Iraqi babies from burning huts. Sniping suicide bombers before they could detonate on a crowded city street. We drew on Hollywood and CNN to develop elaborate scenarios, where maybe, at twilight, during a trek through the mountains of Northern Iraq, bearded insurgents ambushed our fathers with rocket-launchers. We imagined them silhouetted by a fiery explosion. We imagined them burrowing into the sand like lizards and firing their M16s, their bullets streaking through the darkness like the meteorites I observed on sleepless nights.

When Gordon and I fought we painted our faces—black and green and brown—with the camo-grease our fathers left behind. It made our eyes and teeth appear startlingly white. And it smeared away against our gloves just as the grass smeared away beneath our sneakers—and the ring became a circle of dirt, the dirt a reddish color that looked a lot like scabbed flesh. One time Gordon hammered my shoulder so hard I couldn't lift my arm for a week. Another time I elbowed him in the kidneys and he peed blood. We struck each other with such force and frequency the golden gloves crumbled and our knuckles showed through the sweat-soaked blood-soaked foam like teeth through a busted lip. So we bought another set of gloves, and as the air grew steadily colder we fought with steam blasting from our mouths.

Our fathers had left us, but men remained in Tumalo. There were old men, like my grandfather, who I lived with—men who had paid their dues, who had worked their jobs and fought their wars, and now spent their days at the gas station, drinking bad coffee from Styrofoam cups, complaining about the weather, arguing about the best months to reap alfalfa. And there were incapable men. Men who rarely shaved and watched daytime television in their once-white underpants. Men who lived in trailers and filled their shopping carts with Busch Light, summer sausage, Oreo cookies.

And then there were vulturous men, like Dave Lightener—men who scavenged whatever our fathers had left behind. Dave Lightener worked as a recruitment officer. I'm guessing he was the only recruitment officer in world history who drove a Vespa scooter with a *Support Our Troops* ribbon magneted to its rear. We sometimes saw it parked outside the homes of young women whose husbands had gone to war. Dave had big ears and small eyes and wore his hair in your standard-issue high-and-tight buzz. He often spoke in a too-loud voice about all the insurgents he gunned down when working a Fallujah patrol unit. He lived with his mother in Tumalo, but spent his days in Bend and Redmond, trolling the parking lots of Best Buy, ShopKo, Kmart, Wal-Mart, Mountain View Mall. He was looking for people like us, people who were angry and dissatisfied and poor.

But Dave Lightener knew better than to bother us. On duty he stayed away from Tumalo entirely. Recruiting there would be too much like poaching the burned section of forest where deer, rib-slatted and wobbly legged, nosed through the ash, seeking something green.

We didn't fully understand the reason our fathers were fighting. We only understood that they *had* to fight. The necessity of it made the reason irrelevant. "It's all part of the game," my grandfather said. "It's just the way it is." We could only cross our fingers and wish on stars and hit refresh, *refresh,* hoping they would return to us, praying we would never find Dave Lightener on our porch uttering the words, "I regret to inform you . . ."

One time, my grandfather dropped Gordon and me off at Mountain View Mall and there, near the glass-doored entrance, stood Dave Lightener. He wore his creased khaki uniform and spoke with a group of Mexican teenagers. They were laughing, shaking their heads and walking away from him as we walked toward. We had our hats pulled low and he didn't recognize us.

"Question for you, gentlemen," he said in the voice of telemarketers and door-to-door Jehovah's Witnesses. "What do you plan on doing with your lives?"

Gordon pulled off his hat with a flourish, as if he were part of some *ta-da!* magic act and his face was the trick. "I plan on killing some crazy-ass Muslims," he said and forced a smile. "How about you, Josh?"

"Yeah," I said. "Kill some people, then get myself killed." I grimaced even as I played along. "That sounds like a good plan."

Dave Lightener's lips tightened into a thin line, his posture straightened, and he asked us what we thought our fathers would think, hearing us right now. "They're out there risking their lives, defending our freedom, and you're cracking sick jokes," he said. "I think that's sick."

We hated him for his soft hands and clean uniform. We hated him because he sent people like us off to die. Because at twenty-three he had attained a higher rank than our fathers. Because he slept with the lonely wives of soldiers. And now we hated him even more for making us feel ashamed. I wanted to say something sarcastic, but Gordon was quicker. His hand was out before him, his fingers gripping an imaginary bottle. "Here's your maple syrup," he said. When Dave said, "And what is that for?" Gordon said, "To eat my ass with."

Right then a skateboarder-type with green hair and a nose-ring walked from the mall, a bagful of DVDs swinging from his fist, and Dave Lightener forgot us. "Hey, friend," he was saying. "Let me ask you something. Do you like war movies?"

In November we drove our dirt bikes deep into the woods to hunt. Sunlight fell through tall pines and birch clusters and lay in puddles along the logging roads that wound past the hillsides packed with huckleberries and the moraines where coyotes scurried, trying to flee us and slipping, causing tiny avalanches of loose rock. It hadn't rained in nearly a month, so the crabgrass and the cheatgrass and the pine needles had lost their color, dry and blond as cornhusks, crackling beneath my boots when the road we followed petered out into nothing and I stepped off my bike. In this waterless stillness, you could hear every chipmunk within a square acre, rustling for pine nuts, and when the breeze rose into a cold wind the forest became a giant whisper.

We dumped our tent and sleeping bags near a basalt grotto with a spring bubbling from it, and Gordon said,

"Let's go, troops," holding his rifle before his chest diagonally, as a soldier would. He dressed as a soldier would, too, wearing his father's overlarge cammies rather than the mandatory blaze orange gear. Fifty feet apart we worked our way downhill, through the forest, through a huckleberry thicket, through a clear-cut crowded with stumps, taking care not to make much noise or slip on the pine needles carpeting the ground. A chipmunk worrying at a pinecone screeched its astonishment when a peregrine falcon swooped down and seized it, carrying it off between the trees to some secret place. Its wings made no sound, and neither did the blaze orange hunter when he appeared in a clearing several hundred yards below us.

Gordon made some sort of SWAT-team gesture, meant, I think, to say, Stay Low, and I made my way carefully toward him. From behind a boulder, we peered through our scopes, tracking the hunter, who looked—in his vest and ear-flapped hat—like a monstrous pumpkin. "That cocksucker," Gordon said in a harsh whisper. The hunter was Seth Johnson. His rifle was strapped to his back, and his mouth was moving, talking to someone. At the corner of the meadow he joined four members of the varsity football squad, who sat on logs around a smoldering campfire, their arms bobbing like oil-pump jacks as they brought their beers to their mouths.

I took my eye from my scope and noticed Gordon fingering the trigger of his thirty-aught. I told him to quit fooling around and he pulled his hand suddenly away from the stock and smiled guiltily and said he just wanted to know what it felt like, having that power over someone. Then his trigger finger rose up and touched the gummy white scar that split his eyebrow. "I say we fuck with them a little."

I shook my head, *no.*

Gordon said, "Just a little—to scare them."

"They've got guns," I said, and he said, "So we'll come back tonight."

Later, after an early dinner of beef jerky and trail mix and Gatorade, I happened upon a four-point stag nibbling on some bear grass, and I rested my rifle on a stump and shot it, and it stumbled backwards and collapsed with a rose blooming from behind its shoulder where the heart was hidden. Gordon came running and we stood around the deer and smoked a few cigarettes, watching the thick arterial blood run from its mouth. Then we took out our knives and got to work. I cut around the anus, cutting away the penis and testes, and then ran the knife along the belly, unzipping the hide to reveal the delicate pink flesh and greenish vessels into which our hands disappeared. The blood steamed in the cold mountain air, and when we finished—when we'd skinned the deer and hacked at its joints and cut out its back strap and boned out its shoulders and hips, its neck and ribs, making chops, roasts, steaks, quartering the meat so we could bundle it into our insulated saddlebags—Gordon picked up the deer head by the antlers and held it before his own. Blood from its neck made a pattering sound on the ground, and in the half-light of early evening Gordon began to do a little dance, bending his knees and stomping his feet.

"I think I've got an idea," he said and pretended to rake at me with the antlers. I pushed him away, and he said, "Don't pussy out on me, Josh." I was exhausted and reeked of gore, but I could appreciate the need for revenge. "Just to scare them, right, Gordo?" I said.

"Right."

We lugged our meat back to camp, and Gordon brought

the deer hide. He slit a hole in its middle, and poked his head through so the hide hung off him loosely, a hairy sack, and I helped him smear mud and blood across his face. Then, with his Leatherman, he sawed off the antlers and held them in each hand and slashed at the air as if they were claws.

Night had come on and the moon hung over the Cascades, grayly lighting our way as we crept through the forest, imagining ourselves in enemy territory, with trip wires and guard towers and snarling dogs around every corner. From behind the boulder that overlooked their campsite, we observed our enemies as they swapped hunting stories and joked about Jessica Robertson's big-ass titties and passed around a bottle of whiskey and drank to excess and finally pissed on the fire to extinguish it. When they retired to their tents we waited an hour before making our way down the hill with such care that it took us another hour before we were upon them. Somewhere an owl hooted, its noise barely noticeable over the chorus of snores that rose from their tents. Seth's Bronco was parked nearby—the license plate read SMAN—and all their rifles lay in its cab. I collected them, slinging them over my shoulder, then I eased my knife into each of Seth's tires.

I still had my knife out when we stood outside Seth's tent, and when a cloud scudded over the moon and made the meadow fully dark, I stabbed the nylon and in one quick jerk opened up a slit. Gordon rushed in, his antler-claws slashing. I could see nothing but shadows, but I could hear Seth scream the scream of a little girl as Gordon raked at him with the antlers and hissed and howled like some cave creature hungry for man-flesh. When the tents around us came alive with confused voices, Gordon reemerged with a horrible smile on his face and I followed him up the hillside, crashing through the undergrowth, leaving Seth to make sense of the nightmare that had descended upon him without warning.

Winter came. Snow fell, and we threw on our coveralls and wrenched on our studded tires and drove our dirt bikes to Hole in the Ground, dragging our sleds behind us with tow-ropes. Our engines filled the white silence of the afternoon. Our back tires kicked up plumes of powder, and on sharp turns slipped out beneath us and we lay there, in the middle of the road, bleeding, laughing, unafraid.

Earlier, for lunch, we had cooked a pound of bacon with a stick of butter. The grease, which hardened into a white waxy pool, we used as polish, buffing it into the bottoms of our sleds. Speed was what we wanted at Hole in the Ground. One by one we descended the steepest section of the crater into its heart, 300 feet below us. We followed each other in the same track, ironing down the snow to create a chute, blue-hued and frictionless. Our eyeballs glazed with frost, our ears roared with wind, our stomachs rose into our throats, as we rocketed down and felt five—and then we began the slow climb back the way we came and felt fifty.

We wore crampons and ascended in a zigzagging series of switchbacks. It took nearly an hour. The air began to go purple with evening, when we stood again at the lip of the crater, sweating in our coveralls, taking in the view through the fog of our breath. Gordon packed a snowball. I said, "You better not hit me with that." He cocked his arm threateningly and smiled, then dropped to his knees to roll the snowball into something bigger. He rolled it until it grew to the size of a large man curled into the fetal position. From the back of his bike he took the piece of garden hose he used to siphon gas from fancy foreign cars, and he worked it into his tank, sucking at its end until gas flowed. He doused the giant snowball as if he hoped it would sprout. It did not melt—he'd packed it tight enough—but it puckered slightly and appeared leaden. When Gordon withdrew his Zippo, sparked it, and held it toward the ball, the fumes caught flame and the whole thing erupted with a gasping noise that sent me staggering back a few steps.

Gordon rushed forward and kicked the ball of fire, sending it rolling, tumbling down the crater, down our chute like a meteor, and the snow beneath it instantly melted only to freeze again a moment later, making a slick blue ribbon. When we sledded it, we went so fast our minds emptied and we felt a sensation at once like flying and falling.

On the news Iraqi insurgents fired their assault rifles. On the news a car bomb in Baghdad detonated, killing seven American soldiers at a traffic checkpoint. On the news the president said he did not think it was wise to provide a time frame for troop withdrawal. I checked my e-mail before breakfast and found nothing but spam—promises of great mortgage rates, cheap painkillers, increased erectile performance.

Gordon and I fought in the snow, wearing snow boots. We fought so much our wounds never got a chance to heal and our faces took on a permanent look of decay. Our wrists felt swollen, our knees ached, all our joints felt full of tiny dry wasps. We fought until fighting hurt too much, and we took up drinking instead. Weekends, we drove our dirt bikes to Bend, twenty miles away, and bought beer and took it to Hole in the Ground and drank there until a bright line of sunlight appeared on the horizon and illuminated the snow-blanketed desert. Nobody asked for our ID and when we held up our empty bottles and stared at our reflections in the glass, warped and ghostly, we knew why. And we weren't alone. Black bags grew beneath the eyes of the sons and daughters and wives of Tumalo, their shoulders stooped, wrinkles enclosing their mouths like parentheses.

Our fathers haunted us. They were everywhere. In the grocery store when we spotted a thirty-pack of Coors on sale for ten bucks. On the highway when we passed a jacked-up Dodge with a dozen hay bales stacked in its bed. In the sky when a jet roared by, reminding us of faraway places. And now, as our bodies thickened with muscle, as we stopped shaving and grew patchy beards, we saw our fathers even in the mirror. We began to look like them. Our fathers, who had been taken from us, were everywhere, at every turn, imprisoning us.

Seth Johnson's father was a staff sergeant. Like his son, he was a big man, but not big enough. Just before Christmas he stepped on a cluster bomb. A U.S. warplane dropped it and the sand camouflaged it and he stepped on it and it tore him into many meaty pieces. When Dave Lightener climbed up the front porch with a black armband and a somber expression, Mrs. Johnson, who was cooking a honeyed ham at the time, collapsed on the kitchen floor. Seth pushed his way out the door and punched Dave in the face, breaking his nose before he could utter the words, "I regret to inform you . . ."

Hearing about this, we felt bad for all of ten seconds. Then we felt good because it was his father and not ours. And then we felt bad again and on Christmas Eve we drove to Seth's house and laid down on his porch the rifles we had stolen, along with a six-pack of Coors. Then, just as we were about to leave, Gordon dug in his back pocket and removed his wallet and placed under the six-pack all the money he had, a few fives, some ones. "Fucking Christmas," he said.

We got braver and went to the bars—The Golden Nugget, The Weary Traveler, The Pine Tavern—where we square-danced with older women wearing purple eye shadow and sparkly dream-catcher earrings and push-up bras and clattery high heels. We told them we were Marines back from a six-month deployment and they said, "Really?" and we said, "Yes, ma'am," and when they asked for our names we gave them the names of our fathers. Then we bought them drinks and they drank them in a gulping way and breathed hotly in our faces and we brought our mouths against theirs and they tasted like menthol cigarettes, like burnt urinal pucks. And then we went home with them, to their trailers, to their water-beds, where among their stuffed animals we fucked them.

Midafternoon and it was already full dark. On our way to The Weary Traveler, we stopped by my house to bum some money off my grandfather, only to find Dave Lightener waiting for us. He was halfway up the porch steps when our headlights cast an anemic glow over him and he turned to face us with a scrunched-up expression, as if trying to figure out who we were. He wore the black band around his arm and, over his nose, a white-bandaged splint.

We did not turn off our engines. Instead we sat in the driveway, idling, the exhaust from our bikes and the breath from our mouths clouding the air. Above us a star hissed across the moonlit sky, vaguely bright, like a light turned on in a daylit room. Then Dave began down the steps and we leapt off our bikes to meet him. Before he could speak I brought my fist to his diaphragm, knocking the breath from his body. Right then he looked like a gunshot actor in a Western, clutching his belly with both hands, doubled over, his face making a nice target for Gordon's knee. A snap sound preceded Dave falling on his back with blood sliding from his already broken nose.

He put up his hands and we hit our way through them. I sucker-punched him once, twice, in the ribs while Gordon kicked him in the spine and stomach and then we stood around gulping air and allowed him to struggle to his feet. When he righted himself, he wiped his face with his hand and blood dripped from his fingers. I moved in and round-housed with my right and then my left, my fists knocking his head loose on its hinges. Again he collapsed, a bloody bag of a man. His eyes walled and turned up, trying to see the animal bodies looming over him. He opened his mouth to speak and I pointed a finger at him and said, with enough hatred in my voice to break a back, "*Don't* say a word. Don't you dare. Not one word."

He closed his mouth and tried to crawl away and I brought a boot down on the back of his head and left it there a moment, grinding his face into the ground so that when he lifted his head the snow held a red impression of his face. Gordon went inside and returned a moment later with a roll of duct tape and we held Dave down and bound his wrists and ankles and threw him on a sled and taped him to it many times over and then tied the sled to the back of Gordon's bike and drove at a perilous speed to Hole in the Ground.

The moon shined and the snow glowed with pale blue light as we smoked cigarettes, looking down into the crater, with Dave at our feet. There was something childish about the way our breath puffed from our mouths in tiny clouds. It was as if we were imitating choo-choo trains. And for a moment, just a moment, we were kids again. Just a couple of stupid kids. Gordon must have felt this too because he said, "My mom wouldn't even let me play with toy guns when I was little." And he sighed heavily as if he couldn't understand how he, how we, had ended up here.

Then, with a sudden lurch, Dave began struggling and yelling at us in a slurred voice. My face hardened with anger and I put my hands on him and pushed him slowly to the lip of the crater and he grew silent. For a moment I forgot myself, staring off into the dark oblivion. It was beautiful and horrifying. "I could shove you right now," I said. "And if I did, you'd be dead."

"Please don't," he said, his voice cracking. He began to cry. "Oh fuck. Don't. Please." Hearing his great shuddering sobs didn't bring me the satisfaction I hoped for. If anything, I felt as I did that day, so long ago, when we taunted him in the Mountain View Mall parking lot: shameful, false.

"Ready?" I said. "One!" I inched him a little closer to the edge. "Two!" I moved him a little closer still and as I did I felt unwieldy, at once wild and exhausted, my body seeming to take on another twenty, thirty, forty years. When I finally said, *"Three,"* my voice was barely a whisper.

We left Dave there, sobbing at the brink of the crater. We got on our bikes and we drove to Bend and we drove so fast I imagined catching fire, like a meteor, burning up in a flash, howling as my heat consumed me, as we made our way to the Armed Forces Recruiting Station where we would at last answer the fierce alarm of war and put our pens to paper and make our fathers proud.

The Caves in Oregon

The Caves in Oregon

This afternoon, a hot August afternoon, the refrigerator bleeds. Two red lines run down the length of it—and then a third, a fourth—oozing from the bottom lip of the freezer. This is what Kevin finds when he returns home from his job at the foundry and flips the light switch repeatedly without success, when he stands in the half-light of the kitchen and says, "Shit."

Already he can smell it, the blood. And when he draws a steadying breath he imagines he can taste it, too—the mineral sourness of it. He is a big man—a man who spends most of his days with his hands taped, swinging a fifty-pound sledgehammer—and he must bend his body in half to observe the freezer closely. The seal of its underside has gone as red as a tendon. Little droplets are gathering there, swelling fatly, and then, too heavy, they break from their purchase and race for the floor.

Right then he hears his wife, Becca, her car grumbling up the driveway, as she returns home from the community college where she teaches. He hears her keys jangle, her footsteps on the porch, in the hallway. She calls out his name and he says, "In here." She begins to say something, something about the garage door failing to open, her voice cut short by a sharp intake of air when she sees the bleeding fridge.

"Power's out," he says and she gives him a tight-faced look that trembles at the mouth from her teeth taking tiny bites from her cheeks. He can sense her anger coming and it makes him feel as if he is shrinking, small enough to put in his own pocket. "I just got home," he says, his voice coming out in an almost whine. "Like, five seconds ago. I was just about to start cleaning."

She hurls down her keys. Against the Formica counter they make a noise like bottles breaking. "Great," she says. "That's just great. That's *just* what I need." She lifts her arms and lets them fall and stomps her way from the kitchen, into the hallway, bringing down her high heels as if to stab something with every step. He can hear her muttering to herself as she burrows roughly through the closet. A moment later she returns with an armful of beach towels. She throws them down at the base of the fridge and tells him to get the cooler.

"The cooler?"

"Yes, the fucking cooler," she says. "You know, the *cooler*."

He retrieves it from the garage and with some hesitation sets it on top of the towels, watching his wife as he does so, hoping this is where she wants it. She says nothing. She will not look at him. All her attention, this radiant anger he has come to know so well, is momentarily focused on the fridge. For this he is thankful.

These days she is always angry, it seems. All it takes is a dropped dish, the wrong word, heavy traffic, and a switch goes off inside her that sends blue electricity sizzling through her veins.

He retreats from her and crosses his arms, his hands tucked into his armpits. For a moment his wife stares at the freezer, her head cocked, as if listening to something in the far distance. He watches her back, the rigidity of it. A long brown ponytail curls down her spine like an upside-down question mark.

And then she suddenly brings her hand to the freezer door and pulls. At first it resists her, and so she brings her other hand to the handle and leans backward. Then, with a sort of sucking, sort of gasping noise, it opens.

The sight of it reminds Kevin of the time he had his wisdom teeth removed. His dentist had given him an irrigator, a plastic syringe. Twice a day he filled it with salt water and placed its needle into the craters at the back of his mouth—and from them, in a pink rush, came scabs, bits of food. That is what the freezer looks like when its door opens and the blood surges from it—all down the front of the fridge, dampening their photos, glossing over their magnets, until the front of the fridge has more red on it than white.

Becca makes a noise like a wounded bird. She turns her head away from the mess and squints shut her eyes. Her pants, her shoes are splattered with red. A tremble races through her body and then she goes perfectly still.

Kevin goes to her and places a hand on her shoulder and her shoulder drops a little from the weight of it. He feels as if he is touching a banister, a rifle stock, something hard and unbending. "Let me do it," he says. "Please."

The kitchen is loud with the noise of dripping.

"I hate this house," she says, her voice a harsh whisper. "I hate, hate, *hate* this house."

"You go sit down and I'll take care of it. You rest. You need your rest."

She raises her arm, long and thin, her hand gloved with blood, like a stop sign. She will not speak to him, mute with a kind of fury.

"Sorry," he says and his hand falls away from her when she bends over to reposition the cooler. And then, with her arms out as if to hug, she reaches into the freezer. There is a surprising amount of meat in there and she hooks her arms around it, the pile of it, and slides it out all at once. The T-bones, pork chops, bratwursts, chicken breasts splat into the cooler, one on top of the other, a mass of meat along with two ice trays and a sodden box of baking soda. A hamburger patty misses its mark and plops on the linoleum, making a red flower pattern.

By this time Kevin has removed from beneath the sink a sponge, a roll of paper towels, a Clorox spray bottle. His wife watches him when he tears off five lengths of paper towels and lays them in the freezer to soak up the blood pooled there. "That's not enough," she says and snatches the towels from him and lays down several more sheets. "Just let me do it."

He pinches shut his mouth and drops his eyes and holds up his hands, palms flat, as if pressing them against a wall. "Okay."

She plucks the photos and magnets from the fridge and tosses them in the cooler. Then she kneels with a bouquet of paper towels in one hand and the bottle of Clorox in the other. At first, when she sprays, when she wipes, she only smears the blood, making it pinker, making swirls like you see in hair and wood grain. Then the blood begins to come away and the fridge begins to look like a fridge again.

Thirty minutes later, when she at last finishes, she says, "There." She is damp with sweat, with gore. She runs a forearm across her forehead and takes a deep, shuddering breath. Her blouse, once beige, now clings to her redly, pinkly, in tie-dye designs. She strips it off and tosses it in the cooler, along with her skirt, her bra and panties. Her shoes she sets aside. Naked, she goes to the sink and runs the water and soaps up her arms and feet and splashes her face and when she turns toward Kevin her face is calmer, paler, drained of its previous flush.

"Sorry I snapped at you," she says.

"It's okay," he says, raising his voice so it follows her down the hallway, to their bedroom, their bathroom, where she will climb into the shower and leave behind a pink ring at the bottom of the tub as she did several months ago when she began to hemorrhage, when she lost the baby.

The power went out because of the cave.

The cave—a lava tube—runs beneath their house, their neighborhood, and beyond, a vast tunnel that once carried in it molten rock the color of an angry sun.

People say Central Oregon looks like another planet. Mars maybe. The reddish blackish landscape is busy with calderas, cinder cones, lava blisters, pressure ridges, pressure plateaus—much of it the hardened remains of basalt, a lava that spreads quickly, like thin porridge, flowing sometimes seventy miles, its front fed by lava tubes, like their lava tube, one of so many that network the ground beneath Bend, Redmond, La Pine.

Sometimes the caves collapse. A tractor-trailer will be growling along Route 97 when the asphalt opens up—just like that, like a mouth—and the rig will vanish, crashing down into an unknown darkness. Or someone will go to their driveway and find it gone, along with their car, their johnboat, replaced by a gaping hole. Or a hard rain will come, dampening and loosening those unseen joints beneath the surface that send the ground buckling. Imagine five acres dropping several inches, maybe even a foot, in an instant. Imagine fissures opening in your lawn. Imagine septic tanks splintering, sewage bubbling up from the ground like oil. Imagine power lines pinched off and neighborhoods darkened for days.

It's upsetting, not trusting the ground beneath your feet.

Their house is part of a new development called Elk Mound. It is located on a spur of basalt overlooking a coulee crowded with juniper trees that deepens and widens on its way south to accommodate the spring-fed Newberry River that winds through the Aubrey Glen Golf Course on its way toward Bend, just five miles south of them.

Theirs was the last house in the development to sell, a year ago. It had been built over the mouth of the cave. To pass inspection and ensure no vertical settlement the contractor widened the foundation, bolting it to the bedrock with twenty Perma Jack brackets. The realtor advertised the cave as a "natural basement with cooling properties."

In the living room there is an insulated steel door. Somehow, through the cracks around it, the breath of the cave finds its way in, smelling faintly of mushrooms, sulfur, cellar-floor puddles. Beyond the door a steel staircase, nearly forty feet tall, descends into darkness.

Becca teaches in the Geology Department at Central Oregon Community College. She often wears her hair pulled back in a ponytail and khaki pants with many zippered compartments. She keeps a special toothbrush by the sink to scrub away the crescents of dirt that seem always to gather beneath her fingernails. In everyday conversation she uses words like igneous, tetrahedron, radar-mapping. The cave, to her, was the equivalent of a trampoline or fire pole to a child. It was cool. "I know I ought to know better," she said with a smile, when they signed the deed and bought the place for a song.

Three years ago Kevin met Becca when skiing at Mt. Bachelor. She was standing at the summit of the mountain, at the top of a mogul field, when he slid off the chairlift. It was her honey-colored hair that first caught his attention. The wind blew it every which way, so that with the blue sky all around her she looked as if she were underwater. She wore this white outfit that stole the breath from his chest. He unwrapped a PowerBar and hungrily ate it. When she still hadn't moved five minutes later, he approached her.

He asked if she was okay, thinking she might be afraid of the long drop before her, but she only looked at him curiously, completely unafraid, and said, "I'm fine," with the breath trailing from her mouth.

To their north the spine of the Cascade Range continued with the Three Sisters rising through a thin layer of clouds like gnarled vertebrae. Becca pointed her pole at the saddle-shaped place between the South and Middle Sister and said, "I'm just studying that moraine over there."

He had never heard that word before—moraine—and it made him picture a great flood of water, frozen in its tracks.

Then she adjusted her goggles and gave him a smile and took off down the mountain, her skis arranged in a careful pie wedge that curled the powder over, exposing in her wake a broad zigzagging track of blue. He followed, and one thing led to another.

There was a time, not even five months ago, when she would sneak up behind him and pinch his butt and yell, "You're it!" and run from him, squealing as he chased her through their new house, over the couch, under the dining-room table, finally catching her in bed with his hands made into crab claws that touched her roughly all over.

Afterwards they would drink beer and watch the *Late Show* and she would laugh with her head thrown back, smiling so widely he could see her back teeth, her fillings giving off a silvery light.

They were pretty happy.

Then she was late. A few days passed, then a week, then two weeks, before she sent Kevin to the pharmacy. By this time she knew because she had always been like clockwork, had never been this late. But she wanted to be certain. She wanted some bit of proof she could point to and say, "There."

In Aisle 5 the shelves were crowded with dozens of pink boxes. Not understanding the differences between them he randomly selected one—an expensive one with a picture of a rose garden on it—and on his way to the register he grabbed a pack of gum, a Butterfinger, an *Us Weekly*, trying to clutter the register with other things. The checkout girl wore blue eye shadow. He thought it made her look very sad.

At home, when he handed his wife the box, she turned it over and scrunched her eyebrows and read its back as if for nutritional information. "Is this even a good one?" she asked and he said, "Yes. It's very reliable." He leaned toward her and tapped the place on the box where it read *98% Accurate!*

This seemed to satisfy her and she went into the bathroom with the kit and closed the door, and he could hear the cardboard tearing, could hear her swearing when she peed a little on her hand, could hear the muffled roar of the toilet when she finished.

There was a lengthy silence and then she emerged from the bathroom. She had a plastic stick in her hand and she was shaking it and looking at it between shakes like an un-developed Polaroid.

"Well?" he said.

She looked at him with a blank expression and held onto the stick a second longer before handing it to him. He took it with two hands and brought it close to his face. At the end of the stick, in a tiny window frame, there was a plus sign. It was an absurd shade of pink—the kind of pink little girls favored in their dresses and bubblegum. "Plus means what?"

"Plus means pregnant," she said.

His eyes grew larger and he felt at once light-headed and ebullient and fearful. "You're kidding me?"

She pressed her hands hard against her face. "I am not kidding you."

"You're shitting me?"

"I am not shitting you," she said and looked at him through her fingers. "I'm serious."

Kevin, openmouthed, considered her. "You're serious."

"I'm being seriously serious. We're having a goddamn baby."

Kevin works at the foundry, the Redmond Foundry, which produces over 200 alloys. It is a high-ceilinged cinder-block building whose interior is black with dust and red with fire. All around him men wear heavy leather aprons and canvas gloves and tinted goggles. One of his main tasks is shaking-out—breaking up sand castings to get at the metal castings cooling and hardening within them. His sledgehammer is like an extension of his body. When he leaves work his hands are still curled in the shape of it. All through the day he swings it again and again until the weight is nearly impossible to bear, until his face goes as red as the liquid metal glowing all around him and his veins rise jaggedly from his arms. When he swings, his breath goes rip-rip-*rip* and the hammer blasts open the sand casting with a *crack*. A cloud of particles rises from it and sticks to his sweat. And there is the alloy, like a fossil fallen out of mud, to toss in a near-by bin.

Sometimes, if someone calls in sick, he'll work the induction furnace or the electric arc furnace, getting clamps in the right places, arranging molds, making sure they're free of dirt, and then pouring into them the hot metal that looks so much like lava.

His wife thinks he should go back to school—he is capable of so much more, she says—but the pay is good and nobody bothers him and he likes the rhythm of the work, the mindless repetition.

Weekends, they used to explore the cave. They would throw on their jeans and fleece and tie their hiking boots tight and descend into the darkness with their Magnum flashlights throwing cones of light before them. Down here no birds chirped, no dogs barked, no planes growled overhead. Occasionally the cave would pass beneath a road and they could hear the traffic humming above them, but otherwise, their noise was the only thing. Their footsteps, shooshing through black sand or clunking off rocks, seemed so loud. And so they spoke in whispers. And when they spoke—saying, "What was that?" or "Watch your step," or "I love how old everything smells down here. It smells like it's a hundred million years old"—their breath fogged from their mouths.

When a vein of quartz would catch the light, Becca would put her hands to it. The rock would be slick and streaked pink and white, like bacon. She would remove from her back-pack a pick and hand it to Kevin and he would swing it in a short arc and chip some of the quartz from the wall. And she would collect it to take home and stack neatly across her bureau, across bookshelves and windowsills, so that after a while their house seemed to glitter from every corner.

The cave branched off into narrow corridors, scarcely wider than the Korean hatchback Kevin drove, but the main tube reached thirty, forty yards across, like the hollowed passage of an enormous worm. They wondered if it had an end.

Sometimes the blackness would go gray and they would click off their flashlights and pick their way through the gloom until they came upon a sort of skylight, where the roof of the cave had collapsed and now let in the sun. One time they found a dog—a German shepherd—hanging from such a hole. It had been lynched by its leash, its leash tethered to something aboveground and out of sight, perhaps a tree. And the dog dangled there, spotlit by the sun, turning around and around.

There were things—a far-off moaning, a bundle of bones, a dark shape scuttling just past the reach of their flashlight—that scared them. Rocks scared them. Rocks cluttered the cave floor, some of them the size of melons, others the size of elk. For this reason they bought REI spelunking helmets. Sometimes the ceiling would come loose with a click of stone, a hiss of dirt, nearly noiseless in its descent, but when it slammed to the cave floor, it roared and displaced a big block of air that made them cry out and clutch each other in a happy sort of terror.

But that was before.

Becca doesn't like to go down in the cave anymore. Not since the day in July when the bats came. It was early evening, and they were sprawled out on the couch watching *Wheel of*

Fortune. At that time she was four months' pregnant and her belly was beginning to poke out enough that women would stop her in the grocery store and ask. She needed a safety pin to fasten the jeans she wore now. He was drinking a Bud Light and she was drinking water. She let in enough liquid to visibly fill her cheeks, and then swallowed in tiny portions, her cheeks growing smaller and smaller until sunken. He liked watching her drink. She drank water as if it were wine, not as a necessity but as a pleasure, trying to make it last longer. She looked at him looking at her and said, "Do you hear that?"

"Hear what?"

"That."

He picked up the remote and hit the mute button and the applause of the audience fell away and a hush descended upon the room. He heard nothing and said as much.

Becca had her head cocked and her hand raised. "Just wait," she said, and then, *"There."*

And there it was, a scritch-scritch-scritching at the steel door.

For a long time they simply looked at each other and then she pushed him and said, "Go see what it is," and he said, "All right already," and got up from the couch and slowly approached the door and put his ear to it. The metal was cold against his cheek. From here the scratching sound sounded more like the sound of eating, of teeth mashing something into a paste.

Becca said something he couldn't hear and he pulled his head away from the door and said, "What?" and she said, "You think it could be a wild animal?"

"Don't know." Right then he opened the door and the bats came rushing in, a dense black stream of them. They emitted a terrible screeching, the noise a thousand nails would make when teased across a chalkboard. They fluttered violently through the living room, the kitchen, the hallway, battering the walls and windows, seeking escape. Kevin screamed and so did Becca and the noise of flapping, of air beaten in many different directions, was all around them.

Somehow Kevin ducked down and pushed his way through their black swirling color and ran for the front door and threw it open and not thirty seconds later most of the bats had disappeared into the twilight gloom.

Becca was on the couch with an injured bat fluttering limply in her hair. She did not move, except to part her lips and say, "Holy shit." She had a hand between her breasts, over her heart. "Holy fucking shit. What the fucking shit was that?"

The next morning she woke up complaining of cramps.

Even before she was pregnant she would talk about her pain incessantly, saying her back hurt, her neck hurt, her feet hurt, her head, her stomach. If it were touchable—like, the space between her eyebrows—she would touch it. "I think it's a tumor," she would say, completely serious. "Feel this. This does not feel normal."

And Kevin would say, "I'm sure it's nothing."

"I'm sure it's nothing," was what he said when she complained of cramps, when she limped to the shower with a hand pressed below her belly.

"My lower back," she said. "On the right side. I really, really hope I'm okay. I'm pretty worried about the way this feels."

And then she began bleeding. A rope of red trailed down her leg. And Kevin, now in a panic, wrapped her in a bathrobe and with shampoo still in her hair drove her to St.

Charles where she delivered, with a rush of blood, the baby that looked like a baby, a little girl, only too small and too red, the size of his hand.

Becca was convinced it had something to do with the bats. Perhaps she had been bitten or scratched and perhaps some parasite with leathery wings and claws traveled through her bloodstream and did ruin to her. When she told the doctor this, vines of sadness trembled through the skin around her eyes. They ran blood tests and found nothing. No, the doctor said. Not the bats. It was just one of those things.

She didn't like this. She didn't like to think that her own body could turn on her, collapse upon itself. So she said, "What does he know? Doctors don't know anything. One day they say eggs are good for you. The next they're bad. How can they have the answers when the answers are always changing."

Right then Kevin could see the pain between her legs in her face. Still can to this day. Sometimes he imagines a rotten spot inside her, like a bruised bit of peach he wants to carve away with a knife.

Tonight, after they clean all the blood from the fridge and their bodies, after they buy Chinese takeout and carry it into the living room to eat on TV trays, they find a bat. It is tucked into a corner, where the wall meets the ceiling. Kevin can see its heartbeat pulsing through its thin leathery skin. Maybe it is one of the old bats that never escaped or maybe it is a new bat that somehow found its way inside, its tiny brown body crawling through the heating ducts, the walls.

Kevin wants to surround it with something—maybe a glass or a Tupperware container—and carry it outside and release it. When he says this Becca looks at him as if she wants to spit. "I hate this house," she says. "I hate this stupid, stupid house." Then she grabs the poker from the fireplace and holds it like a spear and jerks it forward, impaling the bat.

When the metal moves through it, it makes the smallest scream in the world.

They haven't had sex in a month and a half, not since the miscarriage.

In the back of the closet, on the top shelf, beneath his sweaters, Kevin keeps an old copy of *Penthouse*. He bought it at a gas station several years ago and sometimes sneaks it down to read when his wife isn't home. He likes having something hidden from her, something that belongs to him alone, a small betrayal.

Becca has a rule: if you don't wear a piece of clothing for a year, you get rid of it, and right now she is going through their closet with a garbage bag, filling it with clothes for Goodwill, when she finds the *Penthouse*.

Kevin comes out of the bathroom to find her standing there, with her legs spread apart, the magazine crumpled up in her fist. "What?" she says. "I'm not good enough for you?"

"It's not that."

"Then what is it?"

This is a question with barbed wire around it, and when he doesn't answer she rips the magazine in half and then in half again and throws its pages to the floor and stares at him, panting. The way her anger grows reminds him of an umbrella, a big red umbrella, suddenly sprung.

"Look," he says, exasperated. "You want to punch me? Would that make you feel better?"

Her eyes narrow with anger and he motions her forward

with his hands and says, "Come on. Hit me, why don't you. You know you want to. Do it." He can see her little hand balling into a fist. And then she draws it back and gives him a glancing blow to the shoulder. "Is that all you've got?" he says. "Come on. You can do better than that. You hit like a girl. Hit me like you mean it."

This triggers some switch inside her. She makes a furious little noise and charges forward and hits him again and this time his shoulder seizes up with hurt.

"That's better," he says.

She has a look of complete rage or religious exaltation on her face—he isn't sure which. She is breathing hard. He can hear the air coming in and out of her nose. "What else do you want me to do to you?" she says.

"You tell me."

She points her finger at him and tells him to take off his shirt. And he does. Bare-chested he stands before her, swaying slightly. She reaches forward and twists his nipples—hard—and when he screams she smiles and pinches between her fingers a clump of chest hair and rips it out, leaving behind a pink place where the blood rises in tiny dots. And he screams again. And their eyes hold together like the pieces of a puzzle.

She throws him against the wall and kisses him, roughly kisses him through all their laughing. And they tear the clothes off each other and he picks her up and pushes her against the wall and enters her. And she is bucking her hips against his and he can feel himself losing control, can feel the heat rising in him, moving through the tunnels of him and nearing eruption, when all of a sudden she pushes him away and says, "That's enough."

When he asks what's wrong she absently scratches her

bare breast and stares down at her feet as if the answer lies somewhere underground.

It is easier for Kevin. He can lose himself in the rhythms of his hammer, can smash the frustration from his body. Every day at work he drinks a milk jug full of water and sweats out every last drop of it and it is more than a little like crying.

Right after the miscarriage he thought a lot about the baby, the little girl they never named. How she might have smiled ridiculously at him making funny faces. Or used the coffee table to pull herself up and take her first teetering steps. Then he drank himself to the very pitch of drunkenness, and that was enough. The baby has almost disappeared from his memory, almost.

Sometimes he will say something—maybe he will be watching CNN and maybe they will broadcast a dead Iraqi child lying in the middle of the street and maybe he will make some offhand remark about how lucky they are—and only when he sees the crumpled-up look on Becca's face does he remember and say, "Oh."

She cannot not remember. A playground busy with children. A dirty pacifier abandoned in the aisle at Wal-Mart. The purple teddy bear she bought and set among her rocks on the bureau. On a daily basis all of these things fly into her eyes and thump around inside of her skull, like bats, leaving the poisonous dust of their wings. She keeps her lips pursed around the edge of a pain he can only imagine and she cannot seem to forget.

Midnight. He wakes up to find his wife gone, the shape of her head still imprinted on her pillow. He calls out her name and when she doesn't answer he gets out of bed and walks down the hall and into the living room where moonlight comes in through the windows and makes the quartz set here and there sparkle.

He observes the steel door hanging open—and there, surrounded by blackness, a palpable blackness, strange and horrible, that seems to ooze into the house, stands his wife.

He goes to her. If she hears his footsteps, if she feels the weight of his hand on her shoulder, she gives no indication. She wears one of his T-shirts and nothing else, her feet tight together, her arms at her side.

From the door a cool wind blows, bringing cave smells, of guano and mold and sand and stone. He closes the door and hoists up his wife and cradles her in his arms and carries her to the bedroom, to bed, where she finally comes alive and says, "No," and jumps up and goes to her dresser and opens its drawers. She steps into her panties and zips up her jeans and pulls a fleece over her head and asks, as she begins lacing her boots, whether he is coming or not.

Their flashlights are the only lights. There is no moon down here. Beyond the cones of yellow light there is nothing, everything utterly black. Dark as only a cave can be dark. The longer they walk, the closer the walls seem to get, the narrower the passage.

Becca leads the way—her body tense, her shoulders bunched up nearly to her ears—down a series of unfamiliar corridors, taking a right at each junction so they will know to always take a left when returning. Around a bend, among a pile of rocks, a pair of red eyes brighten, then vanish, and Kevin spends the next dozen yards sweeping his flashlight back and forth, waiting for something to materialize and come rushing toward them.

Becca moves her pale hand along the basalt, steadying

her passage and crumbling away the green-and-gold patterns of lichen growing there. Occasionally she pauses, close-lipped, contemplating something visible only to her, before continuing forward. Her flashlight makes giant shadows that seem to knock against each other.

Then the channel opens up into a space as big as a banquet hall. The floor is strangely clean, absent of rocks. From the ceiling hang roots, like capillaries, groping for purchase. He gives one a tentative tug and when it doesn't give he tries swinging from it and it carries his weight and he flies from one side of the cave to the other, like something out of a Tarzan episode.

Becca has a small smile on her face when she walks the room, touching the walls and looking all around her, as if committing the space to memory. And then she locks eyes with Kevin and brings the flashlight to her face, throwing shadows across it. They seem blacker than the darkness of the cave.

The light clicks off and she becomes a gray shape in the near distance.

He waits a moment, surrounded by his own ball of light, before clicking off his own flashlight. And the next thing he knows a cloud of darkness settles around them. He can hear her feet whispering across the cave floor and then her voice playfully calling out to him, "Marco."

He can hear the saliva popping in his mouth when it rises into a smile. "Polo," he says and moves toward her voice with his hands out before him, his fingers like the snouts of moles, routing through the dark. When he touches stone he hears her voice again, saying, "Marco," behind him now.

This continues for a few minutes, with her always eluding him. He can hear her voice and her footsteps and by the time he races to where she was, he knows she is already gone, but not where, not exactly.

All this time the roots startle him, coming out of the dark to lick his face. More than once he screams. And this is how she finds him. He can feel her hand at his elbow. It squeezes him and rises to his chest and pauses there. "Hey," he says and she says, "Got you."

Both of them click on their flashlights at once. They blink painfully, seeing a yellow light with a few filaments of red running through it. The black liquid of the cave oozes at the edges of their vision as the world takes form and they stare hard at each other for a long time. Then, as if something has been decided between them, she grabs a fistful of his shirt and pulls him down to the sandy floor where she brings her mouth against his. And this time she doesn't stop him when he peels off her pants and explores the slickness between her legs with his hands before climbing on top of her.

Together they move slowly, with the rhythm of a sleeping chest, until they are finished—and this takes a long time—so long that their flashlights begin to dim and eventually black out. And they are alone in the dark, huddling together with the cold creeping into their bare skin.

When they finally untangle themselves and rise from the cave floor he takes off his belt and runs it through his back belt loop only, so that it serves as a sort of leash. She grabs hold of it and follows him as they continue back the way they came. They can hear dripping sounds of water and the hushing sound of wind and the booming sounds of rocks falling somewhere deep in the cave. But they aren't afraid so much as they are resigned to making it home. Kevin reaches his hands before him and moves them in a slow scissoring motion as if clearing the cobwebs from the air. And he lifts his feet high and brings them down carefully and when necessary warns Becca: "There's a big rock here, about knee-high, so don't bang into it."

Every time the cave walls fall away he follows the left passage, groping through the dark, and eventually they find the staircase. They climb it and close the steel door behind them. The air is warmer up here. It feels soft. A patch of dawn sky is visible through the living-room window.

Becca goes to the kitchen and pulls out a gallon of milk and before pouring it into a glass stands there, backlit by the fridge, her face in shadow, looking at Kevin as if wondering, in mystery, how they found their way back.

The Woods

My father wanted to show me something, but he wouldn't say what. He only said I should get my gun, my thirty-aught-six, and follow him. This happened just outside Bend, Oregon, where we lived in a ranch house surrounded by ten acres of woods. I was twelve at the time: old enough to shoot a gun, young enough to fear the dark.

The moment we stepped off the porch, as if on cue, a sound rose from the forest, as slow as smoke. It sounded like a woman crying. I felt my veins constrict and a needle-jab of dread in my chest. "What's that?" I said. "What the hell *is* that?"

"Don't be a pantywaist," my father said over his shoulder. By now he was several steps ahead of me and moving across the lawn. "And don't say hell."

When he reached the place where the grass met the trees, he perceived I was not following him, and turned. "Come on," he said.

In silence, he motioned me forward with his hand and I clutched my rifle a little closer to my chest. Then the noise began again, sharper and louder now than before, reminding me of metal rasping across a file. Even my father cringed.

Once we entered the forest the pines put a black color on things, and through their branches dropped a wet wind that carried with it the smell of the nearby mountains. It was that in-between time of day, not quite afternoon and not quite night, when the air begins to purple and thicken.

We walked for some time along a well-worn path, one of many that coiled through our property like snakes without end. Sometimes loud and sometimes soft, the screaming sound continued, like a siren signaling the end of the world. It overwhelmed my every thought and sensation so that I felt as if I were stuck in a box with only this horrible noise to keep me company. Everything seemed to tremble as it dragged its way through the air.

We hurried along as fast as we could, less out of wonder or sympathy, I began to suspect, than the urgent need to silence it. I hated the noise—its mournful mixed-up music— as much as I feared it.

Then, between the trees, I saw the inky gleam of its eyes, and its huge ears drawn flat against its skull, and then I saw its body. Blood trails oozed along its cinnamon color.

"Man alive," my father said.

It was a four-prong mule deer and it was tangled in our barbed-wire fence, the barbed wire crisscrossing its body like fast handwriting. I remember the blood so clearly. It was *the* perfect shade of red. To this day I want a car—an old-time car—say a Mustang or one of those James Bond Aston Martins—the color of it.

The deer, bewildered, let its head droop and took short nervous breaths before letting loose another wail, a high-pitched sound that lowered into a baritone moan, like pulling in a trombone. A purple tongue hung from its mouth. Its muscles jerked beneath its hide.

I stood behind a clump of rabbitbrush as if to guard myself from the animal. The bush smelled great. It smelled sugary. It smelled like the color yellow ought to smell. By concentrating on it so deeply, I removed myself from the forest and was thereby able to contain the tears crowding my eyes.

Then my father said, "I want you to kill it."

Just like that. Like killing was throwing a knuckleball or fixing a carburetor or tying a necktie.

To this day, some fifteen years later, when I lie in bed in a half-dream, the deer sometimes emerges from the shadows, snapping its teeth, retreating back into shadow as quickly as it appeared. To this day, I dislike the woods, I dislike hunting, I dislike my father.

Which is why, when he called and invited me to join him camping and hunting in the Ochoco National Forest, I surprised myself by saying yes.

I wasn't the only one surprised. "You're sure?" he said.

"Sure I'm sure."

"Your mother just thinks . . . I just figured . . ." His voice fell off a cliff here, uncharacteristically uncertain.

I tried to fill the sentence for him in as diplomatic a way as possible. "Some guy time would definitely be healthy."

"Exactly," he said, relieved, his voice rising to a manly pitch reserved for taverns and locker rooms. "We'll drink some beers and raise some hell!" Here he paused and cleared his throat and his sober tone resumed. "I can't remember the last time we talked, you know. I mean, really *talked.*"

He hit the nail on the head.

East of Bend, the uninhabited country begins as immediately as the ocean begins off the shore. This is the high desert. In a beat-up Bronco, my father and I drove through the sagebrush, the flat yellow dinginess interrupted by the occasional pumice or cinder quarry. Though it was October and though by night the temperature might drop into the forties, thick heat waves rose from the road, shrouding the distant Ochoco hills and making them appear unreal.

I was working in Portland as a software developer and my father was trying to figure out what this meant. For four years he hadn't bothered to ask about my work except to say, "How's work?"

In college, when I announced my decision to major in computer science, he told me flat out he didn't consider it an honest way to make money. He had not gone to college— "Didn't see the point," he said—and worked as a contractor, constructing the luxurious gated communities that continue to sprout up all over Bend, inhabited by retired Californians who moved there for the skiing and golf.

Now, for whatever reason—guilt or genuine curiosity or something else—he asked me in a loud voice, speaking over the noise of the radio and the engine, what exactly the Internet *was*, what exactly a computer *did*.

My father is a big man—with a beard and a keg-of-beer belly—a man who wouldn't look out of place in a truck commercial. What he doesn't understand, he normally labels worthless and sweeps aside with his fist and a few select words. Which is why, when I answered his questions and when I noticed his eyebrows coming closer and closer together in confusion, his knuckles growing whiter at the steering wheel, I decided to change the subject to one he would enjoy.

"How's Boo working out for you?" Boo was a lab/retriever mix he bought about a year ago from an alfalfa-farmer neighbor. He had always wanted a hunting dog and he had been training Boo obsessively.

"Oh, he's a good boy." My father smiled and adjusted the rearview mirror so he could spy on Boo where he slept in the backseat in a horseshoe shape. "Boo?" he said. "Hey, Boo bear?" At the sound of his name, the dog perked his ears and lifted his head from his paws and thumped his tail a few times. "You ready to hunt, Boo?" my father said, and Boo barked sharply.

My father then began to explain at length how raising a dog is no different than raising a child. He claimed a man who fails to sufficiently and constantly train his dog, to test it, to *discipline*—from its weaning to its death—is in for a rude awakening. "Boo wasn't even a month old when I first introduced him to water, to various types of cover, and of course to game birds," he said and ran a hand across his beard, neatening it. "When it comes to dogs, you got to develop their obedience and hunting desire from the get-go or they won't grow up right."

Here he gave me a look full of judgment and love that quite frankly pissed me off, but I pretended not to notice—I kept up my pleasant demeanor—because with him, when things boiled over, it took a lot of time and energy before he would treat you civilly again—and we had a long weekend ahead of us.

He explained how he first coaxed Boo into water. "I took my fly rod, see?" His hand mimicked casting. "And with a pheasant wing dangling from it, I shot it off into the shallow part of the pond and let Boo chase it and sight-point it."

Then he baited Boo with a dead bird, and then a live lame bird. "At first, my pup got afraid when he felt the bottom disappear under his legs, but I got in the pond with him and showed him how safe it was, and now he can, by God, hardly go by a puddle without wanting to jump in it." I remembered him shoving me off a dock and demanding

I tread water for sixty seconds and laughing much as he laughed now, looking lovingly at his dog.

I admit to feeling something like jealousy.

"No," he said, as if responding to some conversation I wasn't a part of, "Boo won't be much help to us deer hunting, but he's good company."

I continued to listen and he continued to speak until the final distance—where the sagebrush gave way to juniper and pine trees—became the near distance and the ground began to steadily rise and the evergreen forest filtered the sun into puddles that splashed across the highway. We turned off the air conditioner and rolled down our windows because here the heat was gone, replaced by a pure cool air that made breathing feel like drinking.

My father was a creature of habit and for as long as my family had been visiting the Ochocos, we made our camp along the South Fork of the John Day River, in the Black Canyon Wilderness. Besides the occasional Forest Service truck grumbling along the nearby logging road, we never saw anyone and my father considered the spot his own.

To remember the exact location, he had blaze-marked a pine with his hatchet. "Keep an eye out," he said, and then, "There!" indicating the tree with the wound scabbed over by hard orange sap. We parked under its branches and tramped through the bear grass and lupin, seeking the cold spring that bled into the South Fork, and next to it, our old firepit, probably with a few weeds growing through its ashes.

We found something else entirely.

Boo ran ahead of us, popping his teeth at butterflies, barking at a chipmunk that chattered a warning from a nearby tree, and then his body went still. "You see that?" my father said, nodding in Boo's direction. "He's sighted something there. Maybe a ptarmigan or a grouse."

It was another thirty feet to where Boo pointed, his body as black and as rigid as obsidian, his snout indicating something hidden among the knee-high grass. "At ease," my father said and the dog relaxed his pose and wagged his tail, but kept his eyes focused ahead of him.

Here was the cold spring—the size of a hot tub—surrounded by willows and sun-sparkled stones, and next to it, our firepit, and next to it, a body.

The man had been dead a long time. So long I could only identify him as male by his clothes—his jeans and flannel shirt—and even then I could not be certain. The vultures and the coyotes and the flies and the worms had had their way with him. I imagined the coyotes howling when they did it, fighting over the juiciest cuts of meat.

After a stunned silence, I ran. I ran and probably made it fifty feet before I stopped and found my cool and steadied my breathing and returned to my father, slowly.

"This is bad," he said. He was wearing a John Deere cap and he removed it now and put his hand into its hollow as if seeking an explanation there. "This is a hell of a thing." He looked like a man who has woken from a nap and cannot find his bearings.

I took my cell phone from my pocket. No surprise: there was no service here, far from any tower. "If we drive to the top of the canyon," I said. "If we get a little higher, I might be able to get a signal. It's worth a try anyway."

"No." My father put his hat back on and straightened it. "Excuse me?"

"No," he said again. "What's the rush?" He lifted his hand and let it fall and slap his thigh. "I tell you something: *he's* in no rush."

I understood this completely and not at all. "Dad?" I said. *"No."*

There was concern on his face, but I genuinely believe this had more to do with having to abandon our campsite than with the dead man sprawled across it. He put a hand on my shoulder and squeezed just hard enough so I knew he meant business. "Justin," he said.

"What?"

"Look. It turned out to be a beautiful day, didn't it?" And he was right—it was—the kind of bright blue day that bleached everything of its color. "How about let's enjoy it?" He regarded the dead man and I noticed his cheek bulge, his tongue probing the side of his mouth. "Tomorrow we'll drive to John Day and tell the police. But not today."

Boo crept toward the dead man, his muscles tense, his body low, as if certain the blackened pile of bones and sinew would leap up at any moment and *attack*. When it didn't, his movements loosened and he panted happily and waded into the spring to drink.

"Okay, Justin?"

I looked at my feet—something I do when gathering my thoughts—and there discovered a weather-beaten pack of Marlboros, the cigarettes that could not kill the dead man quick enough. "Okay," I said in a voice I hardly recognized as my own. "Fine."

From faraway came the sound of a diesel horn, a logging truck rocketing along a distant highway, reminding me that no matter how much this felt like the middle of nowhere, it wasn't.

We made our camp twenty yards upstream from the dead man. While Boo splashed along the banks, chasing the silvery flashes of fish, I set to work digging a new firepit and my father unloaded from the Bronco our rifles and fishing poles and cooler and duffel bags and his old army-issue canvas tent. It leaked and smelled like mothballs and mildew and every night I had ever spent in it, I woke up swollen and sneezing.

That Christmas I had bought him a new tent from REI— one of those fancy waterproof, windproof four-man deals with a lifetime guarantee and a screened-in moonroof.

"Dad?" I said, and he said, "What?"

"What happened to the new tent I bought you?"

"This has been a good tent for us." He patted it fondly. "I like *this* tent." He did not look at me, but set to work unfolding the canvas and planting the stakes.

"You've got to be kidding me." My voice went high and I tried to control it. "That tent cost me nearly three hundred fucking dollars and you're just going to let it rot in the attic?"

He finished hammering a stake into the ground and stood up and straightened his posture to accentuate his six-foot frame. Beneath his stare I felt as if I had shrunk a good five inches, as if my chest hair and muscles had receded—and I became seventeen all over again.

That was the year Mom and I bought him a bicycle for his birthday, an eighteen-speed Trek. "Boy," he had said when he ran his hands along it. "Wow." That night he stripped off every gear except the hardest and from then on rode it all up and down the country highways with a terrible grimace on his face.

A grimace similar to the one he wore now, eyeing me with a hand resting on his belly. "I didn't ask for the thing," he said, "and I didn't want it." He began to rub his belly as if to summon his anger from it like a genie. "And when are you going to learn that quality doesn't always come with a price tag? Just listen to you. You're as bad as a Californian."

Just then Boo came trotting over to us, grinning around a femur bone with a strip of denim sticking to it. My father said, "Release," and took the bone and stood there, holding it, staring at it, not knowing what to do. Boo wagged his whole body along with his tail and my father looked at me. What he was feeling then, I didn't know. His emotion was masked from me, hidden behind his beard.

We plopped our lines in the South Fork and came away with five rainbow trout, each the size of my forearm. We gutted them and threw their heads in the river. We fried them in a pan with a few strips of bacon. We ate and drank and sat in silence. The only sound was the rushing of the river and the occasional *crack* of an opened Coors can. My father was like a still-life painting, his hand on Boo's head, motionless and watching the fire with a detached expression.

I wanted to shake him and hit him and hug him at once. I wanted to get back in the Bronco and return the way we came. I considered sleeping on the bare ground, but the gathering clouds and the nearness of the dead man drove me inside the musty tent.

I woke to absolute darkness and the dull even noise of rainfall. The entire world seemed to hiss. I clicked on my flashlight, revealing a tent that drooped and breathed around me with many damp spots dripping and pattering my sleeping bag.

Have you ever noticed, when you lay your head to your pillow and listen—*really* listen—you can hear footsteps? This is your pulse, the veins in your ear swelling and constricting, slightly shifting against the cotton. I heard this now—a sort of *under*sound, beneath the rain—only my head was nowhere near my pillow. I had propped myself up on my elbow.

There it was. Or was I only imagining it? The rasping

thud a foot makes in wet grass—one moment behind the tent, the next moment before it, circling.

Before I went to bed, as a sort of afterthought, I had tied shut the front flaps. Now they billowed open with the breeze, the breeze bearing the keen wet odor of rabbitbrush, a smell I will always associate with barbed-wire fences, with dying, with fear.

Perhaps the knot had come undone with the wind or perhaps my father had risen to pee. Outside, thousands of raindrops caught my flashlight's beam and brightened with it. I imagined something out there, rushing in—how easy it would be—its shape taking form as it moved from darkness into light.

My father released a violent snore. I spotlit him with the flashlight, wanting to tell him *shh*. His fingers twitched like the legs of the dreaming dog he draped his arm over. His mouth formed silent words, his eyeballs shuddered beneath his eyelids, and I wondered what was going on in there, inside of him.

Morning, a sneezing fit woke me. And after I wiped the gunk from my eyes and pulled on my jeans, I discovered outside the dewy grass trampled down, and before the tent, a boot. Its leather was badly torn and discolored, as if it had passed through the digestive tract of a large animal. I stepped around it, keeping an eye on it, on my way to the firepit. We had stored some wood in the tent with us and I kindled it now with newspaper and boiled water for coffee.

The smell of the grounds woke my father. He emerged from the tent in his white T-shirt and his once-white BVDs. He stretched and yawned dramatically and the noise brought Boo from the tent. Boo promptly picked up the boot with his teeth and presented it to my father as a cat would a dead mouse. "Goddamnit, Boo," my father said and picked up the boot and shook it at him. "Bad dog. *Bad* dog." Boo yipped once and cocked his head in confusion and my father examined the boot before hurling it into the river, saying, "Thing looks like a hay baler got it."

About last night, I mentioned nothing, asking instead if he wanted bacon.

We set off with our rifles strapped to our backs. The rain had left the world dewy with its after-breath, and in the shady spots, a light mist clung to the ground, coiling around our feet, soon to be burned away by the sun. We followed the South Fork until we found a game trail bearing many hoofprints, rain-blurred but recent, and we pursued them up and up and up until we gained the rim of the canyon.

We paused here to get our breath. A small fire—no doubt triggered by lightning—had not long ago burned through this plateau, making the trees sharp and black at their tops like diseased fangs. When I leaned against a pine, its shadow stuck to me.

A basalt cornice jutted from the canyon wall and my father climbed out on it. Far below him, in the spots the sunlight had not yet warmed, vapors floated up and fingered the air. He coughed something from his lungs and spit it over the edge and followed its fall and laughed softly. He was so natural and fearless, standing casually at the edge of a hundred-foot drop, eating his trail mix and peering through his binoculars and cursing the big stags for hiding from him, the goddamned chickens.

Whereas I—with my freshly deodorized armpits and my $100 safari jacket with Velcro compartments and all sorts of zippers and buttons and hooks for hanging knives and compasses—did not feel nearly so comfortable. Add to this the dead man wandering through my mind like a tumor, distracting me, and you have a hunter who hardly knew which end of the rifle to point away from his body.

The trail we followed, after crossing through a dense pine forest, dropped halfway down the canyon and ran into a willow and cottonwood thicket. Springwater made the ground marshy here. This, combined with the forty-degree angle, made me place every footstep carefully—though my father marched along at a fast pace, unaware or unafraid of any danger. Birds called from an unseen place ahead of us and their music had something dark in it. They grew louder, croaking and cawing, and in a small bear-grass meadow we finally came upon them, nearly two dozen crows and magpies and buzzards.

Boo sight-pointed them and my father said, "At ease," and then, "*Sick.*"

With one fluid motion Boo shot forward, barking fiercely. The small birds cawed their surprise and flapped up into the high branches, complaining down on us with their rusty voices. The buzzards remained—hissing, opening their wings—until the last moment, when Boo lunged at them, and then they rose above the treetops, where they wheeled in a tornado formation, but did not depart. Something fell from one of their claws, a rag of gray flannel, and it fluttered between my father and me like a piece of ash.

We knew what it had come from. We did not want to know, but we knew.

This dead man was fresher than the other, no more than a few days old. He lay splayed out in a sort of bloody X. I cannot tell you if he was blond or brown-haired, if he was fat or skinny, because I could not focus on the body for more than a second. I did not cry, nor did I run—but I closed my eyes and pressed my hands to them until fireworks played across my retinal screen.

I think my father said it best when he said, "All right. I'm officially creeped."

I took him by the sleeve and said, "Can we please, please, *please* go home now?"

"Yes," he said. "I think we better."

We were a few hundred yards upstream from our camp when it happened. Somewhere across the South Fork there was a sound—a deep groan—and all three of us went still.

"Quiet!" my father said when I opened my mouth to speak. He had one hand cupped around his ear, while the other held his rifle. When after a moment, we had heard nothing else, I said, "Do you think it's a bear?"

He did not have an answer because right then Boo broke away from us and leapt into the river. It was fast-moving and foaming and pulled the dog a good thirty feet downstream before he made it across. Once there he shook off quickly and rushed the sandy bank and entered the woods, and then a moment later appeared again on the bank, barking terribly at something in the trees. "Boo," my father yelled. "Boo, god-damnit, get over here."

The dog did not acknowledge him but continued bark-ing as he ran in a wide circle and then vanished into another section of underbrush. For a long time, over the noise of the river, we could hear the branches snapping, the bushes rus-tling, Boo barking. Then a silence set in that in this deep shadowed canyon seemed too silent.

Dust clung to the air and drifted across the river. Some of it stuck to my skin. My father could not stop shaking his head. He could not believe it. "I've never seen a dog act like that," he said. "I've seen salmon act like that, when the hook first surprised them, but never a dog."

My father wanted to immediately ford the river and search for Boo, but I suggested to him, since we were so close already, that we might make our lunch at camp, and who knows, the smell of fried fish might bring the dog from the forest.

"Or something else," my father said, and when I said, "What?" he put two fingers to his mouth and whistled a special ear-zinging whistle I have always wished to master. When Boo did not respond he muttered, "Damn, damn, damn," and began marching toward camp with his rifle held before him.

An hour passed and clouds piled up above us. They moved and met each other, closing the blue gulfs between them, like hands slowly weaving a spell of grayness over the day. The sun filtered through the thinner clouds and shapeless sections of light roamed across the canyon floor and walls.

We returned to find our camp not as we left it. The cooler was open, the lawn chairs were tipped over, and my sleeping bag had been dragged halfway from the tent like a stuck-out tongue.

"*What* the hell," I said as adrenaline-soaked panic hummed like Muzak in the background of my brain. "I mean, what the hell, Dad? *What* did this?" I knew this sounded like a line from a bad movie, and I wanted a line from a good movie, but there was nothing else to say. "Dad?"

My father picked up the sleeping bag and smelled it, clearly lost in thought. "Mmm."

"Mmm what?"

"Mmm I don't know. I don't want to talk about it."

"Let's go now," I said. "Can we just go? Now?"

My father pushed the sleeping bag back into the tent and went to the firepit and squatted next to it and began to arrange fresh kindling. "Not without Boo, we won't."

"Look," I said. "We'll go to John Day and—"

"Not without Boo, we won't!" This was said at a scream. A freakish look came into his eyes that I didn't want to argue with, so I lifted my hands and let them fall, seeking an explanation and giving up on one all in the same motion. "We'll eat something," my father said, his voice calm now, "and then we're going to find him. We're going to track him. And if we run into anything else along the way, we'll kill it."

Soon flames crackled and trout filets sizzled in butter and my brain felt as if the clouds had dropped down and seized it.

We waded the South Fork with our rifles held above our heads. Once across, our boots squished and our pants clung to us uncomfortably and we entered the woods and the light fell away as if in a sudden dusk. Birds sailed around us, squawking and inspecting us, but otherwise we saw no living thing when we followed the rain-gutted game trail bearing Boo's prints.

We climbed a steep grade and entered a wooded ravine with a stream trickling through it. It was a tight corridor—filled with shadows and jutting knobs of basalt and stunted juniper trees that somehow grew through the stone, their roots like gnarled fingers ready to scrabble down and seize us—and when we left this ravine and entered a wider gulch, it was with the relief of a deep breath and a loosened belt.

"That's queer." My father was walking ahead of me and stopped, his body bent in half, searching the ground. "Do you see it?"

I saw nothing.

"Boo's paw prints end here." He pointed to the trail. "He's running along at a good clip and then . . ."

I had a natural explanation. "He left the trail and went into the woods." My father did not respond, but kneeled and more carefully examined the rain-soaked soil, as easy to read as print on the page. "What is it now?" I said.

He raised his eyes from the trail and stared back at me steadily. "Boo's paw prints end," he said. "And something else takes them over."

I hunkered down next to him, and among the many hoof and paw shapes he indicated a long thin print—vaguely human—except at its tip, where three toes made a tiny constellation in the soil. I was not surprised. I was beyond surprise. I imagined I heard the ghost of a yelp still lingering in the air.

There was a crashing in the trees close to us and we both raised our rifles. But nothing came out of the dimness except a mule deer, a six-point, a big beautiful animal that ripped through the pines and over the fallen timber and into the open trail where it came to a stand, watching us, swishing its tail, not ten feet away—so close I could smell its musk.

I stared down the length of my rifle. It felt cold in my hand. I remembered the deer tangled in barbed wire and considered firing, but didn't. I didn't have it in my heart—and apparently neither did my father. He sighed and let his rifle fall. The movement sent the deer bounding up the trail and around the corner.

My father continued forward. I stopped him by beginning a series of broken sentences, but each thought lost its grip in the empty air. I became very aware of him staring at me. "Are you done?" he said and when I didn't say anything, he resumed tracking.

A chill wind blew suddenly through the gulch, making the pines send out a roaring whistle. Just as quickly, it stopped, as if the forest had taken a deep breath. There followed a tinkling noise, like a tiny bell, not too far ahead of us. We went to it.

The nylon collar hung from a tree branch, some ten feet above the trail, like a grotesque Christmas ornament. The tinkling came from its tags, knocked together by the wind. For a long time we stared at it, and then my father reached with his rifle and used the barrel to pull the collar from the branch. It was torn in places and its color, naturally red, was made redder by the blood that rubbed off on his hand when he held it.

A wince passed over his face and a flush followed it. I remembered his earlier comment about the hay baler. I remembered the dead men. I remembered my buddy Brandon—my buddy from high school—telling me the story of how one time, on a camping trip in the Deschutes National Forest, he woke up with something hunched over him—a black shape against the starlit sky—and he could feel its breath and he could see its unnaturally large eyes, and just when he was trying to decide to scream or go for his knife, it loped away with hardly a sound.

And I imagined someone, months from now, finding my jacket at the mouth of a cave, torn and spotted with blood. Maybe my bones would lie in a nearby pile, broken, with all the marrow sucked from them.

"No," my father said and twisted and squeezed the collar, as if to wring the blood from it. His face filled with lines of pain and a vein wormed across his forehead. A minute passed before he put the collar in his coat pocket and picked up his rifle, his finger curled around the trigger, his voice wild and fast when he said, "I'm going to . . ."

But he didn't know what he was going to do.

I said, "Dad?" and he looked at me through a fog of shock and anger and fear and confusion, finally saying, "What leaves tracks like that, Justin? Not a bear. Not a cougar. That's for goddamn certain. What leaves a collar of a dead dog dangling from a tree like some kind of message?"

My mind chugged through the possibilities, all of them involving horror movie scenarios of long-armed humpbacked creatures covered in hair, and I began to feel very small and vulnerable on this dark game trail, a piece of meat among the shadowy trees.

"You don't want to say it," my father said, "but you're thinking it."

A tense silence followed his words, broken by a branch cracking somewhere in the distance. Both of us flinched.

He smiled without humor. "Bigfoot? That's what you're thinking, isn't it?" He laughed at this. "You think Bigfoot killed those men."

"Maybe we both think—"

"You think Bigfoot killed my dog." He laughed like someone who never shows emotion, explosively, wretchedly, so I knew it came from somewhere deep inside. His laughter went on and on until it finished with a sob.

I had seen him at funerals—I had seen him break a leg after falling from a tree stand—but this was the first time I had seen him cry. Before I knew what I was doing, I put an arm around his shoulder and drew him against me—and he was utterly overcome.

I thumped him on the back and realized that we had changed places, if only for a moment. It was a strange place to be, just as it was very strange to look back upon yesterday— it lay so distant, so irrevocable. "I'll be glad when we get out of this canyon," I said.

"Tell me about it." He pulled away from me and roughly wiped at his eyes. "We're acting pretty unstrung for a couple of old guys, aren't we?"

"Yes."

From far up the canyon there came a low-throated groan, followed by another, closer by, like a strange series of vapors released from the earth. We held our rifles before us, aiming at nothing and at everything.

My father looked at me, red-faced and hollow-eyed, and I read in his expression what he could never voice out loud.

I knew exactly how he felt. For once we understood each other.

When he started back the way we came, I followed him—and both of us were glad when three hours later we drove from the Ochocos and into the flatter country where among the sagebrush and dry gullies and cattle and knotted systems of fence-line we were no longer surrounded by forest.

The Killing

There is blood on his hands. At the kitchen sink the old man dampens them with hot water and works the soap between his palms, making a pink foam that swirls down the drain with a sucking noise. He dries off with a flour-sack cloth and hangs it from the oven handle and goes to the kitchen table and removes from his belt holster a Colt .45 revolver and opens its cylinder and taps out six bullets—one of them a blackened, empty cartridge—and sets them and the gun on a tablemat before sitting down in a ladder-back chair with a cane seat giving way from years of his weight.

Jim is tall and thin and keeps his long gray hair knotted into a ponytail. His face appears cut from fissured stone. On his arm is a jagged crescent of a scar where a bear once bit him, a bear he shot and thought dead. This is a small scar compared to the other. So many years ago he lost his left foot in Chu Lai and now he wears a flesh-colored prosthesis in the place of it. He can get along fine, but walks heavily to one side.

Through a nearby window he can see the meadow, and the forest beyond it, and further still he can see the foothills that rise steadily into the snow-capped Cascades, the sky above them a cold November blue. A gnarled juniper tree interrupts the view. From it hangs a deer carcass, with a nylon rope strung through its hind hock and over a branch. He shot it with the Colt. He prefers to hunt with a handgun or bow, as it requires marksmanship, the ability to stalk within close range. He thinks it only fair.

The deer is like a hundred before it, and a hundred more to come, all in the same posture of death—its head chopped off, its belly split open and emptied. Blood oozes from it and makes dust into mud. The smell draws the turkey vultures.

At first there are just one or two, drifting overhead, their feathers shining blackly, their wings trembling against the updrafts and wind currents. More soon arrive. Perhaps they too are drawn by the smell of blood. Or perhaps they are drawn from the forest as leaves are swept up into a dust devil, as if summoned, by the endless spinning of the vultures, their cyclonic power.

Jim calls out for his grandson and a moment later the boy appears in the shadows of the hallway, moving into the light of the kitchen. His name is Cody and he is six years old. He wears his sand-colored hair in a buzz cut. A robotic T. rex dangles from his hand.

Jim motions to the chair next to him and with some hesitation the boy sits down in it. Even as he fiddles absently with his dinosaur he keeps his eyes sharp on the gun.

"Look at me."

The boy looks at Jim, then looks away, and Jim says, "I said look at me," and a stare seals between them. He asks if the boy heard the shooting earlier and if he had been scared and the boy alternatively shakes his head no, yes.

"Well. Which is it?"

When the boy makes no response Jim says, "I called for

you earlier. I could have used your help. You don't need to be scared anymore. You're safe here. You understand that? I won't let nothing bad happen to you. Don't you understand?"

The boy sets his dinosaur aside and focuses all his attention on the gun and then reaches for it—just briefly, sliding a finger along its stock—before his hand retreats to his lap. And Jim knows what this small gesture means: the boy will try to be brave.

"Good," he says. "That's good." He reaches for the boy and brings a hand to his buzzed scalp, moving it back and forth, making a sizzling sound that makes the boy smile a little.

Then he asks the boy what he knows about guns and when the boy shrugs Jim lifts the Colt, like a fine piece of jewelry, tilting it this way and that so its metal catches the light. It has a nickel finish and wooden grip. At 10.5 inches in length with a 4.75-inch barrel and a range of 50 meters, it weighs only two pounds, but can knock the biggest animal off its feet and into the next world, Jim says.

His father gave it to him and he will give it to the boy, eventually, when he gets a little bigger.

"I'm big," the boy says, and Jim gives him a thin smile, at once full of judgment and love, and says, "No. You're not."

Outside a vulture screams. The scream is a hungry one. Jim watches it come down from the sky and meet its shadow on the ground. When it lands it sends dust swirling with the air it displaces. It hops over to the deer and fits its head up inside the empty sack of it—to drink—like some great and terrible hummingbird.

Jim gets up from the table and limps to the window and pulls it open and yells, "Hey!"

The vulture withdraws its head from the deer and studies him a moment and hisses before hopping off a short distance.

There it cocks its head and brings its wings together, giving it the appearance of a small man in a black cloak.

Jim returns to the table and sees that the boy now holds the gun with two hands, marveling at the look and heft of it, as if it holds some great significance.

"Careful," Jim says, snapping his fingers. "Give it back."

The boy cradles it close to his body, against his chest, before doing what Jim tells him.

Jim then asks the boy to fetch a rag from the garage. After he retrieves it they work together, cleaning the gun. They unbolt it and remove the springs and slide the rag through its cavities, wiping the oil from the lip of the chamber and swabbing the carbonized residue off the firing pin. Jim checks, and then asks the boy to double-check the chamber, searching for grit or burrs. Then they reassemble the gun. The hammer snaps, the six-shot cylinder clicks and whizzes.

He hands the gun to the boy and tells him to keep his finger far from the trigger. With some awkwardness the boy takes the gun and holds it out before him and squints one eye and aims at the window, at the vulture beyond it, making a shooting sound with a punch of his lips

The vulture is chewing at the deer, tearing away a long fleshy ribbon. Upon swallowing the meat, its head darts into the torso for more, so that the deer and the bird seem but one nightmarish creature—a long bald neck at the end of which dangles an eyeless feathery head with orange antlers scratching the ground.

Jim reclaims the revolver and selects a bullet to fit into its cylinder and once again rises from his chair and goes to the window. The movement startles the vulture. Its head, so impossibly red, emerges from the torso of the deer. Its beak parts and from it comes a series of asthmatic noises meant to frighten Jim.

With difficulty he squats at the window and rests his elbows on the sill and aims and for the second time today squeezes the trigger. The revolver jumps. The report overwhelms all other sound. The vulture does a dance and falls over with only one of its wings flapping and a fist-sized hole blown through its chest.

He directs the boy to follow him outside and a moment later they stand over the bird. "I want you to drag it out to the meadow. Near where the trees begin." He indicates where he means with his hand and then lets it drop to urge the boy forward. But the boy resists, looking up at him. He has a lot of white in his eyes that explains his fear.

"Nothing to be afraid of." Here Jim brings his boot to the vulture and kicks it so that it limply rolls over a few times, the dust sticking to it. "See. It's dead. What's dead can't hurt you."

So the boy goes to the vulture and kicks it once himself and when it does not respond he looks at Jim and Jim says, "Go on now." The boy takes the vulture by the claw and drags it away from the house, to the mouth of the forest, where perhaps the coyotes will eat it or perhaps the vultures will eat their own, quarreling over the meat.

And then together they work on skinning the deer, boning and quartering it while Jim explains how they will roll some of the meat in salt and marinate some of it in honey mustard and take some of it to the smokehouse to lie on a grill with cherry wood chips smoldering under it, soaking the meat with their heavy tang.

All this time a funnel of vultures swirls overhead. Their shadows play across the meadow like a dark rippling water.

His daughter, Anne, lives in Salem, in the Willamette Valley, on the other side of the Cascades, where it rains more days than not and moss clings to the trees like a soft green armor. Compared to Central Oregon, it is another world entirely, so moist and gray, the sky, the sidewalks, as if you could punch your hand through anything and withdraw a handful of squirming worms.

He keeps a photo of her on the mantel. In it she holds a rainbow trout, toward the camera to make it look bigger, her thumb hooked through its gills. The sun is before her, making her squint, but he can see happiness in her crumpled-up expression.

She was the same age as Cody then, and he prefers to think of her like that: talking to dolls; stuffing her feet into pink rubber boots; wading through waist-high clusters of rabbitbrush and pausing now and then to collect something, a black-tipped feather, an arrowhead, an owl pellet busy with fur and bones.

Now she is living with some new man in a double-wide trailer on the Sandy River. There have been many before him, all of them with mustaches and Chevy trucks and sleeveless T-shirts that show off the barbed-wire tattoos that surround the hard bulge of their muscles. His name is Dwayne. All that Jim knows of him is this: he works on a landscaping crew and plays in a band called Poison Monkey and occasionally makes his hands into fists and strikes Anne.

That is why two weeks ago the boy came to live with him.

Jim has lived alone for nearly eight years. He remembers the day Anne left him. He watched her from the porch as she navigated the long cinder driveway. It was midmorning and the sun flamed at the tops of the trees and clouds scudded across the sky, throwing shadows on the ground.

Just before she turned onto the potholed strip of county two-lane, she reached her hand out the window and gave a wave good-bye. Jim copied the gesture and maintained it long after she vanished from sight, on her way to the Willamette Pass, headed up and over the mountains, to Corvallis, where she attended OSU for two years until she got pregnant, dropped out, and moved into a studio apartment above a sports bar with a man named Christopher—a man with yellow hair and a too-big mouth—a man distinguished from the faceless lineup in Jim's mind only because he was the first to betray her.

Then, when she drove away with her pale hand out the window, he felt a cavity opening inside him, as though a sharp long-handled spoon had reached down his throat and carved him out. The sensation was not wholly unfamiliar to him.

Several years before, his wife had left him for the vice principal of Mountain View High, where she then taught English. With him she moved to California, a state Jim now hates with the same sort of illogic that informs hating dogs because a Doberman once bit you.

For her, Betty, he had also stood on the porch. He had watched their old Ram Charger retreat from him, its tires kicking up red dust. But his hand had not risen then, as it did for his daughter, to say so long, good luck. It had remained in his pocket, balled into a fist, his fingernails digging into his palm and leaving behind red crescents.

He prefers not to think of her, his wife. Every once in a while, deep in the night, he'll imagine the taste of her mouth, the way her body arched against his. But mostly her memory is like a tombstone whose inscription has become vague from lichen and frost, a half-remembered someone he refuses to mourn.

Now his home—a single-story ranch with earth-colored siding and basalt stonework along its base—has life in it again.

Here is the boy. His face is like his mother's, only more compact, softer. He looks like she used to look, during those years when Jim would so often cradle her in his arms and thumb the tears from her eyes after she fell and peeled, like a red peel of apple, the skin off her knee.

Her room is as she left it. Dozens of glow-in-the-dark stars decorate the ceiling. Photographs scissored from *Cosmopolitan* hang from the closet door. The colored bulb of a sock rests on top of her dresser, among many half-empty perfume bottles with names like *Fantasy* and *Revenge*. Every few months Jim will vacuum or dust, usually before one of her visits, but otherwise the room remains undisturbed. This is where the boy sleeps, under a glow-in-the-dark constellation that reminds Jim of a phantom net that might descend at any moment and keep the boy here, safe.

Since the boy moved in, he has not cried for his mother or sat mindlessly before the television or followed Jim around, begging for attention, as Jim expected he would. Mainly he wanders through the forest, making pyramids out of stones, pretending pinecones are grenades, notching the trunks of trees with a found arrowhead, flushing out quail and firing pebbles at them with the slingshot Jim gave him.

He is so quiet and so often off on his own that Jim occasionally forgets about him. On one occasion, in the kitchen, he turned around from the fridge and dropped a gallon of milk, startled by the sight of the boy. Jim felt then— off-balance, alarmed—as he sometimes felt when his daughter called and announced she had met or had left somebody.

Right then, with the milk overturned and gurgling all over the slate floor, Jim looked at the boy looking up at him and studied his face as if it might hold some clue to the person that his daughter has become.

Next to his house stands a pole barn, his taxidermy studio. There are no windows, but on warm days he leaves its double-doors yawned open, to let in the breeze and blow out the biting smell of formaldehyde.

Hundreds of mouths line the walls, some with jaws gaped, clenched, snarling, howling. Above them hang a bobcat on a stump, the head of an elk, a buck, a big-horned sheep, the trophy fish he pulled from the Deschutes River—rainbow trout and Coho salmon mostly—their bodies lacquered, frozen in postures of defiance, struggling against imaginary hooks.

Sometimes, when Jim is hunched over a carcass—sewing up its middle or tucking its lips or repairing its skull plate—the boy will come into the barn. He will study the way Jim neatens a fold of fur and runs a needle and thread through it. And then he will go on to explore the stainless-steel counters and industrial sinks, the mounting stands and arm sockets, the tanning machine, the drawers full of scissors and scalpels and pinning needles and fleshing tools and hook scrapers and water-resistant ID tags. He will open up the wooden cabinet where Jim stores the Duo-fast electric stapler and the HVLP blower. He will count the jugs of formaldehyde and the boxes of latex gloves crowded under the counters. And he will go to the back of the barn and wander through the maze of plywood shelves. Here, in tidy rows marching in every direction, are polyurethane figures labeled as mule deer, elk, pine marten, foxes, grouse, quail, German shepherds, Maltese, all of them looking so naked and horrible. Then there are the prosthetic parts, such as tails, glass eyes, arranged by species. At the back of the studio an insulated door opens with a moaning blast into a small walk-in refrigerator that opens up again into a large walk-in freezer stacked floor-to-ceiling with carcasses— about fifty birds, maybe twenty deer, some of them bound and wrapped and tagged for as long as a year before the skin-stuffing process can begin.

It's here where he keeps the foot.

One night in 'Nam, so long ago now, when he was on a week's stand-down at Chu Lai, he was walking around in bamboo sandals, walking to the radio relay to make a call, when he stepped on a nail that went through his sandal and into his heel. It wasn't a deep wound, but it was deep enough. It got infected. Everything over there got infected. It was the humidity that did it.

He didn't get it treated. There were men taking bullets to the stomach and going yellow from malaria. The war was all around him and more often than not the air seemed to shake from artillery shells exploding in the distance. He couldn't complain about stepping on a nail. But then blackness began to creep through his veins and his fever clocked in at a hundred and seven. His foot looked like the foot of a corpse and the rest of him was catching up. So they sawed it off of him, like a cancer, before it took him over.

And he kept it. He keeps it to this day, stored it in a sealed bucket of formaldehyde. When people ask him why, he says, "I wanted it. It's *me,* you know. It's mine. It's not like a nail clipping or a clump of hair. It's my *foot.*"

He supposes it is his way of never growing old, of living forever, suspending his foot in formaldehyde like a bee trapped in amber.

The foot fascinates the boy. He often asks to see it and when he does Jim will take a break from whatever he is doing and drag out the bucket and peel away the lid. They will peer into its pungent waters and see the foot—hairless, maggot white—floating there with a bit of bone poking from its ankle.

Jim keeps a thirty-pack of Coors in the walk-in fridge and he helps himself to one now, as the boy huddles over the bucket with his hands braced on his knees. Jim joins him there. Their faces reflect off the surface of the formaldehyde, Jim's sliding away now and then to sip from his beer. Its coldness brings a warmth to his belly, and along with it, a sort of sentimental sort of fuzzy feeling. He somehow gets the idea that the foot looks horribly alone, trapped in the big white bucket. When he finishes the beer, rather than crush the empty, he tosses it into the bucket. He snorts, maybe with amusement or sadness or a little of both, when the can slowly fills with formaldehyde and sinks to the bottom. And when the boy looks up at him with a puzzled expression, Jim doesn't really know what to say. "It's evolving," he finally says. "Stuff will go in, stuff will come out. It'll be representative." Like some kind of art. "Got anything you'd like to add?"

The boy considers the question very seriously. His eyebrows come together in concentration and his hands root around in his pockets. From them he withdraws some coins and an agate and a porcupine quill and an arrowhead and a ball of lint. None of this seems to his liking. Then his face brightens and he flees the barn and returns a minute later with the framed photograph of Anne, the one where she holds the trout up to the camera. Jim nods his approval.

In it goes.

When Jim gave the boy the slingshot—a Wrist-Rocket purchased at Bi-Mart—he knew it was only a matter of time before the boy killed something.

Today Jim is on the porch, rocking in a rocking chair. He has a Pendleton blanket wrapped around him and his breath rises from his mouth in little vapor clouds. From the rafters hang a dozen wind chimes he fashioned from the bones of cats. They rattle against the cold breeze that carries in it the aspirin smell of snow. Nearby, steps lead down the porch to a pea-gravel path. To either side of the path spreads a rose garden, a thorny tangle, browned and shriveled from the first frost. To keep the deer away he fences in the garden with the thighbones of elk and bear, their color the gray-white of the cottonwoods that wall off the western edge of the meadow.

Right now the boy marches out of the cottonwoods. Leaves, like gold coins, snow around him. With the slingshot tucked into the waist of his jeans he continues across the thirty yards of cheatgrass and along the gravel path and up the porch steps to stand before Jim in his rocking chair. All this time the boy keeps his right hand behind his back. It isn't until Jim says, "What have you got there?" that he reveals his prize. From his hand, upside down and gripped by its hind leg, dangles a dead chipmunk. A bubble of blood grows out of its mouth, and pops.

"Did you kill that?" Jim asks.

The boy admits he did, his smile failing a little.

With the blanket still around him Jim rises from the rocker and it rocks back and strikes the side of the house. "Then you're going to eat it."

Upon hearing this, the boy releases the chipmunk in surprise. It falls to the porch with a plop. Its posture is that of a dreaming dog, laid out on its side before a hot stove.

There is a leaf in the boy's hair, a cottonwood leaf, golden with November. Jim brushes it away and tells the boy to pick the chipmunk up and to follow him.

Together they walk through the living room and into the kitchen. Here Jim shrugs off the blanket and throws it over a chair. From a drawer he removes a stencil blade and tells the boy to lay down the chipmunk on the butcher block.

He shows the boy how to strip its tiny pelt until it is naked and slick, an infant pink. Together they gut it and bone it and dice up its meat to fry in oil and season with garlic and black pepper. They put it on a plate with a healthy splatter of ketchup and take their seats at the table. With his fork Jim stabs a piece of meat that looks a little like a rubber band, but doesn't eat it. "Do you think we ought to say grace?" he says.

The boy looks at him blankly.

Jim has not prayed in years, not since Anne was a child. His wife had insisted upon it then. But when she moved out she took the habit with her. He does not know why the notion comes to him now, but it does, and it seems right. "I think we ought to. Do you know how?"

The boy brings his hands together, making them into a steeple. He looks to Jim for approval.

"That's right. That's exactly how it's done. Now close your eyes and bow your head and think about all the things you're thankful for."

The boy scrunches his eyes shut. His fingers lace together and the steeple collapses into a white-knuckled sort of fist. And Jim cannot help but wonder what the boy is thinking.

"This is the prayer your mother used to say when she was a little girl. I think it's a pretty good one. It goes like this." Jim closes his eyes and sings in an uncertain tenor, "Come, Lord Jesus, be our guest, and let this food to us be blessed."

The sound of his voice in song surprises him and he opens his eyes and sees that the boy has brought his hands to his forehead, his hands joined so tightly together they tremble.

"Can you remember that?" Jim says. "Let's try to sing it together this time."

And they do.

Later that night Anne calls just as Jim begins brushing his teeth. At the sound of the first ring he spits a blue oyster in the sink and hobbles to the phone and brings it to his ear. He can feel the minty grit of toothpaste, like sand, against his teeth and gums, when she tells him, between damp shuddering breaths, what has happened.

"I don't know what to do," she says. "I don't know what to do, I don't know what to do," repeating this over and over until the words blur together, becoming only series of sounds.

Her boyfriend Dwayne has been drinking whiskey. There is something about whiskey, the way its brownness works through him and brings a wild blistering heat to his temper. A few minutes ago he worked his knuckles across her face until she bled from many places. Now he is outside with a bottle in one hand and a shotgun in the other. He is trying to blast the moon from its black place in the sky and the birdshot is hissing down on the trailer roof and Anne, for the life of her, doesn't know what to do.

Jim tells her to call the police, and when she says she can't—it will only make things worse—he tells her to leave, to come home, and when she says nothing he says it again—"Come home."—and then again, until she begins to stuff her clothes into a duffel bag.

Then his daughter says, "Oh no."

And Jim feels his heart clench when he realizes what he hears: a door slamming shut, footsteps clomping across linoleum, the quickened pace of his daughter's breathing.

There is a rumbling sound—a voice—that sounds like a

chair dragged harshly across hardwood, and in response to it his daughter screams, "You bastard, you asshole, you son of a bitch!"

And Jim continues to listen—to the screaming, the noise of furniture turning over, glass shattering—until the receiver is at last set harshly in its cradle and not for the first time Jim feels that she has gone someplace where he cannot follow.

After midnight, from the living room, with a mug of coffee steaming in his hand, Jim watches headlights appear at the end of his driveway. They grow brighter in their approach. This is his daughter. She is driving the same car she was driving when she left him at eighteen—a rusted-out Cavalier he found listed in the *Bend Bulletin* for two grand. Now she parks it before the garage and clicks on the dome light. He can see her, surrounded by a weak yellow light. She adjusts the rearview mirror and observes her reflection and takes out her compact and reapplies some foundation.

Even from here, even under all that makeup, her eyes are blackened hollows and her face appears sunken, rotten, as if there is already something dead about her.

She gets out of the car and climbs up the porch and Jim opens the door and they look at each other for a long minute. One of her eyes is swollen completely shut. An eggplant purple reaches up her nose. Her upper lip looks like someone took a syringe full of water to it. Looking at her, he feels something inside him stir and roll over, like a log with a rotted underside spotted with pale and squirming grubs. He feels the simultaneous urge to hug her and to yell at her for being such a fool, for getting herself into situation after situation.

Before he can act on either, she says more or less the

same thing she said two weeks ago, and two weeks before that, her words as predictable as the creeping progress of autumn, the failing light, the changing shade of the leaves, the cold winds that come howling down from the mountains.

"He was in a rare mood," she says, her voice dampened as if run through wet cotton. "But I talked to him—I just talked to him on my cell phone actually—and he's better now. He's sorry. He feels really terrible." As if all that rage and drunkenness, burned away like mist under the sun, never existed at all.

Not for the first time Jim feels a vast distance from his daughter's life. It is so unmistakably hers. She destroys it and shapes it as she wishes—her mind busy with decisions he cannot begin to understand—and what he says does not matter, not at all.

And so, when he welcomes his daughter inside, he can only give her a tight-mouthed smile that is like an accusation.

Jim cannot sleep, nor can he stay awake, so he lies in bed, lost somewhere in the black canyon of the night, a place where his daughter's face emerges from the shadows to smile at him, and then to hiss. Muddled voices babble in his head and he more than once mistakes the sound of his own heart as a threat—as the ragged report of an assault rifle, as enemy troops stampeding toward him—and he is seized by a terrible panic where the air feels too warm and thick to breathe, like a sick green jungle fog that fills up his lungs and then his skull.

Near dawn he rolls to the edge of his bed and dangles his legs over the side. The stump of his left leg burns, as it always does in the morning, when he sits upright and the blood wants to go where it cannot. He pulls on the flesh-colored shaft that fits his prosthesis onto his leg. He knocks on it and it makes a hollow noise.

He brews some coffee and eats a banana and goes to the living room and clicks on the television and watches CNN. When it begins to loop through the same footage of Iraqi insurgents firing a rocket launcher at a Marine convoy, he gets up and walks down the hall to the closed door behind which she and the boy sleep.

He opens the door and a wedge of light falls into the room, onto the bed. She is lying on her side, on top of the covers, her back to him, with one arm thrown over the boy. She must hear him because she rolls over. He can see her bad eye, the white gleam of it, surrounded by purple tissue, watching him.

"Can't sleep?" he says.

"You know what it's like when you're totally exhausted," she says, "but your mind keeps going around and around in circles?"

"I know what that's like," he says. "But you don't need to think about any of that right now. Just rest."

He stands on the porch and watches the horizon redden. The redness creeps higher into the black bowl of the sky, taking it over. And then the sun arrives and throws light and shadows across the meadow. With its arrival, the air instantly warms, though not enough to melt the coldness in his stomach.

A low cackling draws his attention skyward, where he spots a flock of geese passing overhead. Their spearhead formation, headed south, seems to suggest that change is possible and necessary.

So he clomps down the porch and moves along the right

fork of the gravel path to where she parked her car. He lays his hand on the hood as if over a slain animal before popping it open. He removes a jackknife from his pocket and thumbs open the blade. It gleams, catching the light. He leans over and locates each spark-plug cable where it enters the engine block at the piston site—and then he slices through them with the same precision as when he slices through a band of cartilage, a knot of ligaments.

Her cell phone has been going off all morning. She has her ringer set to play some sad country song he recognizes from the radio. Sometimes she ignores it and sometimes she answers it, and when she answers it she usually ends the conversation by snapping shut the phone and looking around, as if hunting for a cradle to slam it down on.

They are sitting at the kitchen table, drinking mugs of coffee, his third, her second, while the boy plays in some far corner of the house. The heavy silence between them makes his mouth go dry, so he brings the mug to his lips and drinks. The heat of it, its bitter blackness, burns down his throat, a welcome distraction.

Anne has both hands around her mug, as if she is cold and trying to steal what heat from it she can. The cell phone sits between them, like a big bullet, squared at one end and rounded at the other, gleaming silver.

It comes to life. She is bringing the coffee to her mouth when the noise of the ringer startles her. Coffee spills and races down her wrist. She brings the mug to the table in a hurry and shakes the heat off her hand, hissing through her teeth. She looks at Jim and Jim looks at her. She closes her eyes when she snatches up the phone and brings it to her ear.

Dwayne does most of the talking. Jim cannot hear what

he is saying, but he can hear the changes in pitch and volume, the whines that interrupt the growls.

"All right," his daughter eventually says. A pause, and then: "I said *all right*, Dwayne, all right?" She snaps shut the phone and bangs it softly against her forehead a few times.

"Everything okay?"

"Yes." With the back of her hand she roughs a tear from her eye. "No."

"Maybe I should talk to him."

"*No*. Not on your life." She holds the phone away from him as if he planned to grab it from her. "I can take care of myself."

"You and I both know that's not true."

Again her phone chirps to life. Before she can answer it Jim stands and walks to where his daughter sits and grabs her wrist and squeezes it until she releases the phone into his other hand.

"Don't answer it," she says. "Please, please, please don't answer it."

He walks from the kitchen, through the living room, the front door—in his slow clomping way—out onto the porch. The phone continues to ring and fill up the morning with its shrill song. He adjusts the weight of it in his hand and in a windmill motion pitches it across a good thirty yards of meadow to where it strikes a tree and shatters into many silvery pieces.

His daughter screams *no* and grabs at his arm and he turns and sets his gaze on her with such force that she lets him go and begins to cry freely. "I need to get out of here," she says and brings her hands to her face. "I need to go home."

He is surprised by the severity of his voice when he says,

"This *is* home." He points to the porch for emphasis. "*This* is home."

Thirty minutes later Jim is sitting on the couch and the boy is sprawled out on the floor, coloring in his coloring book. The fire is going, a fresh log recently set over the flames hissing and shuddering as the water inside it boils out.

The *Today Show* is on and the camera is trained on an anthropologist with a peppery beard who wears his glasses perched at the end of his nose. His new book has just come out and he is talking about it, about men and the fine line that separates them from beasts. One of his chapters is about New York in the late 1980s. He refers to this time as "The Wilding" and he tells Katie in a solemn voice about the mobs of men who haunted Central Park, their dark shapes scarcely glimpsed between the trees like wolves ranging for food. He talks about the female jogger who was attacked and raped, whose skull was crushed in.

Jim lowers the volume when his daughter emerges from her bedroom, her duffel bag in hand. She crouches next to the boy and pets his head before kissing the top of it. "Mommy is going to go now," she says. "She'll miss you."

The boy does not stop coloring. If anything his crayon moves faster, disregarding the lines on the page, making red everywhere.

Anne stands then and runs her hand through her hair, pulling it back to study Jim with her bruised face fully revealed. The swelling has gone down and the bruises at first glance appear black, but have actually taken on the deeper, greener color of a horsefly. "If things aren't okay, I'll come back. Okay?"

Jim doesn't nod or say okay, as she might read that as

some kind of approval. He only lets his eyebrows rise a little on his forehead to acknowledge he heard her.

And so she leaves them—only to return a few minutes later, her footsteps pounding roughly on the porch before the door swings open. She rushes through it. "My goddamn car won't start." She throws down her duffel with a thump and holds out her hands, palms up. "It won't even make a goddamn noise."

"Huh," Jim says.

"It's like it's completely dead. It won't even make a sound."

"Weird."

"Well. Are you just going to sit there? Or are you going to give me a jump?"

He holds out his hand and says, "Help an old man up."

Outside the sky is a wash of pale blue with a few cirrus clouds interrupting it, the clouds so thin and white, like fish bones.

His truck is parked beside her car, each of their hoods propped open with cables running between them and clipped onto their batteries. He has put on a good show for her, cranking the key, staring with concentration at the engine.

He is leaning under the hood when she creeps up next to him and tucks her hair behind her ears so she can see what he sees. "Any ideas?"

With his thumbnail he scrapes some black crud off the carburetor. "Far as I can tell everything looks all right."

She makes a fist and brings it down on the battery. "I wonder what's wrong with the stupid thing."

"It's an old car. It was an old car when you bought it."

"I guess." She blows a sigh out of her nose. "This is the last thing I need."

"We'll take it into the shop tomorrow."

"Tomorrow? *Today.*"

He unclips the cables from the battery. "Today I'm going to take you fishing."

She retreats from him. "Dad. No. I need to get back to Dwayne."

"The hell you do. You're staying right here. And we're all going fishing. You and me and the boy."

"His name is Cody."

"I know what his name is."

Every week Jim excises the bones from animals and tosses them into a twenty-gallon garbage can. And every week he drags the garbage can from its corner of the taxidermy studio and straps it to his Gator—a glorified golf cart with six wheels and a diesel engine—and drives the hundred yards into the woods to the bone pile.

There are thirty years of bones in the bone pile. Skulls of all sizes, of elk and deer and bear and dogs and cats and birds, all of them with shadowy eye sockets and hairline fissures zigzagging along them. Crows have picked apart the spines into individual vertebrae, hollow white cups the rain runs through. Chipmunks scurry among the slatted rib cages. And there are pelvises, broken antlers, thighbones gnawed in half by coyotes hungry for the marrow. The pile reaches ten feet high in its center and stretches thirty feet wide.

This is what they drive by, when they huddle together in the Gator, on their way to the river, the Deschutes River, which rushes and purls through the eastern edge of his property. His daughter sits beside him and the boy sits behind them, in the bed of the Gator, among the poles, the cooler and thermos and tackle box. They follow a dirt road, rutted and washed out from so many years of snowmelt. They rattle across dry creek bottoms where the hoarfrost remains in the shadows and hollows. Pines loom all around them, and every now and then they duck their heads to dodge a low-hanging branch, as they twist deeper and deeper into the forest and finally arrive at the river.

Some twenty feet wide, the river here crashes into a basalt wall and elbows off at a forty-degree angle. They park at the crook of the elbow. The roar of the water fills up the forest and becomes the only sound after Jim kills the engine and they step from the Gator and stand on the bank and watch the river hurry over boulders. The force of its passage makes the water white and makes the air misty with tiny droplets that swim in the streams of sunlight pouring through the branches of the trees around them.

Jim hands the boy a pole and the boy takes it and holds it out before him and slashes at the air, as if brandishing a sword. The weights loop around the pole, tangling the leader. The boy looks at Jim with a frightened expression as if he expects a knuckled fist to come down on him.

But Jim only shakes his head and says, "You know better than that." He takes back the pole and goes to work untangling the monofilament. "When's the last time you been fishing?"

Anne answers for him: "Whenever it was you took him last."

It's been nearly a year. Since she moved in with Dwayne their visits have been so short, so infrequent, they have little time for anything but a meal, a lazy conversation on the porch, before night falls and morning comes and they pack up their toothbrushes and dirty laundry and follow the Santiam Pass back the way they came.

Jim looks at his daughter directly when he says, "A boy ought to go fishing."

Now the pole is ready and he leads the boy to the river where glacial till lines the bank and makes a chewing sound beneath their boots. He props himself against a log and the boy stands next to him, listening as Jim explains in a fatherly voice the bright-colored rooster-tail spinner, how the current will pull it and make it twirl, how the fish will hurry toward it like moths to flame. He further explains that fall is one of the best times for fishing, as the trout are aggressively trying to fatten up for the winter. Then he asks the boy, if he were a fish, where would he hide—and the boy studies the river a moment before pointing to a fallen pine that interrupts the current. Here the water is still and dark and quiet, separate from the nearby violence of whitewater, and maybe the boy sees in it something that reminds him of the place beneath his bed, the back of his closet.

Jim wraps his arms around the boy and knits together their fingers so that when they cast they cast as one—and the line sizzles—and the lure travels in a long arc before entering the river with a plunk, just above where the water eddies, where the current will take it and spin it.

"Now I'm going to let go and let you take it. If you feel a little tug, give a little tug. And if you feel big pull, hold on tight."

It's cold here, next to the river. The spray dampens their skin and their hair. They pull on wool caps and drink hot cocoa from the thermos. They stamp their feet and bring their hands to their mouths and blow into the cup of them, thawing them. Jim can particularly feel the cold in his stump, where the blood wants to go. There is an itching, needling sensation there, as if several dozen mosquitoes have suckered onto him at once.

His daughter has hiked a short distance upriver to fish. She gives a shout now, barely heard over the noise of the rapids. She has a strike. Her feet are spread apart and her pole is bent into a parabola. She alternates between pulling back and lowering her pole, like Jim taught her to, reeling immediately after lowering the pole, when the fish has moved toward the sudden slackness of the line.

Jim hurries, as best he can, along the riverbank to help his daughter net the fish. It's a Dolly Varden, a seventeen-, maybe nineteen-incher. Pulled from the dark water its belly is as pale as a tuber pulled from the black soil of a garden.

"That's a wall-hanger all right," Jim says and grips the fish—the cold slippery muscle of it—and rips the hook from its mouth. The fish flaps violently in his hand. He takes out his knife and clubs it on the back of the head, once, and then again. Blood comes out of its eyes. Its body goes still. He hands it to his daughter. "That's definitely a wall-hanger."

In her hand the fish comes alive again, with a twitch of its fins, a spasm of its tail. Water droplets fly off it and catch the light before returning to the river or dampening her shirt. Then it is done.

And something happens. Jim is filled with a sense of well-being he doesn't want to let go of—and she must feel it too. Because she's smiling at him. Smiling so broadly that she opens up the scab binding her bottom lip. Even as blood begins to come out of it, red trailing down her chin, she continues to smile.

Late afternoon, he stands in his taxidermy studio, alone. The fluorescent lights buzz hungrily above him. He can smell the fish, gutted earlier, puffing off his skin. And he can see a scale fused to the fabric of his sleeve. It winks at him under the light when he dismantles the Colt revolver and set its parts on the stainless-steel counter before him.

His hands look like the knuckly oak trees common in

the western half of Oregon, but they move with surprising deftness, moving between the bottle of solvent, the bottle of lubricating oil, the cleaning rod and silicone cloth and bore brush, swabbing and scrubbing, preparing the gun.

All this time he whistles.

Then he reaches under the counter and his hand slides through the jugs of formaldehyde until he finds what he is looking for, pulling out a half-empty bottle of Jack Daniel's. He takes the bore of the revolver and stops up its bottom with his finger. Then he pours whiskey into it and brings the muzzle to his lips and drinks. He licks the spice off his teeth and begins to put the Colt back together again.

This is what he tells his daughter:

"Ernie Nelson—you remember Ernie?—the old guy with the beard and the palomino horses?—used to ref basketball?—he just shot an elk at the bottom of a canyon. Big sucker, so he says. Six-point. I'm going to go help him haul it out."

He is standing in the shadows of the hallway and she is sitting on the couch with the boy in her lap, watching *Jeopardy* on the TV. She looks distractedly at him and then returns her attention to the screen. "I didn't hear the phone ring," she says.

"Well," he says. "It rang." Next to him hangs a hat rack, every knob the polished end of an antler. He selects a hat from it, the camouflaged hat he wears bow hunting. He runs his ponytail through the hole above the plastic snap-band when fitting the hat snugly on his head.

With her eyes still on the screen she says, "I thought we were going to watch a movie."

"You go on and watch it without me." He has a backpack

slung around his shoulder and he adjusts its weight when he starts across the living room, to the door. "Have fun."

"What is a gargoyle?" his daughter says at an almost scream.

Jim freezes, his hand halfway to the doorknob. "Pardon?"

On television one of the contestants rings in and says, "What is a gargoyle," and Alex Trebek says, "That's correct. Which puts Steven into the lead by four hundred dollars."

At that his daughter pumps her fist in the air and the boy readjusts in her lap so that he can observe her. On his face is a look of wonder, his eyes big and soft, as if his mom is the smartest person in the world. It's a look Jim recognizes and misses, a look absent from his daughter when she settles her gaze on him now with worried disapproval.

"Doesn't this Ernie guy have a son? Somebody else?"

"He called me, so I suppose I'm it." Her eyes weigh so heavily on him that he suspects he will fly when he gets out of her sight. "Don't wait up. He's way up in the foothills, past Black Butte. We might make a night of it, depending on the how fast we butcher and how cold it gets"

"You're getting too old for this kind of stuff, Dad."

He settles his hand on the knob and turns it. "I'm going to go help," he whispers, a hurt in the whisper. He steps outside, where the sun has disappeared and the trees and the meadow are lost in gray shadows.

On the Santiam Pass, the pines change over to firs and the road grows steeper and the snow piles higher along the shoulder. It is blackened with exhaust and scalloped from the constant wind that makes Jim correct his course with little jerks of the steering wheel. Here and there, draped over the guardrail or glimpsed among the roadside firs, deer lie in misshapen postures of death, some of them split in two by the grills of semis. His eyes jog back and forth, scanning the darkness beyond the reach of his headlights, ready for something to come scuttling toward him.

The farther he drives the more the world seems to narrow around him—the blackness of the sky bearing down—so that it feels as if he is hurtling along a dark conduit. He maintains his concentration on the road while at the same time drifting off to some dreamlike place where the puzzle pieces of his life are rearranged for the better, like the bones of a broken animal he might cast together with screws and glue.

Two hours pass in the black blur of an instant. And then his right signal is flashing. And he realizes he has to follow it, exiting near Turner. The moon has risen and he can see the surrounding countryside: the gray-lit pastures, the silhouettes of Holsteins, barbed-wire fences, and beyond all this, in the distance, the glow of Salem and the steady stream of cars on the interstate heading toward it.

He has been here once before, to pick up the boy. The trailer sits off the road a ways, down a long winding driveway bordered by blackberry vines and thistle. He drives slowly past it and after fifty yards hangs a right down a dirt road that opens up into a clearing next to the river. There isn't another house in sight. A pyramid of half-burned logs and the scattered litter of beer cans and potato-chip bags reveal this as one of those secluded areas where teenagers come to drink and smoke and screw. A pair of panties hangs from a nearby thatch of willows. Spent cigarette lighters catch the moonlight and glow like iridescent beetles.

He kills the engine. Even though his leg, the stump of it, aches from sitting too long, he remains in the truck with his hands on the wheel and his seat belt fastened around his chest. For a time he watches the constellations wheel above him, and then the windows fog over with his breath. Without anything to look at but his hands, their white-knuckled grip around the steering wheel, he feels more fully, awkwardly aware of himself, forced into conversation with the backpack beside him, the gun inside of it.

So he unbuckles his seat belt and pushes open the door and steps into the night. The air is cool and damp, so different than the thin dry air he is accustomed to breathing. It makes him feel as if he is drinking, drowning a little, with each breath. The river hisses nearby. White wisps of mist trail along it.

He waits another thirty minutes. During this time nothing makes a sound, nor moves, except a great horned owl that swoops past him with a huff of its wings and is gone.

He unzips the backpack and withdraws the gun and holds it before him. It seems heavier, somehow, than he remembers it. Its metal gleams blue. Its chamber gives off the faint smell of whiskey. And he is moving toward the river, following the trail trampled along it. The mist, thicker now, creeps through the cattails and gropes for his legs and in his passing swirls and rearranges itself.

His prosthetic comes down stiffly and regularly as he makes his way toward the trailer, its noise out of place in the cool still night, clocklike in the way it ominously ticks off his approach. And he can see now, through the moss-laden trees, the glow where the trailer will be, though not yet the trailer.

Then he sees it. The windows are squares of flickering light cast by the television. Jim waits a minute and when he sees no movement starts forward.

This is one of those luxury trailers—if you could call it

that—a double-wide with a lawn that Jim walks across and a porch that he climbs up and a sliding-glass door he approaches and slides aside. The air has an electric snap to it. A sulfur smell teases around his nostrils.

He is standing in the living room. There is a green loveseat and a vine-patterned couch and a big-screen television tuned in to CMT. Alan Jackson is singing about the Chattahoochee, how it gets hotter than a hootchy-kootchy. The living room runs into a dining area that runs into the wood-paneled kitchen dark with shadows. The only light comes from the TV and from the moonlight streaming in the windows.

Jim notices Dwayne maybe a dozen feet away from him. He sits at a Formica table with peeling edges. He is as dim as a ghost in the blue shade of moonlight. He has a bottle of Miller High Life in one hand and a cigarette in the other. His eyes are closed and his chin rests against his chest. His cigarette is a long red ash crumbling onto the table.

Jim carefully closes the door behind him and moves across the living room to where the carpet gives way to linoleum the color of an old man's teeth. Here he stops and studies Dwayne. He has a thin wiry body and a square-shaped face and a thick broom of a mustache. The mustache has a bead of beer or sweat dangling from one of its hairs. It is odd to see him like this. For so long he has been faceless, bodiless, a dark nebulous force, like a storm cloud that occasionally descends upon his daughter.

His head appears loose on its hinges when he raises it to look at Jim. His eyes are too close together, muddy with drink and confusion. "Who're you?" he says.

There is a shaft of blue moonlight hanging between the two of them. Cigarette smoke ribbons through it. And through the haze Dwayne looks at Jim like he can't quite figure out if he's dreaming or not.

Jim raises the gun. His finger fits over the trigger but doesn't pull.

Right then Dwayne seems to mimic him, raising his own hand, the one with the cigarette pinched in it. He brings it to his mouth. Its ember burns bright when he drags a breath from it. That hand. Jim imagines what it has done and remembers the misery that defined his daughter's voice when she called the other night.

"Who," Dwayne says with the anger rising in his voice. "What the hell are you—"

"Shh," Jim says. And pulls the trigger.

He experiences, in these long subsequent seconds, between the time when the trigger gives and the hammer falls and the revolver jumps with the force of a bullet discharged, a dangling sensation, like the cartoon characters experience when they discover they have stepped off the edge of a cliff, that instant of weightlessness, suspension in time, before the world comes crashing down.

Dwayne watches the bullet blast toward him and screws up his face to absorb it. A softball-size portion of his skull comes off and strikes the wall behind him with a red and gray splatter. He slumps back in his chair and his beer tips over and gurgles across the table in a foaming rush. His mouth gapes open, as if frozen around a silent scream. From it trails a thin ribbon of smoke.

Jim can smell the harsh familiar scent of gunpowder.

It's the smell that defined his time in the 33rd Aviation. He would fly troops out of Manila and drop them off at the Port of Saigon or Cam Ranh Bay in a CV-2 Caribou. When the troops got off, the bodies got on. The bodies were zipped into black bags. Some of the bags were bigger than others and some of them would leak through their zippers. There would be stacks and stacks of them. And there would be a smell coming from them, the rottenness brought on by humidity. It got into your clothes and hair, like cigarette smoke, so badly that a Saigon whore once refused him until he showered, and even then she kept her face turned away.

His entire adult life he has been surrounded by dead things. That is how he saw the black-bagged bodies and that is how he sees the animals he drains and peels and dries and refigures—as dead things. Dwayne is now one, too. The sight of him creates no more emotional effect in Jim than the sight of an elk with steam rising from the bullet wound in its ribs, like smoke from a secret chimney.

He goes to Dwayne and nudges him forward and his body slumps onto the table and some redness joins the yellowness of the beer. With some difficulty Jim digs the wallet from his back pocket, then goes down the hallway to the bedroom and empties his daughter's jewelry case. He shoves the tangle of necklaces and rings into his pocket and opens up all the drawers and throws clothes all over the place.

With a damp dishtowel he wipes his fingerprints off everything he has touched. On the television the country song comes on, the one playing from his daughter's phone, and he pauses in his cleaning to watch. On the screen a weathered Johnny Cash hunches over a piano, singing about hurt.

Jim heads outside, back down the porch, to the lawn, following the dark strip of grass where earlier his feet swept away the dew. The jewelry goes in the river, along with the wallet, but not before he removes the cash from it—a tenner, some ones—to buy the boy some candy on his way home.

Midnight has come and gone by the time he gets home. His daughter has left the porch light on for him. A long time ago, he vaguely remembers, he would come back from the tavern and find the light on and stumble up the porch and crawl into bed and seek out his wife beneath the sheets, her naked body warm and soft, but that was a long time ago. Now he stares at the light so long its afterimage remains in his eyes after he closes them.

He goes directly to the pole barn. The fluorescent lights sputter to life above him when he heads to the back of the studio and withdraws from the fridge the bucket of formaldehyde and unpeels its lid. The smell of stale blood and old fur and powdered latex vanish, replaced by something ammoniac. His eyes immediately water from it.

Alongside his severed foot float the remains of the photograph. The formaldehyde has leached his daughter from the photo paper and flecks of her hang along the top of the bucket and maybe in one fleck he sees what looks like a mouth, smiling or snarling at him, it's hard to tell.

The revolver is shoved into his pants, just above his crotch, and he removes it now and dangles it above the bucket a moment before releasing it. It descends to the bottom of the bucket and knocks against the beer can and photo frame, making a muted clicking noise like some deadly underwater creature.

He seals the bucket and hoists it up and it makes a sloshing sound with his every step. Next to the pole barn is a carport where he stores the Gator. He straps the bucket down in its bed with bungee cords. He throws in a shovel and fires up the engine and starts toward the forest. The moon makes a milky circle on the hood that slides up and up and vanishes in his lap as he follows the weed-ridden trail to the bone pile.

The engine coughs off and a hush falls over the forest. No frogs drum, no crickets chirp. Frost sparkles across the browned bear grass and the bones in the bone pile give off the kind of pale blue light found in sunlit ice.

He digs a hole as deep as his waist and lowers the bucket into it and after returning the dirt to the hole he neatens it with his hand and sprinkles some pine needles here and there. Then he pulls some bones down from the pile to cover the place where the dirt has been disturbed.

Part of this, but not all of this, has to do with evidence.

Afterwards, he sits on the bumper of the Gator, his old muscles aching, his legs painted with dirt. He can feel the moon looking down on him, through the branches, but he keeps his eyes on the forest, on a possum, already shaggy-coated for winter, climbing the trunk of a nearby tree.

"I'm looking at you," the moon seems to say, even as he avoids the white unblinking gaze of it, watching instead the possum race along a branch and execute a clumsy leap into a neighboring pine, where it hisses an evil-sounding song.

He stops breathing for a moment and then starts again when the forest shifts in whispers, when the air trembles into a breeze that rises into a cold wind.

Outside the sky, red with morning, is clotted with clouds. For the past thirty minutes his eyes have traced their passage. He can see them from where he lies in bed, on top of the covers, still wearing the clothes he wore last night. He can smell the smell of earth coming off them.

His daughter is awake. He listens to the noises she makes—the muffled roar of the shower, the clatter of a spoon in a cereal bowl, the babble of morning television. The boy soon joins her, his feet pounding up and down the hallway, his voice high and lovely.

If Jim closes his eyes, if he concentrates hard enough, he can imagine himself out of bed, out there, among them. He will read his newspaper and fold it precisely with every turn of the page. He will sip from a mug of coffee—the coffee steaming in his hand like a gun recently fired—until it is just porcelain against his teeth. And his daughter will splash it full of coffee again. And she will cook him eggs, over hard. And the boy will ask him a question and he will answer with a gruffness that belies the smile tugging at the corner of his lips.

Then his eyes snap open and the dream falls apart. There is an engine outside, growing louder, coming up the driveway. A police cruiser, he feels suddenly certain. And all at once, with a panicked gasp that sounds like a pile of logs collapsing into embers, he is thinking about all the things he doesn't want to think about.

Last night, he must have left something behind—maybe a fingerprint they traced back to his military records—some obvious clue that brings the police to him now. In a panic he rolls over and jumps out of bed. With that first step there is a vanishing beneath him, as if his foot has slipped through the floor. He has forgotten to reattach his prosthesis—and his naked stump comes down painfully against the hardwood. He staggers forward and catches himself against the dresser.

It takes him another minute to fit his stump into its slot, to loop the bands over their hooks—and by this time there are footsteps on the porch, a knock at the door. He hurries out of his bedroom and limps down the hallway and yells, "I got it!"

But his daughter has already answered the door. The latch clicks and her voice calls out, "Hello," at once a greeting and question.

Just then Jim rounds the corner. He expects to see, in the doorway, surrounded by sunlight, two uniformed officers. He is certain of it. He can already picture them lazily chewing their gum, their hands near their holsters. But no.

It's Ernie. Ernie Nelson. Of all people *he's* the one standing there, smiling kindly at his daughter. His NASCAR cap is in his hands. His beard is stained yellow around the mouth from his incessant smoking. It's been a long time—nine years since Anne played guard for the Mountain View Mountain Lions, since Ernie ran up and down the court in a striped shirt and blew his whistle and made authoritative arm gestures indicating a jump ball, double dribble—but they recognize each other and exchange an awkward handshake along with their Good-to-see-yous.

"So how'd it go last night?" she says.

"Sorry?" he says. "Last night?"

"That elk you shot. Getting it out of that canyon."

Ernie smiles blankly at her before saying again, "Not sure what you mean."

Before she can respond Jim pushes his way between them. "Ernie!" he says. "Glad you stopped by!" His words come out with too much spit and he wears a smile not connected to his eyes.

"I was driving by and thought, what the heck, I'll stop in and ask him about that salmon—"

"Sure, sure, sure." He takes Ernie by the elbow and begins to lead him down the porch. "Let's talk in the studio. I'll show you what I'm up to."

They're halfway down the steps when Anne calls out, "The elk you shot, Ernie. The elk you shot last night."

Jim tries to urge Ernie forward without success, as his friend stops and turns and says over his shoulder, "I'm sorry but I just don't have the slightest—"

"Ernie," Jim says.

"It's just that I haven't been hunting—"

"Ernie."

"Not since my knee replacement."

Hearing this Anne doesn't so much blink as snap shut her eyes. "Oh," she says and settles her gaze on Jim. "I must have mixed you up with somebody else."

Jim says, "Come on now, Ernie."

They move along the pea-gravel path. Their footsteps make crunching sounds that sound like coyotes gnawing through bones "What's she talking about anyhow?" Ernie asks.

"It's like she said. She's confused."

"I should come back some other time?"

"No. Don't you pay any attention to that."

"You're sure?" Ernie fits his cap back on his head and rounds the brim with his hands. "Everything's okay?"

"More than okay." Jim thumps him on the back and sends him in the direction of the pole barn. "You go on ahead. I'll catch up with you. The Coho should be on your left, on the counter. I'm about halfway through with her."

Ernie runs a hand through his beard—and a smile appears there, like a card suddenly sprung from a magician's fingers. "She's a beauty, isn't she?"

"She is."

Ernie starts toward the barn and Jim starts back toward the house and as he does the shadow of a cloud passes darkly over the meadow. He flinches and looks up as if he discerns in its shifting shape some enormous sharp-taloned bird that will swoop down on him. But it only drops a few snowflakes before hurrying on to someplace else. All around him the flakes melt and leave behind damp freckles, like a spattering of tears, on the soil.

He keeps his eyes on the ground before him until he reaches the top step of the porch and finally faces his daughter.

"You want to tell me what's going on?" she says.

He holds up his hands, palms up, as if to say *don't shoot.* Her eyes focus in on them and her eyebrows come together. He notices his fingernails, how the cracks that crisscross his knuckles and palms are scabbed over with a reddish dirt that looks more than a little like blood.

He hurries them into his pockets and feels something there—the Snickers bar he bought last night from the gas station. "I got something here," he says and removes the candy bar from his pocket and holds it out before him. "Something for Cody."

She lets his hand hang there without acknowledging it. Her mouth purses around a question she hasn't yet figured out how to phrase. Her eyes are probing his. Her eyes are midnight blue and he sees the remnants of last night reflected in them.

And they, father and daughter, look at each other, they simply look at each other, with Jim standing on one side of the doorway and Anne standing on the other, with the clouds coming together in the sky above them, bringing a dark color to the air.

Meltdown

Meltdown

November 23, 2009 was a bad day. At 8:00 p.m., the crew at Oregon's Trojan Nuclear Power Plant—in accordance with new antiterror legislation, in response to recent al-Qaeda threats—ran a test to see how long the turbines would spin if their electrical supply vanished. Not long, it turns out. Within twenty minutes everything went off-line, including the automatic-shutdown safety mechanisms.

At quarter past eight, the coolant water stopped altogether, the heat increased sharply, and Trojan's managing operator, Rick Townsend, decided to do something about it. He brought the system back online and in doing so caused a sharp power surge, caused a steam explosion, caused the nuclear-containment vessel's 2,000-ton cap to dissolve. Just like that.

Air rushed in, igniting the graphite insulating blocks. Three hundred control rods melted, along with Rick Townsend, and the plant's radioactive core lit up the night sky, replacing the stars with a cranberry glow.

Soon thereafter the president declared the Pacific Northwest, and then the West Coast, and then the Upper Midwest, in a state of emergency. Parades and bowl games and turkey dinners across the country did not happen. Giving thanks was the last thing on people's minds as they drove as fast and as far away as they could, or moved underground, or flew to other countries for extended vacations, afraid of the deadly thing they could not see, could not smell, could not feel, many of them dying weeks later when the poison completed its slow crawl through their system.

You can never really extinguish graphite once it starts to burn. Fourteen days and 20,000 tons of sand, water, clay, and boron later, the fire was controlled, but not out. During this time a hot wind blew east and spiked the atmospheric radiation as far away as Maine.

Five years pass and five million people are dead, the fire is still smoldering, and Darren Townsend, on his Harley Night Train, rips along the mostly abandoned roads of Oregon and Washington with a Geiger counter strapped between his handlebars.

Though radiation will stick to the Pacific Northwest for the next 50,000 years—the government says—give Mother Earth another 1,000 to heal, to purge and dilute the most dangerous elements, and humans can safely begin repopulating the area. In the meantime—the government says—*stay out.*

Darren could care less what the government says.

He gave eight years to the Army. Right after 9/11 he dropped out of Portland State and enlisted—and because the government told him to, he killed men and women and children, some of them by accident, some on purpose. He remembers sending mortar shell after mortar shell into a Fallujah apartment complex believed to house Shiite insurgents. He remembers walking through the chalky debris afterwards, the stone shifting beneath his feet, the body parts rising from the rubble like weird plants. He remembers the flies crawling across the faces of the dead, and then lighting on his own face, near his eyes and mouth, to taste him. If he had not been in Iraq, doing what the government told him to do, tiptoeing around booby traps, dodging bearded men screaming *yi-yi-yi-yi* with plastic explosives strapped to their bellies, maybe by some twist of fate his father, Rick, wouldn't have been at Trojan that night—maybe they would have been sharing a beer or picking out a turkey instead—and then maybe none of this would have ever happened.

Darren doesn't know why he drives 70, 80, 90 mph, the road moving away beneath him as he slaloms past the potholes and abandoned cars, bones—he only knows he likes the way the air whips around him, his body bulleting through its gusts, just as he likes the sting of the occasional hail pellet and yellow jacket splatting his face. Anything that wakes him up, even for a second, he likes.

When he tucks his body into his bike and when he slides along so fast the world becomes indistinct, just a blur of colors, he feels a sense of freedom like a great heaviness shed, and it is as if he is rising off the road, into the pale empty sky, flying.

The noise of traffic, laughter, Muzak trembling from shopping-center sound systems, all of it gone, leaving behind a scary silence that seems to tell him something he strains to hear: life is everywhere and it is nowhere.

Coyotes slink through the aisles of Safeway. Elk engage in rut-combat in Portland's Pioneer Courthouse Square, their horns locked together beneath the vine-choked billboards. In the fields and in the streets are semis and tanks and planes, rust-cratered and woolly with grass, looking like dinosaurs, fallen and decaying, the remnants of some lost existence that no longer matters.

The Dead Zone—as the media has branded it—reminds Darren of *Thundarr the Barbarian,* that old Hanna-Barbera cartoon about a postapocalyptic world where men, the left-over men, become barbarians, their life reduced to fighting beasts, scavenging the abandoned and moss-laden cities. As a child, as a teenager, even as an adult, on the Cartoon Network, Darren enjoyed *Thundarr* for the what-if possibility, dreaming of the day this world—of carbohydrates, of Michael Jackson, of 0% introductory APRs, of turf-eating golf spikes, of laws and contracts and bills that in their collective choke-collar feel more constrictive than all the prisons in the world—would end.

Now, in the summer of 2015, more than five years after the meltdown, that world still exists, elsewhere. Sometimes he considers returning to it—using his veteran status to land a post-office or law-enforcement gig, putting aside some cash, getting married, raising brown-haired athletic children—but only sometimes. Just after he and most everyone else got yanked from the mess in Iraq to clean up the mess at home, he tried that life and didn't like it.

His first assignment: to manage a Texas tent city, one of hundreds of thousands set up to accommodate the newly homeless and to quarantine the newly infected, many of them covered in sores and vomiting blood. Then the dead bodies started piling up. Then the riots started. For obvious reasons he hated it there, but it was a less obvious reason that made him leave. The Texas sky. With no mountains to interrupt it, he felt blotted out, weighted down by its enormous size.

He requested a transfer into toxic cleanup, and got it. It

was the assignment no one wanted. They sent him home, to Oregon, to the place from which everyone else had fled, to join over 100,000 liquidators already there. That's what the Army called the microbiologists and doctors and botanists and cleanup and construction crews: the liquidators. Many of them—some 10,000—have since died from radiation poisoning, the gamma-ray intensity and the long-term exposure about as healthy as a shot of mercury to the jugular.

In a radiation suit straight out of Buck Rogers, Darren helped construct a chain-link barbed-wire perimeter, nearly five thousand miles of it, and then manned its checkpoints with a dosimeter crew, keeping the curious and the crazies and the Mexicans out, treating with chemical showers all those who traveled within. He liked the work and he liked how the world felt empty here—how he felt like the only man alive—especially in the half-light of dawn, when he got up before everybody else and could hear a coyote munching on a field mouse from a half-mile away.

At this time there was a girl, Katie.

Darren was not a bad-looking man, and before—before the world turned upside down—if he was at a bar, sitting at a booth with his buddies, and the right kind of song came on the juke, the girls with moisture shining in their cleavage would single him out to dance. Katie was a private under his command. She had that special shade of hair, sometimes red and sometimes brown, depending on the light. Back in high school he might have ignored her, called her plain, but out here, in the zone, with nothing but men and wild dogs to keep him company, Katie was beautiful.

Now he thinks of her often, the hard bud of her body, her West Virginia drawl like a mouthful of honey, their conversations about everything—about love, for instance. "I love my family," Darren said, "but I don't think I've ever been *in* love. Like, movie love. Like, can't-think-straight head-over-heels love."

In the barracks, in his private quarters, a square concrete cell with a sink and a bed and a bookshelf, she laid on top of him, naked, so small he often joked about putting her in his mouth like a piece of candy. She had an ear to his chest so she could listen to his heart. "Everybody always says they want life to be like in the movies," she said and combed her fingers through his chest hair. "Now it is. Now life is like a movie. But it's the *wrong* movie."

He said, "You said it," but he wasn't really listening. He was too busy with his own thoughts, all mangled in his brain like a snarl of junk metal. He understood love as a theory, but he could not grasp it as fact. He ran a finger up her spine, into her hair, then back down to her lumbar vertebrae, where her shoulders narrowed into her neck. He circled the spot and she hummed and said, "I like that."

He wanted to say, "You shouldn't," but didn't. This circle he traced was a sort of bull's-eye. Here you put your knife if you wanted to paralyze someone. As much as it horrified him, every part of her body he considered both a soft, curved, perfumed thing—and a target. Which gave him a sick feeling at the bottom of his heart he recognized as both the beginnings of love and the opposite of it.

"Sometimes," he said. "Sometimes I feel like I've got this filter, and all the stuff that's supposed to go in and out, between the world and me, it gets muffled."

He had never told anyone this before, but it was true. He didn't know whether it was Iraq or the Trojan meltdown, or both, but physically, emotionally, he hadn't felt anything in a long time. This loss of desire and direction, this mixed-up mood, was maybe why he had returned to Oregon, seeking some source he could shoot with his gun or stomp beneath his boot or blast with a chemical shower.

His heart had all but disappeared into a dark corner of his chest, a tiny flickering speck, and Katie, to give her credit, tried to fan its ember, to purse her lips and blow it into a spark. But when his enlistment ran out, so did he, retreating into the Dead Zone.

When she asked him *why*, he said, "To figure some stuff out. Just for a little while." She shook her head, but didn't question him further, and he appreciated that.

That was three months ago and in one of their FMTVs, a five-ton tactical truck, she drove him and his duffel bag beyond the perimeter, to Ashland, to a Harley dealer he had spotted during one of their Geiger surveys. He broke its window with a rock and stood there with the glass all around him like the thousand jagged and glittery possibilities waiting for him in the zone. Before he stepped inside, he turned to look at her, where she waited in the idling truck.

"Well," he said. "That's that." He blew her a kiss.

"Missed," she yelled, like he was far away, not ten feet from her—and then, unsmiling, she drove away and left him there.

He first fell in love with motorcycles back in high school, when a biker gang showed up at a football kegger. On the porch Darren was kissing one of the cheerleaders, hoping to take things one step further, upstairs maybe, when a great bunch of noise announced a dozen Harleys grumbling up the street, over the curb, onto the lawn, revving their engines in quick bursts so they peeled away the grass beneath them. For a good minute they circled, blasting their motors, making mud scars on the sod, until they knew their presence was known.

Then their engines clattered quiet and they sat there, not saying anything, just grinning.

The football team huddled together and tried to look tough, but that was it, nobody had the guts to say anything when the leathery tattooed men clomped up the porch, into the house, the kitchen, finding there the keg. They filled their plastic cups and drank them and hoisted up the Michelob half-barrel and hauled it outside, dumping it in a sidecar. Then they left as they came, loudly.

"A loner on a Harley?" Katie said when Darren told her where he wanted to get dropped off. "Isn't that kind of cliché?"

"Yeah," he said. "But it's my kind of cliché."

All these years he couldn't get the image of the bikers out of his head. They had such power. Had they showed up in a fleet of Volkswagen Beetles or Mazda Proteges, who knows, it might have turned into a big fight. But with the bikes—with Harleys—that was like carrying a rifle into a shopping mall, announcing to the world in blinking neon lights you were a dangerous thing.

Exactly the image Darren had been cultivating for years, as a sergeant, and now wishes to maintain, as a man alone in a wasteland, with gangs of looters and who-knows-what-else roaming around. Here, outside the checks and balances of society, bad things can happen, he knows.

The Night Train is a big bike, 75 horsepower, with high handlebars and a wide comfortable seat for long road trips. Darren has taken it up to 120 mph on a flat stretch outside Pendleton, and the air became so sharp and clean it made him forget, just for a second, who and where he was.

Aside from one episode of oil starvation, the bike hasn't given him any trouble. From the beginning he knew his way around an engine, but he decided it couldn't hurt to study up, so he stole a few books from Willamette Tech College and has since made some cosmetic upgrades, installing a double headlight, Billet mirrors, six-piston differential-bore calipers, a four-piston rear-brake system, and finally, after screwing around with front- and rear-sprocket combinations, he decided on a 15-front, 45-back combination for the best acceleration for quick getaways, for the best mileage for long hauls. It is a menacing piece of art, a radiant metallic wonder, a revelation.

More important than any other upgrade is the Geiger counter screwed between his handlebars, and when Darren rides, his eyes bounce between it and the road.

Like Chernobyl, Trojan now lies entombed beneath an enormous concrete sarcophagus, containing the radiation. Not that this makes the Dead Zone safe. The damage has been done. The soil, the trees, the animals have been infected. But because asphalt does not retain radiation, Darren knows he is relatively protected here, in the middle of the highway, following the meridian, its yellow-on-black coloring like the poisonous desert snakes he checked his boots for every morning during the war.

When he hugs the shoulder on a tight curve, the radiation doubles. If he leaves the asphalt, with every step he takes the Geiger count will triple, quadruple, and so on. He knows this because he does this, often, to pick up supplies or investigate a fire or poke through a house. He takes precautions, but living in a place like this, precautions are about as superficial as a helmet at 100 mph.

A microrem is a unit of radiation. 1,000 microrems equals one millirem. 1,000 millirems equals one rem. Before the explosion, the average American received—from a combination of cosmic radiation and medical and industrial sources—between 200 and 300 millirems per year. Before the explosion, in the center of Portland, the average radiation was somewhere around fifteen microrems per hour.

During the explosion the reactor emitted between 5,000 and 50,000 rems per hour. A sudden dose of 500 rems is enough to kill a human, whereas it takes over 5,000 rems to kill a cockroach. Needless to say, gamma rays fried to a radioactive crisp anybody within a thirty-mile radius. A good chunk of civilization fell within that thirty-mile radius. A good chunk of civilization can still be found seated in restaurants, lying in bed, curled up at the bottoms of shower stalls. Many remain on their porches, just a bundle of bones, forever frozen in the place they gathered to watch the terribly beautiful cloud blooming from the nuclear reactor, their skin long ago ashed away by the atomic wind or nibbled away by the many wild animals who now roam wherever they please.

Here, along the Columbia River Gorge, the radiation is 200,000 times the normal rate. At night the trees glow a faint red, as if magic, and it is not unusual to see a raccoon as bald as a baby slinking across the highway, a tree-full of featherless birds squawking and hopping from branch to branch, like some poisonous fruit, unable to fly. To step off the road here, to expose yourself to the intense pockets of radiation, would be like stumbling through a minefield wearing clown shoes.

The closer Darren gets to Trojan, the closer to the still-smoldering graphite nuclear core, the more the air feels packed with gunpowder, as if one wrong move, one sneeze, could blow everything to bits. In this way the Dead Zone feels to him like Iraq, full of unseen danger, like one big booby trap. Familiar, in other words.

On his Night Train, zooming across the high deserts of Central Oregon, the rolling green fields of the Willamette

Valley, growling up the Cascade Mountains, diving down Portland's abandoned streets, he feels as if he is entering some nexus, the coordinates by which his family and so many others became ghosts. And though he doesn't think about it much, though he isn't *into* any of that touchy-feely higher-power happy-crappy shit—as he refers to it—he supposes he *is* trying to connect with that wavelength, breathing the same air under the same sky over the same ground.

It's complicated, but to Darren, living with danger, living with ghosts, living with pain and trying to conquer it, *that* feels more like a victory, somehow. That feels more like being alive.

Christmas 2006 was the last time he saw his parents. He was between assignments, on leave from Afghanistan, ready to deploy to Iraq, and he spent a good deal of his holiday eating. Everything from cinnamon rolls to meat loaf to asparagus casserole, everything he could get his hands on and knew he would not taste outside a mess hall for a long time. And sleeping. There was lots of sleeping. His old bed—its mattress cratered to his body's shape, molded to his memory—comforted him, an assurance he always had a place there.

His last day on leave, Darren remembers his father pumping his hand furiously, his version of a hug, saying, "Good for you, you son of a B." He remembers his mother smiling, touching his face and telling him how awfully faraway Iraq was, as if giving a friendly warning. "Aren't you scared?" she said and he said, "'Course I'm scared."

And he remembers that although he checked and checked, and kept on checking on the plane to Los Alamitos, California, as far as he could tell, he was not scared, he was not sad, he was not excited, he was not feeling much of anything, even when months later, he drove a tank through the streets of Baghdad, a torrent of stones and bullets raining all around him, tick-tack-ticking and whizzing and whining, as if to make a song.

Even then.

This numbness still infects him, though he did break down once, when he roared up to his parents' St. Helens home in a storm of gravel. For a long time he stood at the front door, not knowing what to do, studying for clues in the wood grain. When he finally stepped inside he did so with care, to honor the tomblike stillness of the place and also to keep from stirring the dust, which in his lungs would breed tumors like pink mushrooms. Wood absorbs radiation like a sponge and the Geiger reading here was 1,000 microrems per hour.

When he found his mother lying in bed, a gun in her mouth, a family photo clutched in her mummified claw of a hand, a horrible joke came to him, and he said it out loud: "Quite the nuclear family." He tried a laugh, but couldn't pull it off, managing more of a cough. Then his face split open as rocks do when water freezes inside them—and he began to cry.

Outside he paced around and kicked an ash tree and a loose branch fell and struck his shoulder and its black color stuck to him for a week in an oval-shaped bruise that shrunk and paled and vanished.

Darren is not alone. There are others—Mexicans mainly— who live in the Dead Zone. Like him, most are here because they feel they have nowhere else to go. The invisible threat of radiation, the sores that fester on their skin, mean nothing compared to the overcrowding, the joblessness, the blackened economy found everywhere else.

Here they grow their own food. They drive Mercedes

and BMWs. They live in enormous houses. They shop at the abandoned Nordstrom and at Brooks Brothers stores.

Darren sees them when he drives around. Last week he happened upon fifty or sixty people seeding a vast field with what he guessed was corn. The way they were dressed, you would have thought it was a cocktail party. On the edge of the field an old man in a tuxedo rocked in a rocking chair, stroking his long white beard. When Darren turned off the highway and rumbled down the long clay road that led to them, the old man rose unsteadily from his chair, lifted what appeared to be a cane, and fired. A white carnation bloomed from the front of the shotgun, followed by the roar and spray of buckshot that from a good fifty yards' distance pattered harmlessly off Darren's leather jacket. He got the hint and returned the way he came.

Which makes him cautious now, when he parks his bike on the highway shoulder bordering a Willamette Valley farm, where a dozen men hoe in the field. They raise their hands in hesitant waves and cram together in a huddle and finally decide to approach him, slowly, nodding too much and smiling too big, as if trying to convince themselves he isn't a threat. They wear pistols and so does he. The gunmetal catches the light on this sunny May afternoon, advertising the possibility of violence, but they only want to talk, asking him in their broken English what news he has from the outside, if any.

"No sabe nada," he says. Which is true. He knows nothing except what Katie tells him when they speak on his hand-crank CB radio, and their conversations always seem to center around him, what he is doing, when he is coming back. "Just come back," she tells him, and he tells her, "Just don't."

Once the men realize he speaks Spanish, they all start

talking at once, at a million miles per hour, their hands gesturing, flapping like a bunch of brown birds, which to Darren is what they sound like.

He smiles and holds up his hands—like: I give up—and says, "Lento, por favor. Lento." They are too quick and too complicated for him, but once they slow down, he enjoys their conversation, no matter how awkward and halting, their discussion of food, weather, where to find good gas, whether or not the military will hunt them down, kick them out.

"Not for another hundred years, they won't," Darren says and the Mexicans nod and say, "Bien, bien, bien," as if the word were a knife to keep the camouflaged men and their Humvees and helicopters away.

Among the Mexicans there is a man—just a teenager, really—with lamb-chop sideburns and radiation lesions on his face. His arm in a sling, with blood-soaked gauze duct-taped around his bicep. He says his name is Jorge and when Darren asks what happened to his arm a silence sets in like after a dish drops at a restaurant. Jorge brings a hand to the bandage and says, "Los Angeles." And while at first Darren thinks he is referring to the city, he is not.

Los Angeles is why a good portion of Portland has been reduced to ash. Los Angeles is why the state-capital building has *Chinga Te* graffitied in enormous looping letters across its doors. Los Angeles is why Darren nearly ran over, lying upright in the middle of the interstate, a decapitated head, its skin as black as its hair, its mouth boiling with flies.

An old man whose sun-weathered face could use an iron explains this in stuttery English. His hand rests on his pistol as if comforted by it. He says he originally thought Darren was one of them, with his motorcycle, but Los Angeles ride as a pack, as wolves would. "Besides," the old man says, smiling, "They no look like you."

"Like what?" Darren said.

"Like clean. Like football player," he says with laughter and cigarettes in his voice. "Like big American hero guy."

In a matter of seconds the way Darren perceives the Dead Zone has changed the way a flaming match changes the feel of a dry forest. He knows many people live here. He knows almost everyone is armed and a little desperate, a little crazy, or they wouldn't be here at all. But he did not realize a gang of them had organized into a sort of Mexican al-Qaeda.

He asks the injured man why they attacked him.

"Por mi esposa," he says. For my wife. His face tightens like a fist.

Already Darren knows the answer, but he asks anyway. "Y su esposa?"

"Muerto." Once uttered the word hangs in the air and everyone concentrates on their shoes, except Darren, who stares into the man's eyes as if into a mirror.

A rumble comes from overhead and they all shade their eyes and squint up into a sky filled with cirrus clouds that look like pale fish bones. Here they spot a fighter plane. Its sound strikes Darren as sad, something far away and going farther. He thinks of Katie and a moment later the plane vanishes over the Cascade Mountains, its contrail slowly dissipating behind it.

How safe and beautiful everything must look from way up there, Darren thinks, even if it's not.

A couple months ago, back when Darren was stationed along the perimeter, a bunch of dreadlocked women wearing sandals and hemp necklaces pulled up in a van. On its bumper was a faded *Nader 2012* sticker. When the women spilled out of the van, so did the smell of old sweat and herb gardens. They said they were on a mission. They said they had traveled all the way from Connecticut to deposit their art. Their art turned out to be a big egg, the kind in which a horse might incubate, made out of metal, painted white. The egg, they claimed, represented how life would eventually break through the hard shell of pollution.

Darren didn't see the harm. He said all right and they let out a cheer and set down the egg next to the gate, in a nest of salt grass, and there it remains, a hopeful reminder that nature will move on.

Already it has begun—in the weeds creeping through the cracks in the asphalt, the deer bedded down at OSU stadium's twenty-yard line. In a really weird way, Darren thinks, this one-time nuclear furnace has become an Edenish sort of paradise. With hardly any humans to mow and litter and hunt, nature thrives. But nobody—not even the microbiologists studying the area—understands the genetic ramifications of radiation. Darren has heard it all—woolly pigs with tusks like sabers, weird birds silhouetted by the open guts of the moon, an albino bear as big as a Plymouth sharpening its claws on a telephone pole—but who knows . . .

Every now and then he will see something that belongs in a zoo. Parrots roosting in fir trees or monkeys screeching from the Wal-Mart rafters. One night he heard a snarl—like great sheets of tin torn in half—that must have belonged to some big cat. On the Santiam Pass, along the saddle of the Cascade Range, he discovered an elephant, dead from winter or from radiation. It had its legs folded beneath it—it seemed to be kneeling—with its chin resting on its knees. The skin had faded in places and peeled away in others.

Darren put a hand to its chest—to make it real—and his hand kept going. It broke through the leathery skin and into a cavity where everything felt like bonemeal.

But it's the dogs that have become the wildest.

They now run in packs. They live in the woods and in the abandoned houses, probably cozying up to the couches and beds they were for so long forbidden to dirty. They came for him once, near Prineville, at the bottom of a canyon, his engine's noise drawing them from the juniper forest—ears perked, heads cocked—as if summoned. They gave chase, howling like demons, their dark shapes surrounding him. They popped their teeth and he kicked at them and nearly lost control of his bike. They kept pouring out of the woods—altogether there must have been fifty of them. He dodged their bodies like a halfback and zoomed up and up and up the switchback highway that rose from the canyon, until he reached its plateau, a viewpoint overlooking the dry basin of Crook County. He parked and got off his bike, and sure enough, several hundred feet below him, gray and black and brown, the dogs raced along the highway, their own little gang, following his scent.

He remembers this now, when he pulls into a G.I. Joe's parking lot and hears the muffled noise of dogs fighting inside. He came here to stock up on bullets. He did not come here to risk his skin. Under any other circumstances, no big deal, he would have gone on to the next place—but behind all the scratch-and-snarl racket comes a high-pitched and unmistakably human scream.

When he left his liquidator post along the perimeter, he gave up his military-issue 9mm Glock along with his fatigues, preferring the heft and power of the .357. Everywhere he goes he takes the revolvers with him and he withdraws them now, when climbing through the store's busted entrance, its broken glass surrounding him like a snaggletooth mouth.

At the cash registers he pauses. He imagines women with big hair and trashy makeup counting change and flipping through tabloids, and beyond them, construction workers buying claw hammers, ranchers buying udder cream, camouflaged men buying hunting licenses, all of them giving him a nod, all of them ghosts.

G.I. Joe's is one of those whatever-you-need-we-got-it sort of places. Darren makes his way past cross-piled rock-salt bags, past shelves of Shasta soda pop and off-brand potato chips, past display stacks of Penzoil and antifreeze, toward the back of the store, the source of the sound.

Birds squawk and flutter in the rafters. Flies and hornets buzz around his head. Leaves crunch beneath his boots. Spiders have spun webs over everything. He remembers there was once a smell to stores like this—fertilizer mixed with rubber mixed with PVC fumes mixed with hydraulic oil—that was a good smell, no longer, replaced by the heavy stink of an animal's den.

He peeks around Aisle 10 and sees the dogs gathered around a Die-Hard battery kiosk, on top of which squats a Mexican girl, maybe ten years old, maybe ten feet off the linoleum, her long black hair falling to either side of her head. She watches the dogs calmly, as if they are stuffed animals and not something she needs to fear, until one of them, a big standard poodle, stands up on its hind legs and sort of pushes at the kiosk, shaking it. She screams.

This sends the dogs into convulsions, exciting them even more. They jitter and prance and wag their whole bodies and howl like some kind of mob hungry for an execution. Darren counts twenty of them—Rottweilers, German shepherds, Labradors, even a wiener dog. Their coats are knotted and filthy and jeweled with burrs.

"Hey," he says. "Hey, dogs!" At once the whole horde turns to look at him, panting, hesitantly wagging their tails. He wonders if two instincts—those of loyalty and hunger—fight inside them. He doesn't know what to say, so he says, "Bad dogs."

At this some of them peel back their lips, showing their teeth, while others whine and stutter-step forward, as if he were an old friend they hardly recognized.

There are more dogs than there are bullets in his revolvers, Darren realizes, and suddenly he feels vulnerable. The poodle, a mud-caked mess of hair, moves toward him, looking at once ridiculous and frightening, like some four-legged breed of Sasquatch.

"Sit," he says. "Sit. Stay. Roll over." But the poodle keeps coming.

He lifts the revolvers. They seem incredibly heavy in his hands. The poodle lowers its head and begins a sort of hunch-shouldered charge. Saliva swings from its teeth when it opens its mouth to bite him. He puts a bullet in its leg and it screams in a terribly human way before collapsing and rising again and limping fast and far from him, leaving behind a trail of blood.

At the sound of the gunshot—a whipping crack that bottoms out and echoes away—the other dogs scatter, diving down the aisles. Seconds later Darren hears them outside, barking and yowling.

The wiener dog is the only one who lingers, peeking from behind the kiosk. Darren holsters his guns and lifts his arms and says, "Yaaaaah!" and the dog releases a tiny stream of pee before trotting off to join its pack.

Darren looks at the girl and the girl looks at him, looks

away, and then gets brave enough to maintain a stare. She wears a too-long T-shirt, jean shorts, and Velcro tennis shoes. He raises his hand—the universal sign for *hey*—and she does the same. They each manage a small smile. "Speak English?" he says.

Her expression does not change and Darren sees in it the same thing he saw in the wiener dog: a mixture of fear and loneliness that at once makes her want to rush forward and back away. He decides to let her settle down a moment, get comfortable with him.

Nearby is Hunting and Firearms. The glass display case has been busted open and looted of most everything except some lousy grandpa-style pocketknives. Behind the counter Darren pokes around and among the mess of broken glass and spilled cartridges he finds what he is looking for: three boxes of .357 bullets and a handful of shotgun shells. He fills his coat pockets and returns to the kiosk.

"Seriously, you gotta come down," he says. "Down. *Pollado.*" Or is it *derriba?* He can't remember. He motions with his hand. "Down. *Down.* Before they get brave and come back."

She doesn't move, except to blink. She has these eyes, as deeply brown and moist as expensive chocolate. Her eyebrows coming together to form a silent question: is he dangerous?

"No estoy peligroso," he says. "No kidding. I'm a good guy. Yo estoy su amigo."

"I'm not stupid," she says with a soft accent. "I can speak English."

He puts out his hands as if he has given up looking for something. "Okay. This is a good thing." When she doesn't say anything, just keeps staring at him, he speaks to fill up the silence between them: "You're American then? Or Mexican?"

She gives her eyes a theatrical roll and says, "I'm Latina," and Darren thinks: *this* is why I hate kids.

"Look," he says. "Whatever. We need to get going."

Except to sneeze into her hands she does not move.

"Salud," he says and kicks an empty Pepsi can and it rattles a few feet down the aisle. "Where are your parents anyway?" He immediately regrets asking and in his chest gets this jab of dread when she scrunches up her face and starts breathing heavily like kids do before they really lose it.

"Forget it," he says. Before she can second-guess him, he holds up his hands and twiddles his fingers and says, "Come on." After a hesitant moment, she scoots her butt toward the edge, dangles her legs, and falls into his arms.

Outside the sun has retreated behind some clouds. The dogs are nowhere in sight, but his bike is wet with their urine. You belong to us, bub—they are saying—this is our territory now.

"Jeez," he says.

"Gross," the girl says.

He'll wash it later. For now he wants to get away from here. He feels too exposed, in the middle of this parking lot, with the danger of dogs lurking nearby. A wooded lot neighbors the store and Darren thinks he can hear the muffled crunch of footpads there. He straddles the bike. "Will you sit next to me?" With a thumb he indicates the seat behind him.

She tilts her head, but stays where she is, a couple feet away, staring at the bike and then at him, not afraid— Darren doesn't think—but shy, or maybe just disgusted by the sour smell. He notices how skinny she is, her collarbone like a bicycle handlebar. "You hungry?" He removes from his jacket pocket a Snickers bar, unwraps it, and takes a bite. When chewing he makes *mmm-mmm* noises.

She holds out her hand and says, "Please," like a kid at a supermarket checkout. He breaks off a piece and tosses it to her. She snatches it from the air and eats it with smacking open-mouth chews. "You want the rest?" Darren says, "You got to get on the bike." She surprises him with a smile, her teeth just a little buck. Something like agreement or acceptance passes between them. He tries to make his smile as genuine as hers and finds it isn't hard. "What's your name anyway?"

"Roxana Primavera Rivera," she says in a proud careful voice like she might have once used in front of a classroom.

Once again he motions to the seat with his thumb. "Hop on board, Roxana."

This time she does just as he says and gets on the bike, wrapping her tiny hands around him, looping her fingers through his denim belt loops. When the engine growls alive she releases a little scream and buries her head into his back.

They ride—out of the parking lot, out of the town, into the Willamette Valley—and the clouds open up and pieces of light drop down and skitter across the asphalt. He looks for Mexicans, for someone to drop off the girl with, but sees nothing except overgrown fields, tangled vineyards. An hour passes and the low-slung sun burns the horizon into a shriveling purpley brown piece of hot plastic. Night rises from the mountains like smoke, fingering its way across the sky.

In the morning, Darren decides, I'll find someplace for her then.

Just outside St. Helens a mule deer bounds across the highway and springs into the air, so impossibly high, hurdling a barbed-wire fence with a white swish of tail, disappearing into the forest, where the shadows fuse together.

"Did you see that?" Darren yells over his shoulder. She

gives him no response, her head still burrowed into his back, a warm heaviness, a nice feeling. "That was beautiful."

Darren spends most nights in an underground concrete bunker the size of a rich man's closet. His father built it in their backyard—in case the capital-B Bomb ever dropped. That he might drop the bomb never occurred to him. The bunker is dark and dank with a thick lead door and Darren figures it's as good a place as any—it's home, anyway—and down here the Geiger only reads thirty microrems per hour.

Here, in the absolute quiet of underground, he reads himself to sleep with a flashlight tucked between his neck and pillow. He has loads of books—Westerns, science-fiction stories, even romances—stolen from houses and libraries and stores, and he finds in them not just entertainment, but comfort, the comfort of reading about smart people who say all the right things and in the end figure stuff out.

Katie is like that, like someone out of a book. Always saying snappy things that ought to be written down, such as when she told Darren, "If you don't have a home, you've got nowhere to hang your heart." She was right about that. Nights he spends elsewhere, away from the bunker, sleeping under the stars, a vast black continent stretched out above him, he feels lost, erased.

The bunker is where he takes Roxana.

There is no electricity—he uses propane for cooking, candles for light, and a battery-powered stereo for music—and there is no running water. He boils and bottles what he drinks and he bathes in a nearby stream. The water is cold, white with minerals, and comes from the old glaciers way up in the Cascades. When he bathes, huge fish, salmon the size of dolphins, curl around him, flapping their tails as if they own the river. Sometimes they taste him, taking his toes or fingers into their prickly mouths, chewing, and he finds the sensation strangely pleasant. They dart all up and down the river, their reddish scales glowing beneath the water like the magic woods outside Trojan. For a time he worried whether the water was cleaning him or dirtying him—the radiation washed right off the mountains and into his skin—but then he stopped worrying.

He keys the bunker's deadbolt and holds open the door like a bellhop, giving Roxana a little after-you-ma'am bow. She doesn't budge from the top of the stairs. Her expression belongs to someone who just swallowed a bitter pill. "It's no palace," he says with an apologetic shrug, "but hey." He leaves her there and goes about lighting candles, making the place more welcoming, and eventually, when the black bug-filled air gets to be too much for her, she makes her way down to join him.

With the perfect stillness of the bunker air and the red glow of the candles and the awkwardness of sharing a small space with a stranger, a little girl no less, Darren feels weird. He wants to turn on the stereo or get the hell away. When she goes to the bed and plops down on it, he squats in the far corner and examines his hands.

For a long time there is a silence between them until finally she says, "I'm starving." She holds her belly for emphasis.

"Okay," Darren says and goes to a shelving unit stacked with flour and sugar and canned vegetables and soups. "I've got some stuff here I could warm up. Do you like chicken-noodle soup?"

"I want cookies. Do you have chocolate-chip cookies?"

"Cookies," he says. "Are you kidding me?"

She scratches her arm as a response.

Making cookies, to Darren, is like wearing cologne. An extravagance he never would have considered. The world falls apart and who wants to play hopscotch? Who wants to plant a flower garden? Who wants to make cookies? But now that he thinks about it, the other day he *did* collect some bird eggs—he *does* more or less have every ingredient—so he says, "All right. What the hell. Let's make cookies."

She says, "Yay," and tucks her hair behind her ears and gives him a hundred-watt smile.

He doesn't know why, but when he goes about mixing the flour and sugar and Crisco, chopping a Snickers bar into tiny bits, lighting the camping stove, he grins like an idiot. He grins so big his cheeks ache.

The last time he smiled like this, he realizes, was months ago, with Katie, when he told her about this dream he had. In it his parents drove around the Dead Zone on Vespa motor scooters, wearing sombreros and Hawaiian shirts, and when he tried to flag them down, they waved enthusiastically but didn't stop. "You're missing out on all the fun," they yelled, their voices riding the wind.

He asked Katie what she thought about that. She said she thought he was sweet and funny and maybe, just maybe, his parents had a point.

Now he and Roxana make hungry noises and hunch over the camping stove and watch globs of chocolate-chunked dough melt on a pan, and for the first time in a long time he feels something akin to the warm swelling of the cookies.

She takes the bed and he takes the floor. The Pendleton blanket over concrete isn't very comfortable, but that's not why he can't sleep. He rarely sleeps. Nights, a dead man comes to visit him.

Here is the story of the dead man: Darren was working a Karbala traffic checkpoint near the U.S. Embassy when it happened. The day was hot as only the desert can get. He had been searching cars for eight hours, and he was angry and tired and unfocused, until a pistol appeared from behind a rolled-down window. The man screamed something in Arabic and squeezed the trigger. It jammed. Darren's did not. He remembers the man looking up at him, wide-eyed and surprised, his mouth a black O, the kind of look Darren's father no doubt wore when the reactor came apart all around him.

Darren wonders what the Iraqi man saw, what he felt? The cold rush of metal into his mouth. The internal blossoming of blood as teeth and gum and bone evaporated, as the back of his head opened up and ejected what looked like a handful of rotten watermelon. Did he feel the wind whistling through his newly rendered cavity?

Darren killed many others, but none whose faces he saw so clearly.

So whenever he falls into dreams, the dead man emerges from the dark, and Darren wakes up with an asthmatic gasp, squeezing his hands into fists so hard the fingernails cut into his palms little half-moons of blood.

Lying on the floor, he recognizes a similar sort of haunting in Roxana. In her dreams she wails, sometimes softly, sometimes at the top of her lungs, like some air-raid siren.

For a while he just lies there, listening. Then he gets up and paces the bunker, back and forth, back and forth, running his hands through his hair like an expectant father. Every few minutes he stands over her and squeezes her shoulder and whispers, "Roxana? You okay?" But she won't respond. She goes on moaning and he goes back to pacing.

Finally, in a wave of desperation—he wants so badly to silence and comfort her—he scoops her up and holds her in his arms, tight against his chest, rocking her, saying *shhh*. He doesn't know if she wakes up or not, but she calms down.

Her moaning softens to a sort of purr and her muscles relax and after a good fifteen minutes he sets her down and covers her with a blanket and falls asleep kneeling beside her.

Darren occasionally gets the feeling—this dread surging through him—that he is never going to find what he wants, even though he doesn't know exactly what he wants. Before, every goal was so material: I want a fast red car, I want a sexy wife, I want a house with a field out back where I can play catch with my kid. Now every need—besides those of hunger and shelter—has become an abstraction. When he gets like this, usually lying in his bunker with all the lights off, he is left with a carved-out soreness he recognizes as homesickness.

Fed up with the silence and the loneliness, he rides to the perimeter, parking his bike some three miles away. He waits for nightfall and hikes to the checkpoint, keeping to the blue-black shadows when he can, hunkering down behind a moonlit sagebrush. With his binoculars he peers into the barrack windows. The people inside them are like characters on a television screen, drinking and playing cards and Ping-Pong, so unreal to him. Times like these he thinks what he thought when he first pulled up to his St. Helens home: I used to live here.

Inside the barracks—its windows white, pulsing, as if by some miracle a star had been pulled from the sky and trapped there—he sees Katie. She rakes back her hair in a slick brown pile. She has beautiful hair. He wants to kiss it.

Usually that is enough. Seeing her is enough. An antidote to the hollow feeling in his guts. He returns to his bike and speeds off to his own private corner of the universe until the next time he gets that desperate homesick feeling.

Such as now, when he wakes up with Roxana and Katie

coming together in his brain like a constellation he can't quite figure out. He knows this place is no place for a child. And he knows he is not the best sort of man to watch after a child. He will take Roxana to the perimeter. Katie will know what to do with her.

Darren is flying—he is nothing but air—with Roxana curled tight as a shrimp against his back. The road twists over the Cascades and bottoms out in Central Oregon where they find themselves surrounded by ponderosa forests, the trees' bark a scraped-skin red. The bike hums beneath him and the wind is like a woman's fingers in his hair, bearing the smell of sage and sap.

Then he notices a gray cloud of smoke rising in the distance. Too big for a campfire, too indistinct for a burning house or field. And the cloud, Darren realizes, is moving toward them.

He brakes and rolls onto the shoulder with a slurred crush of cinder. Dust drifts up and sticks to their sweat. Roxana says, "Como?" and he holds up a hand that tells her to be quiet. "Something's coming," he says. Up ahead the road elbows into the trees. He focuses his eyes there, as if through the crosshairs of a scope, and the rest of the world falls away.

Roxana says, "What's coming?" and he says, *"Sh."* He is concentrating. He senses, in a certain vibration of the air and the asphalt, engines. Lots of them.

His throat constricts, a lava-hot rush of blood makes his heart do a backflip, and deep inside him big chunks of black matter, stuff that has been lodged there forever, begins to melt away and infect him with a sick feeling. He can't remember ever being afraid in his entire life, but this is fear. Unmistakable, remarkable fear.

Not for him, but for Roxana.

All hopped up with adrenaline, he doesn't quite know how to act, so he acts angry, a state of mind he understands better. He blazes off the highway—into and out of the drainage ditch, its swampish bottom slippery, the bike almost sliding out from under them—and when Roxana says, "Are you loco?" he says, "Shut up! Just shut up!"

Instantly he regrets it and feels his face tighten into a cringe, but he doesn't have time to apologize. He zigzags through the trees like a rabbit under fire. Stiff weeds and clumps of sagebrush claw at the bike, screeching on its metal, and about thirty feet off the road—which seems too, too close—he brings the bike around a fallen tree and lays it on its side and starts covering it with branches.

Roxana hugs her chest protectively and jogs her eyes between him and the road. He can tell by her expression, a sort of scowl, she wants to be angry, but fear is getting in the way.

The fallen tree is a pine, its needles a crisp brown, its bark interrupted by a jagged black vein made by lightning. When he pushes his way into its nest of branches—getting right up against the trunk—his hair prickles, his veins tighten. It is as if he can *feel* the residual electricity. He says, "Come on," and Roxana joins him.

By now a faint growl is audible and they duck down—their bodies bent in half like question marks—and listen to the noise get louder and louder still, and then around the corner comes a train of vehicles: motorcycles, jacked-up pickups, Cadillacs with red flames painted along their sides. All of them cough up oil like outboards, their ruined shocks and cracked mufflers and shrieking brakes rolling together to make a musical noise, like some junkyard circus, surrounded by this mystically blue exhaust that rises up and joins the sky.

On top of one Cadillac, bodies are tied down like trophy stags. If they are not dead they are near it. Blood runs off the roof, down the windshield, where the wipers wipe it away. Darren can see the man behind the wheel, hunched over and squinting through all that redness, smiling. A rosary swings from his rearview mirror.

Just five minutes ago the world seemed weirdly clean and calm. Now, in the drifting fog of smoke, engines snarl and horns beep and mariachi music blasts from tape decks and tattooed men grin into the wind and for a second it's as if the meltdown never happened.

Darren looks at Roxana: her eyes are burning with tears, her mouth is opening and closing without any sound. He sees in her face terrible fear and hatred. She recognizes these men and Darren knows without a doubt what happened to her family. He unholsters his revolver.

The caboose of the nightmare parade is a semi dragging a flatbed. On the flatbed are couches and chairs, arranged helter-skelter, with many men and women splayed out on them. Beer cans roll around their feet. Mexican trumpets blasting from a boom box overwhelm the noise of the diesel engine. Five men circle a woman in a green bikini and dance—slightly off-kilter from drink or turbulence—their hands outstretched like Halloween scarecrows. They are dirty and they are excited.

At the rear of the flatbed a shirtless man swings logging chains above his head. He is as big as an outhouse. With his revolver Darren sights the man's chest, where excess flesh ripples down his rib cage, surrounding his guts, as if he has begun to melt after a too-long exposure to Trojan's furnace. Beneath the noise of the music and the engines, Darren imagines he can hear the chains making a hissing noise, a noise associated with flat tires and snakes, with imminent danger.

Darren's chest is a drum. Inside the drum, the fist of his heart bangs away and he feels clenched and jumpy and oblivious to the reckless stupidity of what he is about to do. His finger tightens around the trigger—in pure reflex—and the trigger gives. The gun jumps in his hand. Time stops. The mariachi music fades, replaced by a thundering crack. With a blue puff of smoke, the bullet tunnels through thirty feet of air and opens up a tiny mouth just below the man's left nipple. He doesn't cry out or clutch his chest—or anything—he just drops. He ceases to live. The physics of the impact work out like this: an ugly twist of limbs thrown from the flatbed, now baking on the hot pavement.

Darren feels certain the semi will grind to a halt—and then the sun will glint off the Night Train's exposed muffler and the woman in the green bikini will point a finger in their direction and yell, "There!" and that will be it—they will be dead.

But no, the gang growls off into the distance, aware of nothing but themselves.

Nearby a bird shrieks *all clear* and the forest returns to its business, twittering and chattering. With a gush of air Darren realizes he has been holding his breath. At first he feels elated, as if he has found something given up for lost, and then he notices Roxana staring at his revolver, and his body suffers some weird jolt—a power surge of guilt—followed by a draining sensation.

He returns the gun to its holster and she says, "You killed that guy."

He reaches out and combs some pine dander from her hair. "Sorry."

There are little gold sunbursts mixed into the brown of her eyes. "I hope you blow all their guts out." She says this point-blank, without a trace of humor or pity, and then takes a few steps away from him, as if to escape the memory attached to her words.

In the Westerns he reads, the heroes spend a lot of time seeking revenge. If somebody, usually a guy with a black mustache, kills a pal or a family member, it is your *duty* to pay him back in lead. It is the just and courageous thing to do, the *only* thing to do.

He wishes he felt this way about Iraq. He wishes dropping bombs and putting bullets into people felt like the only thing to do.

As if the taste of blood has given him a great appetite, he considers lining Los Angeles up and tearing into them, one by one, reciprocating the pain they have caused. Even if they outnumber him thirty-to-one, *even* if his head ends up on a pike, he feels he owes it to Roxana, he owes it to his parents, he owes it to the people, himself included, seeking some sort of absolution.

Whereas before Roxana struck him as scarily adult, she now looks all of ten, just a child, when she tugs at his hand, tugs him out of his thoughts, and says, "Let's go. I'm scared."

He hauls up the Night Train and she takes one of the handlebars and helps him roll it over to the road. They try not to look at the body, the blood pooling around it like an oil slick, as he gets on the bike and she gets on behind him, wrapping her arms tight around his belly, his safety belt. He lets the engine run for a minute, then guns the accelerator, spraying dust and cinder everywhere, and heads due east, his eyes black-bagged and full of pain, like the wounded who return home from a lost war.

Whisper

Whisper

Jacob lay on the forest floor with something broken inside him. When he tried to sit up, his pelvis shifted and released a moist popping sound, filled with pain, so he kept still, listening to the wind whisper through the trees and scatter the last leaves from their branches.

At first he felt cold. Then a hot ache spread from his middle and leaked all the way to his fingertips. He imagined himself lying there, how he would look to whoever found him. With his white hair and rheumy eyes, with his soft belly, his bowed legs, with his liver-spotted skin and the veins beneath it looking like the burned-out filaments of a lightbulb, he decided he would look exactly like a stupid old man who had fallen out of a tree.

He tried distracting himself. Thinking about the Ducks— their so far 5-and-7 season—though he couldn't remember a single game. Thinking about his wife, though he could imagine her face only from a distance, as if through the wrong end of a scope. Every time his mind seemed ready to latch down on something, it escaped him, swept aside by a wave of pain.

A long twenty minutes passed. During this time he felt his stomach and legs swelling with blood, growing tight against his jeans, and he wondered how long it would be, a day, maybe two, before they found him, his body.

He had been sitting in his tree stand when it happened, when the wood gave out beneath him and he fell the fifteen feet to the forest floor and broke. He had built it some thirty years ago, a kind of roofless tree house braced by the Y-junction of an oak's lower limbs. The wood must have rotted or the nails must have come loose and now here he was, fading, like a photograph left too long in the sun. His rifle lay beside him, within reach. He ran a finger along its stock. For a second he considered using it, but only for a second.

Words like *old* and *stupid* and *I wish* cycled endlessly through his head and he began to shiver and rock with the pain, and when he did, the bone splinters branched out into his body like frost across a window. An artery snipped in half. His skin stretched suddenly and painfully against the pressure of blood trying to find a way out, his scrotum swelling to the size of an infant's skull.

He noticed the weight of flannel against his chest, the smell of leaves. He rolled his head around—his eyeballs wild—as if seeking someone to blame. His brother, Gerald. They had fought the other day. About what he could not recall. Something. It was always something between the two of them.

Not long ago they had spoken of death, when trout fishing, when they joked about how the worms they impaled on their hooks would one day get revenge, sooner than later, tunneling into their old bodies once laid to rest.

Jacob could no longer feel his left leg, but above it, all throughout his groin, his skin pulsed as if from the stirrings of some terrible love. Then this hotness transformed into numbness—and the sensation was a quick and refreshing thing, like flipping his face to the cool side of a pillow.

He watched the branches move, the leaves tumbling down, shades of gold and red, lipstick red, riding the breeze, their motion in tune to the passage of time—quick, slow— pausing against the breath of an updraft, then falling, falling all around him. He tried to snatch one. Against the sky his hand looked as pale and crooked as a winter tree.

This was the way he died. And the next day his brother found his body tucked under an afghan of leaves, his eyes open and staring and cracked from the freeze the night before.

Two days later, Gerald sat in his La-Z-Boy recliner, staring through a scope. He had long ago detached it from his rifle and now kept it handy mainly for bird-watching. Out the window, across the mowed space of lawn, he could see the vegetable garden, with its sunken pumpkins and browned vines, edged by the barbed-wire fence, and beyond this, the pasture, where a heifer was fresh. He wanted to watch the birth.

He had a difficult time focusing because of his hand. It had begun to shake two years ago and since then the shaking had grown steadily worse. He suspected it was the beginnings of Parkinson's, but preferred not knowing.

Though it was getting difficult to ignore. Sometimes, when he drank coffee, it dribbled over the lip of the mug and burned his fingers. A few months ago he had given up eating anything with a spoon.

The palsy nested in his right wrist. Last Saturday he dropped the offering plate during mass. "Goddamnit," he yelled when the quarters and bills spilled beneath the pews and the congregation turned to stare at him, their faces pinched with concern.

Now, through the scope, the world shook. The unsteadiness began to nauseate him. When his vision went white, as if from some sudden glaucoma, he pulled his face away from the scope and the world came into focus and he spotted the peacock. It strutted past the window, its head bobbing, its feathers as white as teeth. Five years ago Gerald bought Jacob and his wife, Gertie, two white peacocks as a fiftieth-anniversary gift. "They represent love," he told them. Though theirs was a habitual love, he knew. Even if they said, "Love you," each night before bed, it was a tired phrase, devoid of feeling, as normal and easy as "Sure" or "So long."

So different than what he felt—a pressing heat—even now, gray-headed and dotted with age spots and hunched over with arthritis. "They represent love," he had told them, while looking at her, as he had for so many years.

This was before a clot came loose and traveled through her veins like a tiny dry wasp whose stinger latched itself to her brain and rendered her dumb, her left side immobile. Before Jacob sold his cottage to help pay for the hospital bills, the lengthy stay at the Mt. Angel Rehabilitation Center, the medicine she required. Before they moved into the farmhouse with Gerald, who told his brother, "Come. Please. That way we can all look after each other."

The peacock let out a warbling scream—*eey*aw-*eey*aw-*eey*aw—and with one flap of its wings lifted itself into the low branches of an oak tree, some fifteen feet off the ground, the distance his brother had descended.

He didn't want to think about it. But he couldn't *not* think about it. The body sprawled out on the ground, the bones broken inside it like the shards of a plate knocked off a table by a careless elbow. The body now drained of blood and filled with formaldehyde, lying on a metal tray in a refrigerated locker. The body, his brother's.

Gerald searched around inside himself and tried to find some emotion, whether happiness or sadness or guilt, but found only a black space, like a closet with a busted light. He didn't know what was in it, not for certain.

In the kitchen, his niece, Jackie, molded the crusts of apple pies. He listened to her bang some pots around, hum an old-time polka tune he used to dance to. Used to, he thought. These days everything is *used to*.

Now Gerald raised the scope to his eye again and watched the heifer turn around in a circle, lowing in pain. He wondered if his brother had made a similar sound in his final moments.

The heifer slowed in its turning, finally pausing to lower its snout to the pasture. It began to graze, chewing at the browned clover, seemingly unconcerned as two spindly legs sprouted from her backside, groping for purchase. Blood and embryonic fluid leaked down her hindquarters. A contraction made the heifer stiffen her neck and wall her eyes. There was a surge of fluid. Now half a calf hung from its mother, the two of them appearing in profile like some grotesque Siamese twin.

Another minute and the calf slipped out completely, falling to the pasture, a wet and bony heap with a placenta hanging around its neck like a muddy shawl. A shower of blood and excrement followed.

Gerald yelled, "Jackie," but his voice was weak and the word fluttered down the hall to die. A minute later and he tried again. "Jackie?"

"Yes?"

"She done birthed another one."

"What?" He heard water running and what sounded like a wooden spoon put down on the counter.

"Why don't you come in here when I'm talking to you?"

Outside the heifer licked the calf and the calf tried to make sense of its muscles, struggling in the grass like a tangled marionette.

He heard heavy footsteps on the linoleum, and then a whispering on the carpet announced her presence. His scope filled up with her checkered apron and he put it down to see her standing before him. She kept her hair short, combed up in a brown poof maintained by a lot of hairspray. "What, Gerald? What's the fuss?"

He handed her the scope. "Look, that's what."

She did—and promptly passed it back. "Another cow. How many hundreds of cows?" She frowned and folded her hands over her poochy belly like some disapproving school-teacher. "I don't have time for this. I have to hurry and have the pies ready for the wake."

"Should we tell Gertie?"

She cocked her head. "Tell her what?"

"About the cow, of course," he said.

"You'd think you'd have more important things on your mind besides cows." Her eyes grew moist and her mouth began to quiver and she turned to go, saying over her shoulder, "My father is dead. Your brother. Doesn't that mean anything to you?"

She retreated from Gerald, who sat frowning in his chair, listening to the wail of the white peacocks, that wavering cry he had always likened to the sound of suffering women.

The wake was about to begin and the kitchen was full of stout old ladies, all of them with hair like dandelions gone to seed. They hovered over the food they had brought, rear-ranging it and warming it and sneaking tastes of it. On the counter the percolator hissed and popped with fresh cof-fee. Next to it the Crock-Pot simmered with pulled pork for sandwiches. There were stacks of whole-wheat buns. Jars of pickles and pickled garlic and pickled beets. Cheese plates. Slices of onion, green pepper, summer sausage. Radishes. Jell-O salad. Silverware clattered as it was arranged into cups like in a cafeteria. On the kitchen table, a legion of pies—apple and pumpkin and blackberry—the blackberry looking a little like congealed blood.

An hour ago Gerald had trucked in a load of aluminum folding chairs from St. Anthony's and positioned them in the living room. This was where the men sat, waiting for their wives, speaking in low voices about the weather and the alfalfa crop and Jacob. "A hell of a thing," they said. "Hell of a thing." They fell silent when Gerald negotiated his way through them, helping Gertie to the couch.

He was wearing a black suit and she was wearing a black dress and they had their arms wrapped tightly around each other. Essentially he carried her. It wasn't grief that immobilized her, but the stroke. Her face appeared molten on one side, the eye half shuttered, the mouth drooping as if arranged in a permanent scowl. The muscles had gone slack there and all along her left side, her leg a dead branch that dragged behind her.

"Here's a place," Gerald said and lowered her onto the couch. "There now. This is just the place." When he uncoupled his arms from her, he did so slowly, already missing the warmth of her pressed against him.

With her good eye she observed him moistly. "Cookie," she said. It was all she could say. At first, when she came home from Mt. Angel, everyone thought she meant she wanted a cookie. Jacob would bring back from the grocery store Chips Ahoy, Oreos, Toll House, Mrs. Fields, pressing each variety to her lips only to have her turn her head away like a sullen child. "Cookie," she would say and he would say, "That's what I'm trying to give you. A cookie. Don't you want it?" until he understood this was the only sound her mouth recalled. It meant nothing and it meant everything. "Cookie," she would say. "Cookie." And her audience would nod encouragingly as if on the verge of understanding the word and its repetition, like some code that could be translated if only studied long enough.

"Cookie," she said now to Gerald—in thankfulness or accusation, he didn't know.

Soon the room filled up with the remainder of the family and friends invited, maybe thirty of them, all of them bowing their heads as Father Armstrong began his prayer.

Gerald didn't listen to a word the father said. He concentrated instead on Gertie breathing next to him. And the walls, their vine-patterned wallpaper cluttered with clocks and photographs. Most of the people in the color photographs, he noticed, now sat in the room, whereas the grainy black-and-white images mainly contained the dead. His parents, smiling in their Sunday best, probably the same clothes they wore now, buried in the Moccasin Hollow Cemetery, a spattering of tombstones on the outskirts of town, a place where teenagers went to smoke and kiss. The Bobcat would be at work there tomorrow, its shovel peeling back the earth in the shape of a rectangle only a little bigger than a casket.

The prayer finished and Father Armstrong asked if anyone wanted to share anything about Jacob. It was quiet for a time. Then Sam Ritchie raised his hand. The father called on him and he stood up and in his nervousness rubbed his palms together in a way that sounded like sandpaper hissing. He was a big man and the flannel shirt he wore barely surrounded his bulk. "I remember when Jacob and I was kids," he said and brought his lips together tightly. "When we was kids, we used to go down and catch pollywogs together in Jasmine Crick." All of a sudden he released a doglike yelp and put his hands to his face and wept into them and everyone concentrated on their shoes, embarrassed to see a large man look so small.

Father Armstrong walked over and patted Sam on the shoulder and Sam said, "I'm okay, I'm okay. Just a second. You've just got to give me a second. All right?"

"Of course," the father said.

All around them the clocks ticked away the seconds it took for Sam to rough the tears from his eyes and take a deep steadying breath. When he finally opened his mouth to say something more, Gertie filled the silence for him. "Cookie," she said. And then again: "Cookie."

From her place on the couch she observed them all with her good eye, saying, "Cookie, cookie," in an even tone—perhaps speaking in a ciphered tongue about her late husband, perhaps speaking nonsense, no one knew for sure. But as she continued to speak they all bowed their heads, pretending her words into a kind of prayer.

Because Gertie could not bathe herself, Jackie would come over every evening to splash soap in the tub and fill it with hot water, as she did now.

A minute ago Gerald stood in the kitchen, holding a jar of pickled beets leftover from the wake, but the roar of the water had drawn him into the hallway. He tiptoed across the hardwood as if it were ice, trying not to let it groan beneath his weight and reveal his presence. He stabbed the beets with a fork and pulled them out of the brine and into his mouth and chewed at them messily and stared at the bathroom door. Jackie had not closed it completely and a crack of yellow light ran along its side. Gerald went to it.

His eyes took a moment to adjust from the dimness to the brightness—and then he saw her, in the tub, Gertie. Her silver hair hung damply around her shoulders and her freckled breasts folded over her belly like lumps of warm clay. The water steamed and white tendrils worked through the air, as if ghosts had invaded the room.

Jackie stood a few feet away, oblivious to him. From the drawer beneath the sink she took a washcloth and kneeled next to the tub to test its temperature before knobbing off the water. Her mouth moved, perhaps lullabying, as she wet the washcloth and wrung it out and began to clean her mother—her face, her arms, her breasts and belly— gently—wiping the folds of skin that appeared as delicate as damp paper.

And all the while Gertie sat there, motionless. His eyes traced the lines of her body, the blankness of her face. She wasn't wholly there and neither was he, lost somewhere inside the emptiness of his head, a hollow filled with the shadows of yesterday—remembering her almond eyes, the wet budding of her lips, her once-dark hair splayed across a pillow—remembering his brother, too.

There had been a time when they were alive—really *alive*—their teeth white and their skin tan, their arms and legs ropy with muscle. Back then they would rise clear-headed from their beds at 4:30 and throw on their coveralls and happily step out into the moonlit morning, into the pasture, where the cattle lowed. They would whistle and clap their hands and herd the cows into the barn and set up their wooden stools and aluminum buckets. This after dancing until midnight at the grange hall, dancing so hard their feet blistered and their jeans grew dark with sweat.

This was before Jacob left the farm. Before he joined the Merchant Marines and earned his college degree and became a schoolteacher and married Gertie and moved to Eugene—at once thirty minutes and a whole world away.

For the brothers to have been so similar for so many years, sharing the same chores, the same chipped glassware and soiled mud boots—and then for Jacob to turn out so differently, seeking a life separate from Gerald—it felt like a betrayal.

Now the mist from the bathwater crept into the hall. A milky, swirling nothing from which a finger reached out to trace his cheek. At that moment his hand began to tremble so horribly that he lost his purchase on the jar. Against the hardwood it shattered. He startled at the sound and sight of it and lurched backward, reaching for something to steady his balance against—the wall.

Like a shallow-breathing animal he watched as a red line of beet juice bled toward the bathroom door. In the moment before it opened, before Jackie stared at him wonderingly, he felt an overwhelming sadness, like he had lost something— something vital and substantial—his life—his opportunity to do more with it than simply rotate crops and urge milk from a cow's teat—all the possibilities of what-could-have-been scattering like fragments of glass across the floor, like bones inside his brother's body, something that could not be reassembled.

He did not love her—not exactly. He was not certain if he was capable of love, as he saw the women and men around him more as accessories, like the Phillips screwdriver he kept in the silverware drawer or the stereo he installed in the cab of the tractor, something to serve or amuse him. *Want* was a more accurate word. He had always wanted her. But she belonged to his brother.

Over the years he had wanted many women and made

them his, the first time when he was seventeen. At the county fair, while he was showing cattle, he spotted in the audience a girl wearing a sunflower-patterned sundress. She stood out among all the denim and flannel, a yellow flame that trembled at the corner of his eye as he led his Holstein around the ring to polite applause. Later, he sought her out and found her in the midway, laughing with a group of girls. He pulled her away with small talk and cotton candy. They went for a walk together and he led her behind the barn, away from the crowds. There he lurched forward with the hunger of a starved animal, wrestling her to the dirt with ease. While she kicked her legs and punched her fists helplessly against him, he pushed his way through her dress, her panties, and attached himself to her body. It was the first time he recognized that sex had a life of its own, separate from resolve, independent of a person. Pure reflex. Like breathing. Some unknown chemical or wire within him made it happen. This was why he never felt guilty afterwards. He knew he couldn't help it.

This same scene played out in closets, stairwells, bathrooms. Once a backyard. A living room. The bed of a truck. Sometimes it was premeditated, other times it simply happened. He spotted a woman on her knees, with a trowel, clawing through the dirt of her garden. Or he passed a woman in the supermarket whose flowery perfume overwhelmed him. It could be the swell of a breast or the blueness of an eye. He would follow them until the moment presented itself.

And though he would begin—when he found himself a crushing weight between their thighs—with a rapid jerking, he would soon slow his thrusts, creating a slow push and pull, a slow burn, wanting to feel every fraction of every second, the heat that gripped him moistly and ultimately choked from him a sudden swelling gush that left the bottom of his stomach feeling punctured, an empty space of air. And then he would hear, for the first time, the sobbing of the creature beneath him. Their body split in half by the impact of him.

It had been a long time since the last one. But he remembered. He remembered all of them. He carried around their memories like precious stones clicking softly in his pocket, something to finger now and then.

Except her. He could only watch and imagine her above and below and beside him.

Sometimes, after he finished his chores and ate his supper and the sky darkened with evening, Gerald would drive to the outskirts of Eugene, where his brother and Gertie lived. Their home crouched in the middle of an oak forest. He would park on a nearby haul road and hike through the woods, picking his way through a blackberry bramble, stepping carefully over mossy logs with slugs jewelling their surface. And then he would smell woodsmoke and maybe something cooking and in the distance he would spot a brightness that grew more and more distinct, floating out of the night, the orange square of a window.

When he reached the place where the woods stopped and the mowed grass began, he would hunker down behind a stump, its rich damp wood giving off a smell not unlike a woman, a whiff from between her legs. From here he would stare at that window as you would stare at a fire, mesmerized by its ragged orange color, the way its heat plays across your skin.

To bring her closer, he would carry his rifle with him and position it on the stump, staring through its scope, waiting for her figure to pass before the window or settle into the couch in the living room. The scope of the rifle would fill with the image of her, sometimes showing all her teeth in a smile, sometimes pursing her lips in anger, sometimes wrinkling her forehead or biting her thumbnail or bringing a mug of tea—two-handed—to her mouth. Staring down the length of a rifle, he imagined his body a bullet that would crash through the glass and enter her.

At times like these his breath and his pulse would quicken and in his mind sound together like waves crashing closer and closer to a sand castle abandoned on a beach.

Something he experienced again now, so many years later, when standing outside her bedroom, his fingers tracing the wood grain of the door, finally settling on the knob, turning it. The hinges made a noise like a dying bird when he pushed his way into the darkness of the room. A blue rectangle of moonlight fell from the window and onto her bed.

At that moment he noticed her eye. She had these big blue eyes with plenty of white in them, and though one of them drooped closed, the other shone in the moonlight, watching him. "Cookie," she said.

"Yes," he said. "Cookie."

He slowly moved across the room and slowly sat at the edge of the bed he and his brother had carted into the house three months ago. He ran a hand along the quilt and fingered a loose bit of string. Then he lay back, settling his weight into the mattress, and when he did he noticed beneath him the hollows and dips, shaped over the years by Jacob. Now he's got a new place to rest, Gerald thought, imagining a coffin's satin upholstery, the contours his brother's body would mold within it. At that moment he felt closer to his brother than he had in a long time, as if they had become, even if only for an instant, the same person.

He felt his hand move away from him, crawling across the mattress like a pale spider and seizing her fingers and weaving them together with his own. She gave him a squeeze that could have meant *hello* or *please, no.* He rolled on his side and raised himself up on his elbow so that his face hung over hers. He had for so long imagined them together, and now here she was—so close her breath played across his face—but he could only breathe in as she breathed out, filling his lungs with the heat of her.

Seventy-five years old and he still milked his own cows and planted and harvested his own fields, his only help a hired man named Tom Mullet. This morning, after the scraping and spraying that followed the first milking, Gerald stood in the open doorway of the barn and watched Tom negotiate the four-wheeler through a huddle of cattle, on his way to the far side of the pasture, where a barbed-wire fence needed mending.

Above Gerald, in the hayloft, the peacocks cooed, their soft gossip reminding him of how Jackie sounded on the telephone all day, these past few days, telling the same story over and over as she accepted condolences and explained that Gerald would prefer not to speak with anyone presently. He cocked his head and listened to them a time before trying to mimic their sounds, but it was more of a groan that escaped his lips and upon its utterance the peacocks went quiet.

He would have to go inside soon, to shower and shave and dress for the funeral mass. But first he would feed the penned calves. With their gray tongues they licked the grain from his shaking fingers and left behind a film of spit. When he finished with them, he latched the gate to their pen and sealed the grain bucket and sat down on it. The calves stuck their mallet-shaped heads through the bars and bit down on his coveralls, tugging at him, still hungry.

"You cows," he said, "are a bunch of damned pigs."

His words, once spoken, sounded distant from him, as if they belonged to someone else. And he realized he was straddling two worlds—as he often did these days—breathing the air of the past and present at once as his mind fogged over with memory:

It had been a long day. He and Jacob had milked and lugged wood for the woodstove and pitched hay out of the loft and scrubbed the cellar walls and applied to them a fresh coat of whitewash. In all of this time they paused only to eat a few ham biscuits and drink a jug of water from the cold pantry. Now it was four o'clock and nearly time to milk again and their mother wanted them to slaughter a hog for Christmas supper the following day.

They chased after it, both of them laughing, slipping in the snow, with the hog trotting just ahead of them. Jacob finally tackled it, struggling as it tried to bite and hoof him, while Gerald stood nearby with a sledgehammer raised above his head. "Steady, Jacob," he said. Down came the hammer and the hog lay still with a dent behind its ear.

With a carving knife they opened up its throat and the blood spread lavishly in the snow. Gerald remembered it looking as though it would taste good. They folded their arms and waited for the animal to bleed out. After a minute Jacob got bored and packed a snowball out of red slush. He tossed it in the air and caught it, then cocked his arm back and slung it at Gerald. It hit him in the face.

Immediately he felt a terrible anger rising in him. Some of it came from exhaustion and some of it came from the snowball, but most of it concerned the announcement Jacob had made the day before—about his plans to leave the farm. The courage that took, the freedom that came with it, made Gerald clench his teeth so tightly his jaw popped. When he wiped away the snow, it left his hands red, as if the blood had come in anger to the surface of his skin.

So he charged and tackled his brother to the ground and they fought—they *needed* to fight—punching each other all over, everywhere but the face, and when they grew tired they lay in the snow, resting, their breath escaping their mouths in gray clouds that mingled together.

Then they gutted the hog in silence. Gerald remembered the terrible reek of their butchering—so different than that pleasant odor of things newborn, of baby calves, their smell somewhere between warm milk and chicken soup.

The memory belonged to both of them, but now only Gerald remained to remember it, sitting alone in the barn, his right hand trembling like the leg of a dreaming dog.

A crow perched on top of the bell tower at St. Anthony's. It flew off, when Gerald pulled up, as if to tell someone he had arrived. The parking lot was full of Chevy trucks and Buick sedans and Gerald found a place among them and made his way along the sidewalk and into the foyer, where a crowd of men in black suits and women in black dresses drank coffee from Styrofoam cups and ate powdered doughnuts off napkins. When he shouldered his way past them, they smiled tight-lipped smiles, nodding, reaching out to touch him reassuringly on the back.

With no more thought than he put into washing his hands he reached for the holy water and traced a large cross from forehead to breast and from shoulder to shoulder before entering the main chapel. Here the air smelled heavily of dust and aftershave and carpet glue, with a hint of something sweeter, the pollen of the flowers crowding the stage. Two stained-glass windows framed the alter, swarming with a colored light that revealed the long-headed hollow-eyed

Christ that bloodily presided over a closed coffin, glossy and white, almost translucent, like a pane of soap about to be blown into a bubble, the bursting of which would unveil his brother, floating and turning in the air.

Gerald made his way down the aisle and knelt with some difficulty next to the front pew, again making the sign of the cross, this time muttering, "In the name of the Father and the Son and the Holy Spirit." He took hold of the pew and his old joints popped when he hauled himself up and took his place next to Gertie, who wore a black shawl and sat crookedly, leaning against her daughter Jackie as if for support. If he had not known her fatigue—the familiar slope of her shoulders, her eyes shut and her mouth a black O—he might for a second have thought her dead.

Gerald didn't turn around to look, but he could hear the church filling up, as the air filled with the shuffling of sleeves and tissues, the creaking of pews, the low murmur of voices, the occasional cough and sniffle. He counted the flower arrangements—twenty-seven in total—and felt a mild irritation—all this pointless decoration for the dead reminding him of the white peacocks, somehow.

Eventually Father Armstrong took his place at the pulpit and gave the introductory rites in a solemn voice. This was followed by the Prayer of Confession. And then the organ shouted the refrain from "Amazing Grace" and everyone stood and sang at first falteringly and then with greater confidence as their throats warmed up. Everyone except Gerald, who moved his mouth but made no noise.

After the Liturgy of the Eucharist and the Prayer of Intercession, the ushers passed out small white candles with cardboard shields around their middle. Father Armstrong took a candle from the candelabra and walked down the aisle, lighting the wicks of those closest to him, asking everyone to share their flame with their neighbor. Before long, fire glowed from every corner of the church and Father Armstrong ascended the alter once again.

When he began the invocation—"Holy God, holy strong One, holy immortal One, have mercy on us"—the congregation raised their candles to their foreheads and then lowered them to their stomachs and then extended them back and forth across their chests. In her right hand, her good hand, Gertie gripped a candle of her own and perhaps consciously—or perhaps not—she too traced the pattern of the cross and in doing so ran the flame across her shawl.

Just before she howled in pain, she struck Gerald as so beautiful, her face taking on a look of rapture as fire rose around it in an orange halo.

At the Aurora Sinai Medical Center, Gerald sat in the corner of the room, watching her sleep. Her face, enfolded in bandages, moved every now and then, contorting itself secretly beneath its wrappings. A black gap indicated where her mouth was, but otherwise her features were unavailable to him.

A few minutes before, Jackie and her husband Bill had been there. Neither could stop moving, sitting down and then standing up a moment later, rubbing their hands together and breathing deeply.

"You should have known not to light her candle," Jackie said to Gerald at one point.

"What are you yelling at him for?" her husband said. "It's no more his fault than yours or mine or anybody else's."

Her expression softened and a few tears raced down her cheeks. "I know, I know," she said. "You think I don't know? I'm upset. Aren't I allowed to be upset? I mean, considering?"

Gerald watched her pace back and forth and thought,

I held you when you were wet and purple and screaming, only a few hours old. I could have dropped you then and silenced you.

She stopped in her manic pacing and looked at him. "What did you say?" she said.

"Nothing," he said, not knowing how much he had said aloud. "I'm just an old man mumbling."

She brought her hand to her forehead, as if checking her temperature. "God, I don't know how much more of this I can take." She raised her face to the ceiling and raised, too, the volume of her voice. "There's only so much a person can take!"

For another minute they all watched Gertie, her chest rising and falling beneath a white sheet. Then Gerald told them to go get a cup of coffee, a breath of fresh air. He told them he would look after her. "You'll feel better," he said.

"Maybe that would be nice," Jackie said. "A nice cup of coffee."

"Go," he said, and they left him there.

He waited a minute and then rose from his chair and approached her, bending over the bed, over the guardrail, to kiss her. His mouth opened and briefly covered her own. Her head twitched at his touch.

In that moment, when their lips came together, his mind went elsewhere as he remembered her as she was, the glimmers of another time. She was running out of the ocean, her heavy breasts swaying inside her bathing suit. She was laying down a picnic blanket in the park and weighing down its corners with rocks so it wouldn't flap in the wind. She was skating toward him on a frozen pond. Snow fell and the motion of it made the sky seem as if it were lowering, pressing down on her with its immense gray weight. On all of these occasions he knew his brother had been there, too, but in his mind he had excised the memory of him as if with a pair of scissors.

Then he pulled his mouth away from hers and she was just a body barely breathing in a bed.

His hand began to quiver. He crossed his arms, tightening them across his chest in an effort to stop the shaking, holding himself as it grew steadily worse. But he was unable to stop it.

When he climbed awkwardly onto her bed, he was only vaguely aware that for the second time in as many months his body was behaving beyond his control. Perhaps if his brother had stayed on the farm, if he—Gerald—had been the one to pursue some other trade. Perhaps if he had thrown a suitcase in the back of his pickup and moved far away from here and not had to endure fifty years of watching from a guarded distance a life unavailable to him. Perhaps if he had found a woman of his own—and married her—perhaps that would have satisfied something and rendered the darker parts of him impotent. Perhaps then he would not have climbed the tree—the lush oak whose limbs hung over a busy game trail—and loosened the nails that held the stand in place and waited for the day it would collapse beneath his brother.

He ran his hand along her belly, her breasts, rubbing her, as if to arouse some life from her, but her body remained silent and expressionless. He peeled away the sheet and folded it over the base of the bed. Then he drew back her gown over her knees, her vein-riddled thighs, until he revealed the silver triangle of her pubic hair. He laid his cheek to it, as if it were a pillow, its down tickling him. He could smell her. She smelled like iodine. And his ear, pressed against the soft mound of flesh, could hear the pings and gurgles of her insides. Among them he thought for a moment he could hear a voice calling to him—his brother's—yelling his name from somewhere up inside her. He imagined pressing his lips to her sex, breathing into the tunnel he had always dreamed of sharing with her, with his brother, moving his tongue and lips, whispering to them both the secrets he had kept tucked away inside for so many years.

He remained that way until he heard the door click open behind him, heard the sharp intake of breath and the thump and slosh of coffee as it fell to the floor and finally the footsteps coming toward him.

The Faulty Builder

The Faulty Builder

What bothers John most is the sight of his own tired face staring back at him in the mirror. His eyes are red-rimmed, watery. His forehead, the broad plain of it, is road-mapped with wrinkles. His skin is a yellow shade of pale. His hair has almost as much gray in it as brown; his wife says it makes him look *ex*tinguished. His lips appear pinched and they shudder now and then as if he were holding his breath to the limit.

This is March, and in Bend, Oregon, that means winter has six more weeks. The snow continues to fall and the snowdrifts continue to pile higher against the windward sides of homes. Windows remain sealed shut with frost so that the world outside appears always foggy, as if seen through a cataract. Icicles the size and shape of spines dangle from gutters. Blue jays and magpies flit from garbage can to garbage can, searching for something to scavenge, while emaciated deer stand, wobbling, on their spindly hind legs to seek out the seed from bird feeders, to peel the bark from low-hanging branches. The air is so thin and dry it makes nosebleeds common, so much so that it isn't at all unusual to see someone—in the grocery store, on the sidewalk—with blood all over their chest and a Kleenex shoved up their nose like a candlewick, a wet red heat burning through it. And the sky, the permanent cloud cover, bears down with a gray weight, like a low-slanting ceiling that makes John duck his head for fear of bumping against it, giving him a permanent slump-shouldered posture.

He has had enough of winter and enough of his job. He works in the Investment Products Department of Northwestern Mutual. Every day, alongside his coffee and bacon, he gulps down his Lipitor and Ramipril pills and drives to work in an egg-shaped Windstar minivan and settles into a windowless office that smells like carpet glue and doughnut glaze. On the wall hangs a diploma from OSU, and next to it, one of those motivational posters that across its bottom reads, DREAM. Above the word a dolphin leaps out of the sea, carving an arc through the sunset.

Here, in his orthopedic leather chair, he drinks Diet Pepsi after Diet Pepsi while talking to clients, reviewing accounts, typing up contracts and refiguring investment units, taking conference calls with financial representatives, the Securities and Exchange Commission, the IRS. He keeps his Internet browser open to the New York Stock Exchange. His eyes track its numbers, so many numbers, their black shapes swarming through his head like a stirred ant pile. All day long he speaks of things looking bullish and bearish, of tax implications, late trading, market timing. He so often says, "Effective with the close of business this afternoon" or, "Effective at the close of the following business day" that in his mouth the words have taken on a rolling rhythm and become a sort of song.

He needs to get away.

Consider this. The other day his doorbell rang at 4:00 a.m. When he went to answer it, his boxer shorts hastily tugged on backwards, his bathrobe billowing open in the cold winter air, he found a policeman waiting for him.

"Do you own a white minivan?" the policeman asked. His eyes were narrow and his shoulders were dirty with snow.

After a foggy second, John told him yes, rubbing the sleep from his eyes. Yes, he did. Why? Had it been stolen?

No, the policeman said. It hadn't been stolen. It had been left running. During the night he had driven through the neighborhood several times, each time noticing the cloud of smoke blasting from the tailpipe.

The policeman moved aside, allowing John to brush by him and step onto the porch. And there, in the driveway, next to the police cruiser, sat his car. Its tank had burned through its fuel. Its headlights glowed weakly under a scrim of snow.

John scratched the back of his head in the way of embarrassed men. "I'll be," he said. "I must have—when I came home from work, you see, I was going to jump back in the car—I left the engine running—I was going to go to the supermarket—and I must have—since I decided not to—forgot."

The policeman removed a flashlight from his belt and clicked it on and studied John a moment before saying, "Are you feeling all right, sir?" with "all right" seeming like a substitute for *drunk*.

"Yes." John raised a hand to shield his face from the light. "I'm fine. Everything is perfectly fine."

His doctor—a gaunt man with white wisps of hair combed carefully across his scalp—tells him a different story. "You're fifty pounds overweight. Your blood sugar is all over the place. Your systolic pressure clocks in at 150 mm Hg."

His doctor sits in a chair with his legs crossed and a

clipboard in his lap. Aside from his mouth moving he remains perfectly still, like a propped-up cadaver. "Do you know what that means, John?"

John sits across from him, his legs hanging off the examination table. He doesn't wear a shirt and his belly rests in his lap like a garbage bag full of warm milk. In response to the doctor's question his shoulders rise and fall in a shrug.

"To top it off." The doctor consults the clipboard. "Your triglycerides are up to 260 and your LDL is up to 330." He doesn't say these numbers as most would—in quick bursts—as two-sixty, three-thirty. He instead draws them out, laying heavy emphasis on the *hundred*.

There is a disapproving silence that John interrupts by shifting his weight, the sanitary paper beneath him crinkling. He tries to find something to concentrate on besides the doctor and settles on his hands, his wrists. He imagines a thin yellow gravy rushing through their pipe-work.

The doctor continues: "I'm only half-joking when I say I have obese seventy-year-olds with numbers not much different than these."

John tries to sound cheerful but his voice comes out sounding like it has a bad back: "I don't feel old. I don't feel age."

This is a lie. His eyes are black-bagged with exhaustion. His joints feel like pockets of broken glass. The staircase to the second floor of his house leaves him out of breath. His penis, when erect, droops like a scythe.

Because of his belly, the weight of it, his wife, Linda, prefers to be on top. Lately, inevitably, he slips out of her—and they either give up, if she can't push his softness back inside her, or she makes him finish her with his mouth.

"I don't feel old," he says and his doctor recognizes the lie by bringing together his white eyebrows and scraping his teeth across his lip. "I'm going to be perfectly honest with you. You *must* begin eating better, exercising more, working less." For each of these things he taps his finger against the clipboard.

"Or?"

The doctor gives him a tight smile. "Or." He slowly lifts his hand to his neck and makes a slitting motion.

Mid-March his wife, a fifth-grade teacher, has spring break—and John has saved up his vacation days to correspond with hers. They will be staying in Depoe Bay, at the Inn at Otter Crest, a mossy-roofed gray-sided hotel that hangs over a cliff hanging over the ocean.

There is something about the ocean. All that blue-green water stretching off into the horizon, uncluttered by flashing lights and concrete buildings and ringing phones. The way you can bring binoculars to your eyes and find, without looking very hard at all, a humpback or a gray whale breaking the surface of the water—a long black U sliding in and out of sight. And the waves roll over with a boom and sizzle their foamy white tongues along the sand. And the spume lifts off the water—and the wind smells of salt and algae—and he could spend all day crouching beside tide pools filled with bright-colored anemones, crabs, urchins.

It's always been that way for him. Nights, when he plops down on the couch and cracks open a can of Coors and sips from it, he often watches the Discovery Channel. He likes to see the sharks darting through schools of tuna, the squids blackening the water with their ink, the whales calling to one another. He likes to imagine himself floating someplace deep underwater, an underworld where fish would slither over his back and brush by his belly, where hunger would be his only concern.

Next to his bed he keeps a sound machine. It has all

sorts of different settings. Birds chirping. Frogs drumming. Thunder booming. Waves crashing. And he keeps it tuned in to this, the ocean setting. It's on a timer so that for fifteen minutes every night waves turn over next to his head, easing him into sleep. His wife complains that the waves don't sound like waves at all—they sound like paper torn slowly, she says—but to him they sound like the most beautiful thing in the world.

He doesn't know why he feels this way, just as he doesn't know why he used to eat dirt as a toddler. Certain people just feel drawn to certain things. And for him the ocean represents a kind of afterlife. The mere thought of it—the days he ticks off the calendar as his vacation time approaches—helps get him through his workweek. His dreams are there. Lost hopes and romantic possibilities and forgotten memories are there. Peace is there. Everything missing, everything he can't explain about his life, is there, washed up on the sand.

Which is why, the day before they leave for Depoe Bay, when Linda calls him into the living room and bumps up the volume on the television and points to the screen where the Portland weatherman talks about a major storm system moving toward Puget Sound, the *slight* possibility of it sliding south and coming to a head against the Oregon coast, he says, "So?" with some hatefulness in his voice.

"I think we should cancel," she says. "I don't think we should go."

"We're going."

"There's a 24-hour cancellation fee. That means we've only got—" she glances at her watch for emphasis "—another couple hours."

"It'll be fine."

"What if it isn't? Some vacation that will be. Sitting inside some moldy motel room all day. We could go to my mother's instead. I'd really like to see her. She's so lonely these days."

"Linda." Here he holds up his hand as if to block the words coming from her mouth. "I said it'll be fine and it'll be fine."

The next day they drive toward the wall of the Cascades. John can barely make out the mountains from the sky, the mountains covered in snow and the sky full of slow-moving clouds. Sagebrush lines Highway 20. Their white huddled shapes remind him of the ghosts of dwarves. He is happy to see them go, when near Sisters the trees thicken and the road steepens and the Windstar begins its slow crawl up the Cascades, toward the saddle-shaped dip between the North Sister and Mt. Jefferson that will mark the beginning of their descent into the Willamette Valley, where spring has already started.

Snow falls. Old-growth firs—sixty-, seventy-feet tall— loom close to the road and the snow weighs down their branches so heavily that blobs of white fall and splat against the minivan's windshield, swept away a moment later by the wipers. The wind blows, pushing the minivan toward the centerline. Ice crystals rise in whorls off the drifts and the sun catches them and makes them glitter.

Every now and then a blue sign will appear—advertising the Metolious River Recreation Area, the Hoodoo Ski Bowl—and a road will branch off the highway, a quick glimpse down it revealing cross-country skiers, snowshoers, snowmobilers, people dressed in bright-colored parkas from REI, people who spend so much time in ski goggles they have raccoon-like tans, people who enjoy winter. John doesn't understand them.

Semis park along the shoulder to put on chains. Enormous plows, like prehistoric beetles, scrape the snow from the road with their broad steel shovels and drop cinders behind them, making the road appear dusted with paprika, helping tires find purchase on the slick asphalt.

Linda yells at him, tells him he's going too fast. And he is. He can't seem to help it, his foot weighed down by the desire to leave all this behind.

Eventually they rise over the hump of the Cascades and follow the long winding highway down and down and down—and then something happens, the changes begin. The water begins to run off the icicles and the ice in the river breaks apart and glimpses of green emerge from the snow-drifts and eventually take over. He notices leaves unfurling from the branches of the oaks and ash and maple, and among them, clusters of trillium and bloodroot and white wild onions. Songbirds flutter between the trees.

He turns off the heat. He rolls down the window and lets in a warm wind. Two hours and he feels as though he has fast-forwarded two months. It's nice.

He can hear her voice, but barely, like an alarm heard through the mist of a dream. Then she hits him, a punch to the shoulder, and at this he jerks his head to look at her, his eyebrows shooting up as if to say, What was that, honey?

"I *said* I have to pee. I said so twenty minutes ago." Tall and sinewy, she is forty-seven and looks it, her pale skin dotted with age spots and finely lined with wrinkles. Under each of her eyes there is a purple patch. Today she wears a green hooded sweater, blue jeans that taper at the bottom, white tennis shoes. She has a bony nose. Her hair is the color of dead leaves.

"So we'll stop," he says.

"That's what I said. I said get in the right lane or you'll miss the turn, is what I said." She points emphatically at a roadside sign that reads, Rest Stop, 1 Mile Ahead. She rolls up her magazine, one of those women's magazines, as if to strangle it. "Jesus, do you ever listen?"

He cannot recall the last time he felt in love with her. Not that he doesn't love her now. It's just a different sort of love. Not that *in-love* love, that falling-off-a-cliff feeling that used to exist between them. He remembers how, so long ago, before they fell into the rhythms of their careers, before middle age bowed their backs and thinned their hair, Saturday mornings, she would wake him up with her hand—and afterwards, they would shower together, not minding the coldness and awkwardness that came with shifting their bodies beneath the thin stream of water. The cup of her elbow, the hollowed-out dip behind her knee, he remembers those places, how he would run his tongue along them and how their salty flavor and their pearly color reminded him of the soft mantle of an oyster shell.

Then she would cook breakfast in the nude, a damp towel wrapped around her head like a turban. The bacon would hiss and sputter and occasionally she would shout when a bit of grease popped off the pan and left a red spot on her belly, her thigh. And he would sit on the couch, jogging his eyes between the newspaper and the ripe curves of her body.

He remembers her like this: with a window behind her, and beyond it, a birch tree with the light filtering through its leaves. The small pleasure of seeing her just so, framed like a photograph, made him smile then—and now.

And she maybe senses this because she looks at him and smiles briefly before returning her attention to her magazine.

The rest area, a good quarter-mile off the interstate, consists of a dark-wooded building circled by an unkempt lawn speckled with fat dandelions. There are two rotten picnic tables, a garbage can, and mounds of freshly overturned dirt, the work of moles. The parking lot is edged by fifty-foot firs and oaks half their size, both covered with fluorescent green moss.

Theirs is the only car. He stands where the asphalt meets the grass, waiting for Linda, staring off into the woods. The sunlight that spills through the branches reveals the ragged mat last year's leaves make on the forest floor.

He has the same feeling here as when he walks into a church. The air is at once static and loaded, as if there is some kind of *under*sound his ear can't quite decipher. Like after a bell rings.

He has his head cocked. He is listening. His shadow falls across the lawn before him, drawing his eyes downward. In the grass something stirs, the blades shifting as if blown here and there by an absent wind. He bends his body in half to get a better look. There—the source of the small sounds—a moist black eye—a spade-shaped head—a leathery brown back spotted white—glimpsed not once but many times over. The entire lawn is alive with them—salamanders—dozens of them. The noise they make, barely discernable, is the noise of many tongues moving damply inside of many mouths.

He has heard about this kind of thing before. His grandfather grew up in Peoria, Illinois. There, before a tornado hit—the old man told him more than once—the birds went quiet, the sky turned dark as a bruise, and the salamanders and worms boiled out of their underground dens, drawn to the surface by the sudden shift in pressure.

Right then Linda appears beside him. "What on earth are you looking at?"

He isn't sure how to respond, and before he can, a salamander darts out of the grass and onto the asphalt. It pauses before her shoe, actually reaching out with one webbed foot to touch her—before retreating to the cool slivers of shade offered by the grass.

Her eyes don't actually grow bigger in her head, but they seem to, a small expression of horror he recognizes from the time, five years ago, when she visited the doctor complaining of chronic stomach pain, a stabbing sensation that had bothered her on and off for several years and had only recently become unbearable. X-rays revealed an ectopic pregnancy.

They had long given up on having a baby. And now this, a fertilized egg in one of her fallopian tubes had grown into a child the size of a salamander. When the doctor removed it—it had a black thatch of hair and a scrunched-up face, teeth—he determined that it had been inside of her for many years—dead—curled up in the dark muddy pocket of her belly.

Sometimes, when John burrowed his head between her thighs and darted his tongue in and out of her, he imagined he could taste the child. It was a sour pasty taste. Horrible enough to make him pull his head away, fighting the urge to gag. He always tried to hide the gagging with his hand or a quick wipe of the washcloth they kept on the nightstand, but one time she caught him, and he saw the look in her eyes, and it was heavy with a pain he had never seen in her before.

A sudden wind picks up, ice in its breath, chasing them back to the minivan. Once inside they watch the treetops nod and the branches sway as if something big is about to disentangle itself from the woods. An empty potato-chip bag swirls through the parking lot.

When John keys the ignition and pulls out of the rest

area and onto the highway, he can see, in the far distance, clouds, a thick black tide of them churning up over the green coastal mountains.

"I don't like the looks of this," Linda says.

As if on cue lightning flashes, a white zigzagging vein that lingers on his eyes.

He reaches for the radio, but her hand is already there, snapping the dial. She races through the channels—with pops of static between them—until she finds what she is looking for, the studied baritone of a broadcaster's voice, telling them about the low-pressure system that has unpredictably settled over the region, drawing the storm farther south than anticipated, into Oregon. Gale-force winds are expected. Maybe funnel clouds. Certainly hail.

"I think we should turn around." She rakes a hand through her hair, drawing it back to fully reveal her face, pinched with worry. "John? Why can't we turn around?"

"Because we're going on vacation."

"Can't we go somewhere else? We can still make it to my mother's by dinner. I could call—"

"No. The reservation's made." He makes a karate motion with his hand. "It's done. We're going."

"Don't make me say I told you so. I don't want to say that."

He almost says, "Yes, you do," but doesn't. Once her mood sours toward him it can take hours, days, to win so much as a smile from her face.

"It'll blow over. I'm telling you, by the time we get there it'll be all done and spoken for."

He snaps the radio off and lets his hand drop to the soft cooler that rests between the driver and passenger seat. He unzips it and rifles through it and pulls out a Diet Pepsi. He pops the tab and lets it run down his throat. Then he grabs a snack-size bag of Doritos. He tears it open with his teeth and pushes a handful of chips into his mouth and crunches them down to a paste, repeating the motion over and over until the bag is half empty.

"Chip?" he says to Linda.

When she answers him with a curt shake of her head, he continues to crunch his way through the bag. "Suit yourself." A minute later, finished, he licks the orange dust off his fingertips and runs his tongue along his teeth, hoping to find one last crumb, just a taste, that might somehow minimize what he recognizes as dread rushing through him, that old familiar feeling he thought he left behind.

Right then one of those Asian cars you could fit in your pocket—a black Mazda Miata—appears in his rearview mirror and a second later shoots past him, swerving in front of the minivan while going ninety at least. Its tailpipe is drilled to make a sound like growling. "Fucker."

"Excuse me?"

The car disappears around a bend, hugging it so tightly the tires leave a thin black strip of rubber on the road, and John makes his hand into a gun to shoot a bullet after it. "I was talking to that guy."

"I should hope so."

He tries to think of something more to say to her.

For the past thirty minutes—through Albany, Corvallis— Linda has leaned against the door, her head turned away, as if determined to maintain a separate space. He can see her reflection in the window. Her eyes are narrowed, focused on the storm gathering ahead of them. The sky hardens into blackness, as if slowly mineralized.

"Hey," he says. When she does not respond he says, "Hey," again, this time reaching out his hand, hesitantly touching her thigh.

Their eyes lock in the window.

"Hey," he says. "It's going to be fine. Seriously. Don't worry so much. It's going to be a great weekend. I'm really looking forward to it."

She does not respond except by raising her eyebrows a little higher on her forehead, as if they don't quite believe him.

At that moment he veers into the left lane to pass a semi. It is hauling a livestock trailer filled with a hundred panicky hogs. Through the ventilation holes John can see their snouts and shadows. When he is almost past the semi, its horn blares. Linda makes a gasping sound and John looks up to find the trucker looking down at them.

He has a cardboard sign duct-taped to his door. "Show Me Your Hooters," it reads. Above the sign, in the window, a big bearded man looks down on them. He wears a cap and in the shadow thrown by the brim of it his eyes appear as black hollows. A hand rises up and gives John and his wife a little wave. They continue like this for a few hundred yards, side by side, glancing between each other and the road, before John lays his foot on the gas and the minivan growls forward.

John remembers a story his grandfather told him—about a storm. It was the worst Peoria, Illinois, ever saw. Balls of lightning rolled down chimneys and exploded in living rooms. Hailstones the size of softballs crashed through windows. Pigs flew. Salamanders writhed. Straight-line winds sucked fence posts from the ground, daggering them into houses, barns. Funnel clouds came down from the sky and vacuumed up the earth.

On the outskirts of Peoria there was an underwear factory. The storm peeled off its roof like the lid to a tuna can. When the funnel clouds finally shrank and the winds died down and the sky lightened, everyone emerged from their basements to find the town turned inside out and garnished with panties.

There were panties everywhere—hanging from tree branches, telephone poles, car antennas—everywhere. And the survivors could only shake their heads and rest their hands on their hips, their mouths set in tight thin lines that expressed at once their shock and amusement.

The semi grows smaller in his rearview mirror and the storm grows larger before him, muttering and grumbling with thunder, darkening the air beneath it with skirts of rain, not close, but closer than before. Its clouds seem to ripple blackly and powerfully, like ocean swells.

Sometimes Linda got in these moods.

He would come home from work and find the lights off, a single candle lit in the living room. The orange glow of it would reveal her lying on the sofa, the pillows propped up behind her, a glass of Merlot in her hand. He would stand over her and she would seem barely able to turn her head, to lift her eyes to look at him, as though there were some invisible net draped over her body, holding her down. The kind, amused expression she normally wore would have melted away, replaced by the face of someone he only vaguely recognized. On her cheeks tears would have left behind a salty rime. On her lips, the dried blood of wine.

One time her vibrator was lying on the coffee table, another time a butcher knife.

He never knew what to say in these situations. Usually nothing. Usually he just shrugged off his suit jacket, knelt next to the couch, and petted her hair until she asked if he wanted to order a pizza. But not long ago—when was it?—sometime after the holidays, when the loneliness of winter had set in—he said, "You okay?"

In response she moved her shoulders in a sort of shrug, as if to ease away some pain.

And he put a hand to her cheek and said he didn't know if this was what was bothering her, but if it was, she should know that he thought it was a good thing they never had children. That was what he told her. It's probably for the best, he said.

He tried to make his voice buoyant, but the word *probably* weighed it down. "Reason number one," he said. "I just read this article in the *Wall Street Journal,* and you know what it said? It said that in twenty years, at the rate of inflation, it's going to cost 200 grand to send a kid to college. Can you believe that? Think of all the money we've saved." He held out his hand then as if they were being introduced for the first time. She looked at it, but didn't take it. "And there's nothing holding us back. You know how it is with all our friends. They can't go on vacation. They can't go out to dinner. They can't, they can't. For us, the sky's the limit. We can do whatever we want to do and we can go wherever we want to go."

On her face the patterns of the wrinkles and the shadows revealed her sadness. "What have we done?" she said. "Where have we gone?"

He almost said, "Depoe Bay," but caught himself, recognizing that it was time to stop talking. Each of his words he understood as a hollow canister containing only absence.

If they had looked into fertility treatments—if he had drunk less alcohol and eaten more vegetables—if she had angled her pelvis upwards, after he filled her with semen, letting it stew inside of her—if they had only tried a little harder and a little earlier—and if her fallopian tube hadn't clogged up with a carnival strangeness, the kind of thing you see preserved in formaldehyde—then maybe the architecture of his life would feel more substantial, less the product of a faulty builder whose craftsmanship had constructed around their marriage a windowless room where they invariably ate dinner on TV trays while watching *Entertainment Tonight*, where they drank whiskey sours on Fridays and got their oil changed every three thousand miles and carefully studied the Crate&Barrel catalogue and went to see the latest Tom Hanks movie and wore sombrero-looking hats when gardening.

He remembers what a friend of Linda's once said to them: "You have a lovely home. Now all you need are some children to mess it up." She had two boys, both of them red-faced, fat-legged toddlers who left their toys all over the yard and screamed when they didn't get their way. At the time John had laughed good-naturedly at what she said, thinking she was jealous and he was lucky. Now, without the possibility of children, he feels like a man standing at the edge of an oceanic void, at the jumping-off place of his life, with nothing to tether him to this world.

Now he and Linda huddle into their seats and say nothing. The sun moves in and out of the clouds. The trees to either side of the road vanish as they drive out of the forest and into pasture where cattle lick salt blocks and barns huddle against the windbreak of hills, and then past vineyards, and then alfalfa fields for ten miles, twenty, with the alfalfa swelling into trees and the trees closing in once more—like fingers—allowing only a thin strip of sky overhead that soon becomes clotted with blue-black clouds. Thunder rumbles. The air takes on a twilight dimness and John leans forward in his seat and clicks on his lights. They cast a colorless glow. A big burst of lighting comes, followed by thunder that sounds like a great chair dragged across the floor of the sky.

"I'm sorry," he says and she says, "I'm sorry too," and he isn't sure what she refers to, their bickering, their vacation, their marriage, all of it.

The wind swells, groaning against the windshield. Trees nod back and forth, leaning toward the road, some of them bent nearly in half. A branch snaps and crashes to the road before them and John revs the engine and swerves onto the shoulder and back into his lane to avoid it. "Shit," he keeps saying under his breath.

A drizzle starts, dotting the windshield. The drizzle thickens into a rain, coming down in gray sheets the wipers can't keep up with. And then the air blurs and thickens with swirling white as the hail begins. The world takes on a big rattle. In an instant everything grows as white as winter. He takes his foot off the gas and slows to forty, to thirty. The hailstones drum against the hood and the roof and the windshield, and he can feel the vibrations in his fingers—his fingers wrapped tightly around the wheel, fighting the wind and the uncertain surface of the road. Under the many-voiced roar of the hail he swears he can hear his heart beating—the deep-toned bu-bump of it like the notes drawn hurriedly from the center of a drum.

He is only dimly aware of his wife. When the words "Maybe we should pull over" finally register, too much time has passed to acknowledge them. All of his attention is crushed down into the thirty feet of road before him. Every time lightning flashes, every hailstone seems to pause in its descent, looking like a white beaded curtain that a moment later crashes to the ground. He tries to blink away the lightning—its afterimage sticks to his eyes—but every few seconds, there is a brighter flash, a louder rumble.

At first, between those hard blinks meant to bring his

eyes back into focus, he isn't sure what he sees in the near distance: red eyes, a black humpbacked silhouette that becomes not a monster, but taillights, the frame of a car. The Miata, he realizes, from earlier. It has slid off the road, into the ditch, coming to a rest against a tree.

At first—he can't help it—he feels a burning delight. In a life that has not turned out the way he expected, something has finally, in one violent instant, turned out the way he expected. The driver was going too fast and now he has paid for it. The sight of the car, its hood crumpled, makes John feel—for the first time in a long time—as if there is a certain logic to the universe. A comforting thought.

There are branches littering the road and with tiny jerks of the wheel he dodges the minivan through them. His eyes rise again to study the Miata, now twenty yards ahead, and there, by the side of the road, he spots the driver. The man—in his late teens, early twenties—just a boy, really—watches their approach. Through the driving hail, John can see his hair is an unnatural shade of blond. He wears a black leather jacket and black baggy jeans. He has blood on his face, and the blood stands out brightly against all that white. He holds his hands above his head and scissors them back and forth. The minivan closes in on him steadily. There is a glittering intensity to his eyes that John recognizes: confidence. Even after wrecking his car, the boy stares at John with confidence, certain he will stop.

And maybe this has something to do with why John hesitates a second—his foot rising off the accelerator, hovering over the brake—before trying to stop the minivan and finding out he can't.

"What are you doing?" Linda says.

John continues past the boy and spies the tilted vision of him in the rearview mirror. The boy turns to follow them, his mouth a big black O, still waving his arms, now with a kind of frantic disbelief that John finds reassuring.

"John?" his wife says. "John, what the hell are you doing?" There is a high urgent tone to her voice. "Stop. We've got to stop."

He says, "It's not safe," and it's not, with the trees, blown by the wind, leaning dangerously close to the road, their limbs like thick arms swatting at them—but still, it would have only taken a second to stop, to throw open the door and allow the boy inside. "He'll be fine."

She throws up her hands and lets them fall to her thighs with a slap. "He'll be fine, it's not safe? John?" The way she breathes—roughly through her nose—is a conversation in itself. *I can't believe you,* she's saying. He doesn't look at her, but he knows she is looking long and hard at him. He can *feel* her eyes, as if they carry heat in them.

"We've got to think of ourselves," he says and hits the steering wheel to drive home his point or express his regret, he isn't sure.

"*Your*self. That's all you've ever thought about."

"I'm happy thinking about myself."

"Yeah, you're happy." She gives him a cold look that carries the weight of their marriage in it.

"Listen," he says. "I might not be the best person in the world, but I think I know a thing or two about life and making it in this world and . . ."

Midsentence he turns to her and she meets his eyes easily, her stare ugly and penetrating. All of a sudden he cannot find any more words. In place of them he takes a deep breath that sends a cold wind whistling through the caves of his heart.

Outside, hail rakes at the windshield like an endless series of fingernails trying to claw their way in, and he begins to feel he is a part of it, the storm, separate from the minivan and from his wife, the blood icing up in his veins like a November river, his mind a white blur.

He tries to find distraction in the radio, clicking it on, and then, recognizing the song—"Sloop John B"—he turns it up. "Hey, this is from that record we used to play all the time. Remember?" Even as he white-knuckles his grip around the wheel and tries to negotiate a slick corner, he shakes his head back and forth and does a little dance in his seat.

The music fills the minivan and he finds himself momentarily lost in the sound, the syncopated three-beat, five-beat tapping of a drum, the high innocent voices of the Beach Boys. He hears in this music a certain vibration of meaning, of notes that seem to carry color in them—bright yellows, pale blues—like the starfish hugging the bottom of the ocean.

Then the radio cuts out. And the hail softens into freezing rain. Within a few minutes mittens of ice have formed around the wipers. He rolls down the window. Immediately a cold wind fills the minivan. His eyes water when he reaches outside and stretches his arm around the windshield and in a desperate grab lifts the blade off the glass so that when it snaps back the ice shatters.

When he seals shut the window, she says, "I can't believe you did that. I can't believe you just left him there."

John says nothing, only gives his head a little shake as if he can't believe it either.

"We need to stop," she says. "Do you hear me? Or *we're* going to be the ones on the side of the road."

"I know that, okay?" His voice has the high-pitched whine to it that he always tries, and fails, to suppress when he gets angry. "Just please, please, please shut up."

She touches her fingers to her neck, in that hollowed-out dip at the base of it, something she usually does before she cries. "We *need* to stop."

"Where? You show me a place to stop, I'll stop."

As if on cue they turn a bend and in the distance spot an Amoco station. It is a long rectangular building with windows that run its length and reflect the brightness of the lighting in the sky. Before it there are four gas pumps, behind it a shed, and next to it an abandoned truck eaten up with rust and blanketed with a thick coat of moss, with hail clinging to the moss, like clotted cream.

"Stop," she says. "Please."

The slush in the road is calf deep. When he brings down his foot on the brake, the back tires kick sideways before finding traction. He hangs a slow right into the station and parks before its entrance and shuts off the engine and a second later the windshield ices over. They pull on their jackets and zip them to their necks and jump out of the minivan to race through the lashing rain. Every step is a sliding uncertainty. John holds his arms out for balance. He breathes heavily, not used to moving with any kind of speed, and his breath curls away from him in the wind.

Linda makes it through the door first and doesn't hold it open for him. He catches it when it swings back, and with a grunt pushes through, into the dim light of the store. He stomps the ice from his shoes and leans against the wall and takes deep breaths and puts a hand to his chest and feels his heart, stopped up with white pockets of fat and awkwardly somersaulting at the top of his rib cage, but still pumping, by God. Another moment and he collects himself enough to take in his surroundings, a rack of T-shirts with eagles and wolves silk-screened across them. A display case of lacquered logs with clocks built into them. Grocery aisles crowded with candy and potato chips. There are antlers hanging from the walls, white-tipped, as sleek and sharp as knives. Behind the register hangs the largest set, like a tangled rack of bones, made not of bone but of dried blood vessels. Beneath them stands Linda, trying the phone on the counter and hanging it up with such force that John startles at the sound, a shriek escaping his mouth.

He looks around, worried someone might have heard, but there is no one. The store is empty, the attendant gone, perhaps at home, hurrying to close up his windows against the storm that gathered so suddenly in the sky.

At the storefront, with a good six feet between them, John and his wife stare out the windows. For a second the storm seems to die down, and John feels hopeful, wondering if this is it, the end—and then the wind puffs and groans and stirs to life once more. In the sky the clouds whirlpool, as if sucked upward into some cosmic plug hole.

"Not the worst I've ever seen," John says, "but right up there."

"Please. When have you ever seen—" She says something else, but thunder follows lightning and takes away her voice.

In a rush the rain hardens into hail. It comes down heavily, seeming to erupt from every inch of the sky, filling the world and whitening it, pouring down in an endless curtain so that the air seems to contain more ice than air.

John listens to the drumming against the roof, the windows, the asphalt, a sound he can feel as much as hear, the sort of rattle that might rise up among a thousand snakes. The hail makes dents, like tiny mouths, on the hood of his van.

Beside him Linda wraps her arms against her chest, as if hugging herself, and stares intently into the storm. "Something's coming," she says.

Outside, through the rattle of hail, John can hear things crashing about, knocked against the side of the store by the terrible wind. And under this he can hear a humming that grows steadily louder, an engine. Through the ragged holes glimpsed between the falling hailstones, he sees a light flare, then disappear, then flare again. These are hazard lights, blinking a warning against any fast-moving cars. They belong to a semi. It crawls along at no more than ten miles per hour. Slush fans out from beneath its tires when it pulls off the highway and into the parking lot.

John can hear the semi moan as it downshifts, and its brakes shriek in complaint when it finally comes to a halt at the edge of the parking lot. And there it idles. The engine seems to growl, waiting for him.

The semi is carrying a load of hogs to slaughter. When the lightning flares John can see them through the ventilation holes—their pink snouts, their shifting bodies—and then the door swings open.

There is the driver—an enormous body, nearly as wide as it is tall, dressed entirely in denim—climbing out of the semi cabin. A beard curls around his jaw. His cap perches high on his head.

From behind him comes another. Dreamily—and then in a panic—John recognizes the peroxide hair, the black leather jacket, the boy. He can feel his muscles gathering around his spine like a fist around a knife. There is such tightness in his posture he thinks he might break. "Oh no."

"Oh, thank God," Linda says. And then, concern creeping into her voice: "What's the matter with him? Something's the matter."

The boy, with a hand to his stomach, seems to fight a doubled-over posture. The truck driver loops an arm around his shoulder, helping to redistribute his weight, and together they limp toward the store, wading through the several inches of hail that has accumulated. Pain has replaced the confident look on the boy's face. He gnashes his teeth and every other step he closes his eyes for a long second, moving slowly through the hail, the stones popping off his skin and leaving red marks. When Linda opens the door for them, the wind lifts the hair from John's scalp.

In the middle of the store, in the center of the aisle, they stand like this—John, Linda, and the truck driver—the three of them making a half-circle around the boy. The boy lies on the linoleum floor, his head propped up by a bag of rock salt. Linda hunches over, resting her hands on her knees, as if she wants to crouch next to him and comb her fingers through his hair, but can't quite bring herself to do it. "We've got to help him," she says. "Poor thing."

John notices the trucker looking steadily at Linda. He is a sun-yellowed man. His beard has a pubic quality to it. The sight of him studying Linda makes John feel a little disgusted and jealous at once. When he clears his throat, both of them swivel their heads in his direction and wait for him to say something. This is what he comes up with: "I don't suppose you have a cell, do you?"

The trucker reaches into his breast pocket and pulls from it not a phone but a pack of Marlboros. He shakes out a cigarette and brings it to his lips and smiles around it, the smile aimed at Linda. "Do I look like the type would own a cell phone?"

John recognizes the look she gives the trucker—a long quizzical look, as if feeling him over with an invisible antenna—trying to figure him out. "No?"

The cigarette bobs in his mouth when he says, "Sorry."

The center aisle leads to a door bearing a sign that reads STAFF. The trucker goes to it and tries the knob. It opens and he moves through the doorway, disappearing into a rectangle of shadow, reappearing a moment later. "It's safer back here." His voice is like gravel. "You should come on back here. In case those windows go."

The boy must have broken his nose against the air bag. It seems to hang on him crookedly. A fan of dried blood spreads across the bottom half of his face, the red shadow of a beard. He has his eyes closed and John and Linda hover over him another minute before following the trucker.

When they peer in the doorway they find a Coleman lantern burning in the center of a Formica table. On the walls, illuminated by the dim orange light, hang trophy fish and posters of women in thong bikinis. Cigarette butts lay everywhere, their ash smudged blackly into the floor. A pile of cracked car batteries. Newspapers. In the corner, a mop clotted with chewing gum and candy wrappers. The ancient smell of mold rises from it.

Linda brings her hand to her nose, giving her voice a hollow quality, when she asks, "What are we going to do?"

The trucker drags an aluminum chair from the table and sits and indicates that they should do the same. "Take a load off."

"What about the boy," Linda says. "Shouldn't you do something?" A temporary truce, she looks to John for help, and he gives it, saying, "We really ought to do something."

"What else is there for him to do but rest? I'm no doctor. You think of something to do, do it."

She brings a thumb to her mouth and peels away a hangnail and seems to lose with it her apprehension. There is a cupboard in the corner and she fetches from it a bowl. She fills it with warm water and throws a washrag over her shoulder and returns to the center aisle, with John trailing behind her.

On her knees, next to the boy, she dampens the washrag and wrings it out and runs it across his forehead, his cheek, his chin, with such gentleness, wiping away the blood the way you would peel an orange, hoping not to break the skin. "There," she says when she dabs the last bit of blood from his chin. "Better?"

The boy has his eyes open and he gives her a small smile that bends into a grimace. "My ribs hurt," he says and clutches his chest with both hands.

John leans in and over her shoulder says, "He says his ribs hurt."

She stiffens, but doesn't turn to look at him. "I know what he said. Don't tell me what he said. I'm right here." Her voice grows immediately kinder when she addresses the boy. "I'm going to lift up your shirt, okay? Just to see." John recognizes the tone as the tone she uses when her fifth-graders occasionally call their home, confused by homework.

She parts his leather jacket and peels back his T-shirt and gives a gasp. The right side of his chest looks like an arthritic fist, the bones pressing in knuckley bulges against his skin with a brownish gray color in between them. The boy looks down at the damage, then up at them, his face broken up by pockets of shadow and light.

The trucker appears in the doorway, leaning against its frame. Smoke surrounds his words. "I seen this happen before," the trucker says, shaking the red cherry of his cigarette at them. "The steering wheel punched him." He takes the last drag off his cigarette, burning it down to the filter, then lifts his boot to stub out the ash out its sole. "This ain't good," he says and continues to say under his breath. "No. Not good."

Linda says, "Will you please be quiet?"

The trucker takes off his hat and looks into the dark mouth of it before returning it to his head. "Bite my head off."

The way John is standing apart from everyone with his legs shoulder-length apart and his arms hanging stiffly at his side, he must look like a metal swivel rack crowded with beef jerky, maybe a pyramid of soda, part of the store. His heart feels as if it is turning over in his chest, and right then, maybe the boy hears it because he raises his head and looks at him. His expression hardens.

"You're the one drove by, left me standing there."

John says nothing. There is a heavy silence broken by thunder.

Five minutes later, Linda is telling John in a hushed, pressing voice that they need to do something, they need to get the boy to the nearest hospital.

"What can I do?" His voice comes out as an almost stutter, a beat between each word. "We're in the middle of nowhere—in the middle of a storm—and you want me to take him back out there? In *that?*" He gestures to the window. "We'll both end up dead."

She looks ill. "I should have known better than to even ask."

He hates how she stares at him—the black patches under her eyes like runny mascara—how she thinks she knows him so well. He is older than her. He has done plenty of things she hasn't been a part of, wild gutsy things. He used to run—he placed 515th in the Seattle marathon. When he was in high school he gutted a deer in the middle of a snowstorm. Another time, from the roof of his apartment building, he overturned a garbage can full of water on his landlord, five stories below. Or how about in college, when he and his friends took a road trip—down through California—into Mexico? There he lost his virginity to a whore with purple eye shadow. At the hotel, out on the balcony, he pushed her up against the railing and seized her wet crotch with his hand. They fucked right there, right in the open, where anybody could have seen them.

This was all before Linda knew him. What they had become together seemed separate from that, almost like an intrusion. Remembering how he was before makes him feel a little more alive, somehow.

He asks what she wants to do.

"I want to scream," she says.

He says he knows the feeling.

John is standing at the front of the store, looking out the window. Now and then the glass seems to wobble against the force of the wind, shuddering like a thin sheath of ice beneath a mad current.

The trucker lights another cigarette. "Hey," he says and blows a thin jet of smoke. "You better get back from there. That window is liable to go."

John regards the trucker before returning his attention to the window, then holds up his hand, like a dare, and lays it on the glass.

Right then the wind rises up as it never has before, with a moan. The hail swirls in hypnotic designs and all around them the trees dance. A soft violet light surrounds anything metal—the minivan, the semi, the gas pumps, even John's wedding band—and his hair rises on end. Little balls of electricity dance between the branches of the trees and the air has a sparkling quality to it, like what sunlight does to river water. The sparkles focus into a whip of lightning that uncurls from the sky and takes hold of a nearby tree.

Instant daylight.

A white vein runs down the tree's middle and turns into yellow fire and the thunder explodes, louder than the force of ten cannons fired at once, the noise bottoming out into a rumble that gets hushed away by a blast of wind.

There is a far-off sound—a wet snap—like a broken bone—and a branch from the tree missiles through the air, striking the parking lot, skipping once before settling into the slush and skating toward the store, the front door. With a crash the glass there opens up into a knee-high hole with a broken branch jutting through it, already oozing sap.

John takes his hand off the window and looks at it in disbelief, like a pistol accidentally fired. It's just an ordinary hand, with soft pink palms, a dark stripe of hair along the knuckles, certainly not capable of anything remarkable. He puts it in his pocket and looks at the trucker, who still leans in the doorway and calls out in a teasing voice, "Told you so."

He is so certain of himself. How can he be, with his frayed jeans and his fingernails carrying crescents of dirt beneath them? Even at this distance, ten yards away, beneath his beard a smile is evident. His lips are unnaturally red, the red of a poisoned apple. John imagines being bitten by him. His throat constricting, his heart seizing up with poison, and after his last breath stills, maybe his face will be transfixed with a final look of peace unavailable to him now.

The boy is coughing—big damp coughs that rattle around in his lungs and make him draw his knees against his chest. John can hear them and he can hear the wind rushing through the trees and crying through the hole in the door and rustling the magazines in the magazine rack.

The boy is coughing and John has his back to him, his hands jammed in his pockets. He watches, curiously, as the dark round shape of a raccoon emerges from the nearby woods, waddles across the parking lot, and squeezes through the hole in the door, lured to the warmth like people lured to whatever they're lured to. It shakes the dampness from its fur and stands on its hind legs and sniffs the air before scurrying down the candy aisle, disappearing into some dark corner of the store. No one seeks it out with a broom, not with the storm as their common enemy.

The boy is coughing and finally John turns to look, and when he does, he observes his reflection in the glass doors of the soda cooler. It never fails to surprise him. In his head he still looks as he looked in college: flat-bellied, square-jawed, his muscles tight and surging beneath his skin, all the arrogance in the world suggested in his expression, the way his mouth always hiked up on one side. Not anymore. That John is buried beneath a mask of fat that he wouldn't mind carving off with a penknife. He looks back and forth between the boy and his reflection, momentarily unbalanced, realizing some resemblance between them.

The boy coughs and some blood dribbles down his chin and his tongue darts out to taste it and when he coughs again John feels the blood rattling in his own chest. He takes off his jacket and goes over to the boy and lays it over him. After all these minutes of feeling powerlessness, it feels good to find something he can do to help.

He tries to think of what to say. "We're going to get you help," he decides on.

The boy has the gray kind of blue eyes that seem forever weighed down with sadness. He turns his head to the window, with the hail streaking down it, and says, "Now he wants to help."

John flips through magazines without really reading them while the hail outside softens into rain, then hardens to hail once more. Everything turns bright—followed by a darkness that eases into dimness once again—and thirty seconds later sounds a thunderclap that makes him duck his head a little.

In the silence that follows the rattling boom, he looks around self-consciously to see if anyone saw him flinch. From the end of the aisle, as still as a statue, stands the trucker. He is looking at Linda. Linda is hunched over the boy. Her back is arched and her bottom is provocatively raised. John knows what is going on inside the trucker's head, as if a window revealed it: Linda unclothed, his thumbs hooked inside her buttocks, parting them so that he might slide inside of her easily.

John can see this clearly—can hear the moan escaping both their mouths—as if it were happening in front of him. And, as strange as it seems, the possibility of it thrills him: someone might want what is his.

A kind of caffeinated excitement works through his veins. He can feel an erection pressing against his pants. And then something else, a jolt. He grabs his arm, pained by what feels like the lingering effects of lightning: small twinges of electricity running up and down his veins. This isn't the first time this has happened, so he doesn't feel particularly alarmed. He walks around the store until he locates the shelf crowded with aspirin and pops open a bottle of Bayer. He punches through the foil seal and rattles the pills out in his palm and dry-chews them down to a bitter paste and listens to the murmur of the hail, rising and falling in gusts, like the murmur of surf, and he tries to let the sound take him away from here.

But there is a torn-open feeling in the place just above his stomach. It makes him grab desperately for a nearby shelf.

He grips its metal as tightly as the pain that clutches his torso. He shuts his eyes with such force that fireworks seem to explode across the inside of his eyelids, and when he opens them again, the white and red lights linger in his vision and play across the faces of his wife and the trucker and the boy, all of them a few paces away, watching him.

"What's your problem?" his wife asks. There is wariness in her eyes and then concern. She takes a few hesitant steps toward him. "Are you okay?"

He tries to answer but cannot. His lungs won't push air up his throat. And his tongue is a dry hard muscle in his mouth. He does not notice until he reaches for her that his hands are trembling. She takes a step back from him and his hands, seeking some sort of purchase, swipe clumsily across a nearby shelf and knock to the floor several boxes of Whoppers, which break open, releasing dozens of chocolates that roll around like pool balls seeking a pocket to die in.

If only he could draw a deep breath and maybe drink a cold glass of water, then he might feel better.

His legs give out and his weight drags him to the floor while over and over his wife asks, "What's the matter?"

What's the matter? He is simply and horribly afraid. Afraid of the pain that has taken hold of him, the needles stabbing through his arm, his chest. And accompanying this fear is a many-sided sense of shame—for collapsing in front of everyone, for living a life he sees as so small and insignificant, so devoid of value and purpose, and for strangely, suddenly, desperately wanting it to continue, more than anything. All the black things in his life—all that is doubtful, fearful, hateful—seem to have pooled themselves into a single feeling, the burning weight in his chest.

Even with his wife looming over him, he feels strangely deserted. Through their legs he spots the boy, lying a few feet away. For a moment they only stare at each other, each of them curled up to the linoleum and dampening it with their pained sweat. Little trembles go through their bodies. The boy closes his eyes and when he opens them, where his eyes should be, there is only blackness, the kind encountered at the bottom of a well too deep to draw a bucket from. Then he blinks again and his eyes return, staring at John.

The hail continues to fall and John imagines he can hear in its hissing rhythm the ocean, the waves turning over, the tide pulling them in and out, their slow rhythm like an enormous clock that indicates its time through the movement of water. It seems to work against the beating of his heart.

He imagines himself on the beach—near dawn—an early fog hanging over the water. He hears the long mournful cry of a foghorn. Way out past the breakers, ghosting in and out of sight, fishing boats troll for halibut and salmon. He steps into the surf, half in, half out, and it would be so easy to let the tide carry him out, to sink to the bottom of the sea, a place where plankton drifts by like clouds.

The fantasy is agonizingly brief. One second he can feel the waves lapping at his skin and then suddenly they are gone and he is on the floor again. His wife looks searchingly into his eyes and he unlocks his gaze from hers to stare over her shoulder where hail spills through the hole in the window, spilling through in a continuous stream, like blood pumped from a ragged heart.

Somebody Is Going to Have to Pay for This

Somebody Is Going to Have to Pay for This

David works for the city, the water division. He spends his days driving around Pine, Oregon, in a pumpkin orange Chevy Astrovan. He's done the math: every day, on average, he puts a hundred and fifty miles on the odometer. That's an eight-hour day, five days a week, for the past ten years.

He clocks in at seven each morning. He drives around until ten. Then he selects a hydrant and cranks it open, letting its water rush into the street. This is called hydrant flushing, and it's necessary because rust and sediment settle at the bottom of the pipes that interlace like veins beneath the ground. He does four or five hydrants a day, and each job takes only ten minutes or so. While the water roars—thousands of gallons coming out brown, then yellow, then white, then clear—he waits in the van, reading the newspaper. He reads every page, even the classifieds. When David wrenches off the water, a hush falls over the street. The only sounds are the drip and gurgle of water, the distant blaring of car horns, and the squeak of his shoes as he returns to the van and settles his weight into it. Depending on the time, he may hunt down another

189

hydrant, or take his lunch break, or just drive around some more.

It's a job. And at fifteen dollars an hour, it's a good one, giving him more than enough to cover the rent and pay for the Coors that runs down his throat every night when he sits in front of the TV watching nature shows where big animals tear apart little animals.

Joe is his supervisor. He's an old guy, closing in on seventy, with a pack-a-day habit and too much weight piled on his small frame. His nose and eyelids are a mess of broken blood vessels and his cheeks permanently carry the beginnings of a white beard. For four years he's been threatening to retire. Instead he sits in his office with the blinds closed. He smokes cigarettes and reads old copies of *Field & Stream* and listens to talk radio.

Today he waves David into the fluorescent buzz of his office. David hesitates a moment, and winces. The last time he went in there was nearly six months ago. It looks much the same. Stacks of newspapers yellow in the corners. A nudie calendar, several years old, hangs from a nail. On a desk in the middle of the room there's an unfinished game of solitaire, a Yosemite snow globe, and an ashtray piled high with cigarettes.

Joe pulls out a rumpled pack of Marlboros. "Smoke?"

David shakes his head, no. He is wearing a Trail Blazers ball cap and he pulls on its brim, bringing a shadow to his face. Then he sits in a chair facing Joe and spreads his hands flat on the tops of his thighs. Out of nervousness—wondering why he is here—he drums out a song with his fingers.

Joe shakes out a cigarette for himself, lights it, and says through a cloud of smoke, "You know Johnny Franklin, right?" He's talking about the fire chief, a broad-shouldered guy with gray mutton-chop sideburns.

"He's got a son," Joe says. "Just finished a twelve-month deployment with the Army National Guard in Iraq. Now he's back. Johnny asked me to do him a favor. I said I could help."

"You're letting me go?" David's voice comes out as a croak.

"No, no." Joe neatens the cards on the desk and smiles. "I'm giving you a partner."

David leans back in relief, and when he raises his hands their sweat leaves two gray prints on his jeans. He smiles, but the smile fails a little when he realizes that he will have to share his life with another. He feels like an only child whose parents have announced the imminent birth of a brother. "Thing is," he says, "with the work I'm doing, I don't know that I need somebody—"

Joe cuts him off. "I told him to show up at seven-thirty." Smoke tusks from his nostrils. "Should be here any minute. You'll show him the ropes for me, yeah?"

"Sure." David nods his head and mumbles through his lips. "I can do that for you."

"That's good." Joe gets up heavily from his swivel chair and they shake hands.

A birthmark obscures the right side of David's face. His whole life, when he walks into a room, it seems as if everybody swings around at once to give him a long stare, heavy with curiosity and disgust, the way you might look at a broken leg or a homeless man shouting at a cat. The purple skin is raised and coarse. It looks like blood spilling down his cheek from a gash in his forehead. He walks around with his head ducked, his ball cap pulled low, trying to keep his face hidden. It's a little like being held hostage, riding in the Astro van with the right side of his face exposed.

The man seated next to him, Stephen, has a boxy jaw and

a blackish buzz cut that glistens like a wire brush. His skin is deeply tan, and his shoulders are rounded with muscle. They've been tooling around Pine, with the radio filling the silence between them. David isn't used to talking. He is used to driving. So he answers most of Stephen's questions in an abrupt barking way, concentrating on the road before him as if this were an unfamiliar city.

"So this is it?" Stephen says, all the vowels stretched out in a Central Oregon drawl, each word a lazy sort of song, clipped off by a hard consonant. "We just drive around? Every now and then flush a hydrant?"

"Pretty much."

"Nice."

David tends to notice the ugly things about people, itemizing them in his head, creating a checklist that brings him some kind of comfort. Now he takes note of Stephen's hands. The palms are yellow and callused, the tops hairy, knotted with veins. They look like hands you might dig up in the desert, long buried.

Stephen studies David too—not so subtly. "You ever watch any of those *Dr. Phil* shows?" Stephen says.

David jerks his head to look at Stephen straight on, wondering if this is the lead-up to a joke, but Stephen appears sincere, his forehead puckered with concern. "That's one of the things I missed most. TV. No TV over there. Ever since I got back, I watch everything. I can't get enough of it. Even the Food Network. Can you believe that shit? I don't even cook. The other afternoon, I'm watching that *Dr. Phil* show and I see somebody had the exact same deal as you. They zapped him with a laser, cleaned him right up."

David feels his hand, like something separate from him, rise to his cheek. He traces his fingers along the birthmark, shielding it partially from view. "Really?" he says in a half-whisper.

"Just like that. Clean as can be." Stephen's hand polishes an imaginary spot from the air. "Like they wiped wine off a counter."

David isn't sure how to feel, until he realizes that no one has ever been so direct with him. It puts him at ease, unlike those people who look at him out of the corner of their eye, their mouths pressed into self-conscious frowns. He glances at the road just long enough to say, "Could never afford something like that," and then his eyes shyly meet Stephen's again.

"It's free. The show does it. Can you believe that shit? And hey, hope you don't mind, but you should look into it. You're not an ugly guy, you know. Under all that."

David says, "You think?" but Stephen doesn't hear him. He's talking about some guy named Cody—a first sergeant from Tennessee. "Prettiest man alive. Truly. Looked neat even in his fatigues. Anyway, one day, routine patrol, IED rips his Humvee to shit. Flames everywhere. Humvees look tough, but they burn like crazy. Thirty seconds and you're up in smoke. That's what happened to Cody. Poof. God knows how, but he ends up living. Third-degree burns—or whatever the worst degree is?—first-degree maybe. You know what I mean. The kind of burn where you can't tell muscle from skin. I went to see him in the CSH. Downtown Baghdad. Dude was fucked up. Looked like a skeleton glopped with red paint." He goes quiet for a minute, and when he speaks again, his voice comes out soft, gray-hued. "What I'm trying to say is, you got a birthmark, so fucking what? You know?" Stephen punches David in a desperately friendly way. "You know?"

David feels his mouth curl into a smile, tentatively, and he gives Stephen a tiny nod, the smallest of movements.

The next few weeks, things get better, not all at once, but incrementally, so that the change doesn't really register with David, like the air that slowly cools as September turns into October. He doesn't feel happy, not precisely, but he does feel something new, a sting, a want.

They drive along North Avenue to Seventy-sixth Street, to Kenwood, and up into Pharaoh Butte, where retired Californians live in three-story homes, set back in their own spaces of lawn with wraparound porches and American Beauty rose gardens surrounded by Japanese maples. River-rock pillars flank the front doors. Chandeliers hang in the entryways.

"You ever visit Saddam's palaces?" David says.

"Nah," Stephen says, as if he wishes he had, not wanting to disappoint. "Drove by one once. Real nice place."

"Yeah?"

"A regular Taj Mahal." Stephen nods at the homes sliding past their windows. "So what—lawyers, doctors—what do you think these cocksuckers do?"

"Don't know," David says. "Important stuff, I guess."

They turn around and drive along Grand Avenue to the Parkway, to Mayfair Road. They dip under a rust-stained bridge and zip past the dump, where seagulls and crows circle the pale wash of the sky. In Moccasin Hollow, a collection of trailers hidden among the pine trees, Dobermans, tethered to the ground by chains, bark when they pass. Children in soggy-bottomed diapers throw pinecones as if they were grenades. A three-legged deer leaps awkwardly across the road and they swerve to avoid it.

They know a week in advance what hydrants they will flush, and part of their job is contacting local businesses and residents, letting them know the water pressure will drop, advising them not to do laundry during this time because stirred-up rust can stain clothing. This week they're assigned to the Moccasin Hollow neighborhood. They knock on doors and talk to a bloated woman with five squalling children, a war vet with a mechanical hook attached to a putty-colored stump, an ancient man with hair growing off the end of his nose, and a big Indian who chases them off his porch with a ball-peen hammer.

"Jesus," Stephen says at the end of the day, "I hear Baghdad's nice this time of year."

Time passes, and like a couple settling into a marriage, they figure out a routine. They flush a hydrant. They stop for coffee at 7-Eleven. They flush a hydrant. In the back of the van they set up a makeshift bed, a pillow and blanket. Stephen takes a nap while David drives, then David naps while Stephen drives. They flush a hydrant. They eat lunch at the Bald Butte Drive-In, where they down Cokes and eat mushroom-and-Swiss burgers and waffle fries, a cold splat of mustard along the edge of their plate. They flush a hydrant. They swing through the ExxonMobil, and when the attendant asks, "What'll it be?" they say, "Fill it with premium," and smile at each other like kids getting away with something. They flush a hydrant. Every now and then, they steal construction barricades and set them up in the rich neighborhoods of Pharaoh Butte, Horse Back Butte, and Paiute Creek, blocking off streets and driveways. In the background, always, music plays—KICC 100 and 95.5 The Oink mostly—making them nod their heads and purse their lips in a whistle, filling the space between their conversations.

These are the kinds of things they talk about:

"Did you know hydrant pressure is indicated by the color it's painted?" David says. Red, yellow, and green, with green being the most powerful, letting loose one hundred pounds of pressure, enough to knock a man down and blast him across the street if he isn't careful.

"No shit?" Stephen says. He brings his hand to his mouth and chews at the callus beneath his forefinger, then peels it away with his teeth and eats it, seeming to pleasure in the salty taste. "Did you know a whale penis is nine feet long? Did you know a pig orgasm lasts ten minutes? Did you know before 1850 golf balls were made of leather and stuffed with feathers?"

"No shit?" David says with laughter in his voice, the laughter cut short when Stephen says, "Did you know I once shot a man in the face?"

His smile is not a smile. His eyes are dark circled. One long minute passes before he continues. "It was at a traffic checkpoint. Everybody was supposed to stop, but he didn't stop. He kept coming. Even after I shot out his tires, he got out of the car and kept coming. He was yelling something, crazy Arab gibberish. I didn't even realize I did it. Pure reflex. You get to that point. A jet flying overhead sounds like a bomb, a car backfiring sounds like a bomb, a bomb sounds like a bomb. I was jumpy. So I shot him. His head jerked back and his hands went up to it and came away red. His jaw wasn't exactly gone—but basically. I could see all his teeth and into his throat, and he kept coming toward me, going nuuuh, nuuuh, nuuuh."

Behind them a truck honks. David sees that he is going only ten miles per hour. He stomps his foot down on the gas and the van growls back up to speed. "Did he have a bomb strapped to his chest or something?"

"Wouldn't you think that?" Stephen massages the bridge of his nose, sorting through the memory. "No. He didn't." David says nothing. He thinks the conversation is over. But Stephen says, "I guess he was just mad," and his hand falls from his face and turns up the volume on the radio.

The slanted light of early evening is coming in the windows, and on the television a lion gnaws on a gazelle while hyenas slink about, waiting for their turn at the corpse. David squeezes an empty beer can. It crumples grudgingly, the metal splitting open in places, slicing the skin beneath his thumb. He places the can on the floor, among four others, similarly deformed, and then brings his hand to his mouth, sucking the blood absently while watching the screen.

He punches the remote until he lands on a triple-digit network airing a *Dr. Phil* repeat. He has never seen the show before and he listens now as the doctor—a big bald man with a heavy Texas twang—yaks it up with a young couple experiencing sexual problems. At first he makes small talk with them, joking around, hoping to make them forget about the cameras so they'll trust him, so they'll open up and he can get down to business and solve their problems by offering advice in a loud no-nonsense voice. "What you need to do is," he says, "you need to move away from where you've been and toward a new beginning." He likes this advice so much he repeats it, motioning from left to right with his hands: "Away from where you've been and toward a new beginning."

The audience applauds and Dr. Phil says to the camera, "Don't you go nowhere, you hear? Be back before you know it." The screen goes blue with white lettering—listing a web site and a California studio address—while a baritone announcer's voice says, "Would you like Dr. Phil to solve your problems? Send an e-mail or letter to the listed address for the opportunity to be on our show."

David gets up, dodging through the beer cans and dumbbells, and goes to his bookshelves, where he pulls down the phone book and flips through the white pages until he arrives at F. His finger runs down the names, pausing and tapping Franklin, Stephen. David writes the address on the back of his hand, where the ink looks a lot like stitching.

The drive takes ten minutes. He has trouble, with the beers in him, focusing on the numbers hanging above doorways, and he circles the block several times before spotting the ranch house with the chain-link fence around it. He parks a hundred yards away, on a side street. When he gets out of his truck and walks steadily toward the house, his snow hat, pulled down low over his face, makes him feel invisible. The houses all around him appear scorched in their darkness.

The living-room window is an orange square of light. Inside it Stephen sits in a green recliner, drinking a beer, watching *Fox News*. The screen flashes between Bill O'Reilly speaking forcefully into the camera and insurgents who shake their fists and throw stones at soldiers and fire rifles into the sky.

David creeps up the porch for a better view. A few minutes pass, and a woman appears next to Stephen, her blond hair in a ponytail. She wears gray cotton shorts and a tie-dyed tank top and she spreads her feet and puts her hands on her hips in a Wonder Woman pose. This is Stacy. David knows because Stephen talks about her nearly every day, sometimes saying things like, "She's got this peach of an ass. I just want to shove my dick in there and break it off," and at other times saying things like, "Swear to God, she never stops nagging. I thought I was done with taking orders. But look at me, saying I'm sorry about drying shit of hers that shouldn't get dried, getting my pubic hair all over the bathroom floor. I mean, Jesus."

They met a few months before his battalion was activated, and when he asked her to marry him she surprised him by saying yes. When he came back alive, she was the one surprised. Now she says something that makes Stephen stand up so forcefully the recliner nearly tips over. They yell at each other and make stabbing motions with their hands until Stephen throws his beer bottle against the wall. It explodes in a star of foam and glass that quickly loses its shape, trailing to the floor.

From where he stands David can barely see the flattening of her lips as she says, "Fuck you," and stamps her foot down, grinding it into the carpet as if crushing out a cigarette. Then she leaves him, disappearing down a darkened hallway. Stephen stares after her for a time before settling into the recliner again. He brings his hand to his mouth and begins to gnaw at its calluses, spitting shreds of skin onto the floor.

A moth bangs against the window before fluttering off into the night. The noise draws Stephen from his recliner, his black silhouette filling the window. David crouches down and stays perfectly still, so close he could punch his hand through the glass and grab Stephen by the wrist.

The next morning Stephen comes to work a paler color.

"Something wrong?" David says after they snap their seat belts into place.

Stephen regards him with eyes that are only partially lit. "Rough night is all. Didn't get much sleep." He gives a smile that appears to ache from the effort of making it happen. "Mind if I smoke?"

"I didn't know you did," David says. "Smoke."

"What do you know about me? I'm not asking that. I'm asking if you mind."

"Be my guest."

David turns up the heat and puts the car in gear and drives through the back lot. Gravel pops beneath his tires when he crawls past the postal jeeps and school buses and orange construction vans and trucks parked there. He pulls onto the highway and clears his throat. "It's your girl, isn't it?"

"The fuck do you know?" Stephen's mouth curves into the shape of a scythe.

"Sorry."

"I said it's nothing and it's nothing. Mind your business." Stephen stares at him very closely, hardly moving, with a look of obvious disgust on his face. David feels a familiar panic grip him, hating to see someone seeing him that way.

"Sorry," David says and pulls his hat a little lower on his head. "I was just—sorry."

For the next hour, Stephen stares out the window while David drives, stealing glances at him. Then, all of a sudden, Stephen brings his fist down on the dashboard and says, "Bitch."

David darts his eyes between the road and Stephen, not knowing whether to say anything.

"Yeah," Stephen says, as if they have come to some sort of agreement. His face brightens. "You know what? Fuck her."

He playfully punches David a few times in the shoulder, saying, "Fuck her," with every punch. The touch of his hand sends a charge through David that burns inside him and makes him say, "You know, if you ever need a place to crash, you can always crash with me."

"Yeah?"

"Yeah. Whatever. I mean, I've got plenty of room."

"We'll see," Stephen says, but he sounds contented.

In the middle of Pine, there is a cinder cone, Bald Butte, dotted with sagebrush and rabbitbrush and the occasional stunted juniper tree. A poorly paved road swirls around and around it, all the way to its summit, where teenagers park at night and tourists snap photos during the day and the city fires off fireworks on the Fourth. This morning David drives there and pulls out of the glovebox a half-empty bottle of Jack Daniel's.

"Breakfast," he says, and they each throw back a mouthful of the dark liquor. It tastes like gasoline, but it seems right to drink, as if they are celebrating something, or mourning something. They get out of the van and climb onto its roof and watch the town redden under the sun, the shadows dissolving, while they pass the bottle back and forth for half an hour. "You must be pretty bored," David finally says. "After all you've been through—over there—this job must bore the hell out of you."

They sit there, comfortably silent for a long time, before Stephen says, "Actually, that's not the case at all. It's kind of familiar. The driving. Feels like that's all I did over there. Drive. And wait. Wait for somebody to shoot at me, wait for an IED to go off, wait for my commanding officer to tell me some bullshit." His voice has that sincere wistful quality men normally reserve for taverns and locker rooms. "Being over there, it's just a job—with bullets, of course—but still, it's just a bunch of sitting around, trying to figure out what's next, what the fuck's the point."

Weeks pass. Fall deepens. The birch trees go gold, and in the failing light the world seems to take on sharper angles. In early November a water main breaks. Joe comes on the CB and sends them over to help. It is one of those new neighborhoods where all the houses look like they came from the same box and BMWs crawl the freshly paved roads.

When they park at the end of the block, a guy wearing a yellow polo shirt tucked into his khakis bangs open his front door and starts down the driveway. He moves with a prowling intensity that betrays his anger before he starts yelling. They can hear him from where they stand across the street as if he were right next to them. "I called two hours ago," he says.

He spells it out for them: a) he tried to take a shower and now he smells like somebody else's shit; b) he started up the dishwasher and now his plates and glasses are streaked with mud; c) he just put sod in and now his front lawn is a fucking swamp.

He is wearing boat shoes—no socks—and he brings down his right foot for emphasis. A crown of water splats up around it. "Somebody is going to have to pay for this," he says.

David could probably break the man over his knee if he wanted, but he presses his mouth into an apologetic frown and casts his eyes downward, toeing through the grass until he finds the cap to the water valve. He flips it open and goes to the van to retrieve the key, a long metal rod that reaches deep into the earth. He fits it into place and spins it, and with a rusty creak, the water ceases to flow.

A truck full of Mexicans arrives. They wear jeans and orange reflective vests spotted with flecks of tar. One of them sets to work with the jackhammer while the others huddle around and watch it bite through the asphalt. Then a semi pulls up with a backhoe resting on its trailer bed. One of the Mexicans climbs into its cab, and it growls to life with a clattering of metal and diesel. It rolls down the ramp, and its shovel peels away the blacktop, the gravel, and the dirt just a few inches at a time, taking care not to strike a gas line. "It's guesswork," David explains to Stephen, his voice nearly lost under all the noise. "Nobody really knows what's underneath us."

Once the shovel strikes metal—with a cling—the backhoe quits digging and scoops up a ten-by-ten steel brace to lower into the soggy square hole it has fashioned. This is to keep the walls from caving in on David and Stephen and the rest of the men when they climb down and set to work with their shovels, exposing the main so they can apply a clamp over the crack.

David digs deep with his shovel, dragging the blade through the mud, tossing it over his shoulder, enjoying the damp smells of the earth. In the cool November air his breath puffs out of him in short-lived clouds, and his sweat gives him a chill. The effort feels good, the blood burning through his body. It feels substantial, like his job is a real job.

While they work, the polo guy paces back and forth, smoking his way through more than a few cigarettes— menthol, by the smell of them. When David and Stephen climb out of the pit for a water break, he says, "Done? I hope so. For your sake."

He flicks his cigarette in their direction. It arcs through the air and lands on David, on his forearm, just long enough to burn him. He brushes it away hurriedly and says, "What's wrong with you?" his voice coming out genuinely hurt.

"What's wrong with your face?"

David looks at him uncertainly for a second, and then at Stephen, who does not return his gaze, but squints across the expanse of mud at the man as if at a target.

Then Stephen leaves them standing there and climbs into the backhoe. He keys the engine and fiddles with the levers, not so different from the levers of a tank. With a roar, the backhoe comes alive. It crushes a path across the sidewalk, the driveway, the lawn, eating up with its tread the grass and mud.

When the man tries to intervene, waving his arms in a fury, the backhoe swings around like a scorpion, its shovel knocking him down. An accident, everyone agrees.

The first day of deer-hunting season in the fall is an unofficial holiday in Deschutes County. Stephen invites David to hunt on his father's property, out near Sisters, twenty acres of big pines that run up against the Black Butte wilderness area. They set off early in the afternoon, wearing jeans and blaze orange jackets. The sky is a copper color, and the air is sharp enough to make their breath ghost from their mouths.

The forest swallows them, whispering and snapping, before disgorging them in a clearing of fireweed and browned strawberry beds. They head toward a cluster of thick-waisted junipers that surrounds what looks like a clubhouse on stilts. Ten or so feet off the ground, it has a slanted steel roof and a camouflage paint job. This is a high seat, the penthouse of tree stands. Beneath it is a trough, baited with salt licks, rotten apples, corn.

They climb a ladder and push through a trapdoor. Inside there are army cots, a cooler filled with Coors, a wood bin, a woodstove, and aluminum chairs set before sliding-glass windows. On the wall is a poster of a big-breasted woman in a bikini bent over the hood of a Camaro, both the woman and the car oozing with soap suds. And next to the poster, the charred corpse of an animal is nailed to the wall. It is the size of a small child, its legs curled up against its torso and its teeth visible in a small snarl. When he was eleven or twelve, Stephen explains, he baited a steel-mesh cage with jerky and trapped a raccoon that had been getting into their garbage. He released it, but only after dousing it with gasoline and sparking a match. There was a foomp sound, and the coon took off like a comet, zigzagging through a dry field of crabgrass, setting it aflame in strange orange designs Stephen stomped out with his foot.

When his father discovered what he had done, he nailed the coon to the wall of the high seat as a reminder. "That way maybe you'll think twice before you pull the trigger." Never firing off a round out of boredom—at a jaybird, a jackrabbit, a doe—hungry to kill something, anything, as boys often are.

"Jesus," David says.

Stephen breaks the silence by kicking a folding chair. "Best seat in the house," he says. The chair faces a window that opens up into the forest. "All yours. Just keep your eyes on that game trail." He winks. "Fish in a barrel."

They take their chairs and cradle their rifles in their laps. They don't speak for a while, their silence deepening with the shadows in the woods. Then Stephen gets up to pull a beer from the cooler and offers one to David, who pops the tab and, after slurping at the foam that comes boiling out of it, says, "Hey, did you know a whale penis is nine feet long?"

Stephen gives him a blank look. "I'm the one who told you that, man."

"Are you?"

"Yeah."

"Oh. Sorry." David feels his grip tighten around his beer, the metal giving way. "Things any better with Stacy?"

Stephen returns to his window and looks out it. "So-so."

"Just so-so?"

"Let's put it this way," he says, keeping his voice at a low volume. "Are you still good on that offer? If I needed to, I could crash at your place?"

"Sure." David tries hard to control his voice. If there is too much excitement in it, he can't tell.

"Just in case," Stephen says.

"You're always welcome. Stay as long as you like. There's plenty of room."

Stephen twists the tab on his can until it snaps off. "Good to know."

They fall silent again. David finds it difficult to concentrate on the woods and throws a glance over his shoulder every few minutes to check on Stephen. It feels different, sitting here with him and not moving, not listening to the engine hum, not watching the world slide by. It feels good— permanent.

Time passes and his vision blurs and the forest falls away as he imagines the two of them as young boys, dirt under their fingernails, carrying in their hands slingshots and BB guns, darting through the trees, headed toward where they heard a chipmunk chattering minutes ago. The false memory makes him feel so close to Stephen, his friend, he wants to reach out and touch him.

He glances over his shoulder then, just in time to see Stephen snap off the safety and bring the thirty-aught-six to his shoulder. He rises from his chair, slowly, the metal complaining only a little. David follows the line of Stephen's rifle. There, at the edge of the meadow, less than thirty yards away, a buck untangles its antlers from the forest and moves cautiously toward the trough.

Halfway there it pauses. It swishes its tail. It raises a hoof and puts it down again. Maybe it smells them, or maybe it smells the blood in the grass. David holds his breath, anticipating the shot. When it doesn't come, he says, "What are you waiting for?"

"I don't know," Stephen says.

David gently pushes him aside and nestles the stock against his cheek and sights the buck through the scope. Right then it raises its head and looks at him. The blood in his ears buzzes, like a wasp loose in his skull. The rifle kicks against his shoulder. The gunshot fills the world.

The buck jerks its head around in a half-circle, as if curious where the shot came from, and then it collapses and a flock of swallows swirls from the forest, over the meadow, dappling it with shadows.

A few minutes later, they stand over the body. When David nudges it with his boot, its hind leg quivers, then goes still. Since the gunshot, the air has gone quiet except for the rhythmic knocking of a woodpecker's beak against some distant tree. The woods are softly colored with the gloom that comes with twilight. The hole David has blown in the deer's side is big enough to put his hand in, and he does. Hot, moist. It reminds him, with a sick kind of pleasure, of a woman. When he withdraws his hand, gloved in blood, it steams a little. He smears its redness against his left cheek and says, "There. Now I match."

Stephen laughs as if he is trying not to. "I'm glad you took the shot," he says, his smile fading. "I don't know what's wrong with me."

"Nothing's wrong with you."

Some blood oozes into David's mouth and he spits it back out. It occurs to him then—with blood on his lips and the woods darkening all around them—that he has never been happier.

The next Monday morning, David arrives at work fifteen minutes early and waits for Stephen on the loading dock, an elevated concrete platform with a steel ramp leading up it. Nearby, a poplar, stripped of its leaves, shakes against the wind that comes howling down from the Cascades. A rime of frost coats its branches. With the sun still low in a sky full of torn clouds, the air has a gray quality that carries little warmth. David paces back and forth and stamps his feet, trying to keep the cold out of them.

Eventually Stephen pulls up in a Chevy Cavalier with an Army National Guard sticker on its bumper. Rather than park along the chain-link fence, next to David's truck, he kills the engine at the bottom of the ramp and hops out.

"Hey, Stephen," David says, and Stephen says, "Hey." He steps onto the ramp and pauses there with David hanging over him, obscuring him with his shadow and a big breath of mist.

"Something wrong?" David says.

Stephen brings his hand to his mouth and chews hungrily on it. "Maybe." He sighs deeply, and in a halting voice that seems bothered—by nervousness or excitement—explains that he has been asked to be part of a task force. He and fifteen other soldiers will work as an embedded training team to mentor the Iraqi Army.

"What do you mean?" David says.

"I mean I'm not working here anymore," Stephen says. "I'm going back." He examines his palm. Blood and saliva dampen it. He wipes it on the handrail. "Next week, I'm on active duty. I just came to say my good-byes and pick up my paycheck." He studies David a moment and irritation creeps into his voice. "Well, aren't you going to say anything?"

David doesn't know what to say, so he says, "What about Stacy?"

"What about her?"

"You can't just leave her again, can you?"

"What do you care?"

"I don't know." His voice has a fine crack in it. There is a pain in his forehead. It makes him think of insects eating away at the space between his eyes. He squeezes the bridge of his nose.

"I better go talk to Joe," Stephen says. He moves up the ramp another two steps, and from here David can see the redness in his teeth, the blood from his chewing.

"I'm in your way, aren't I?" David says and steps aside and makes a motion with his hands, ushering Stephen onto the dock. "Sorry."

Stephen doesn't say anything else, but just before he pushes through the double doors, David yells after him to wait a minute. Stephen pauses, half inside, half out, as David takes a few lumbering steps toward him and offers his hand. It hangs there a second, then Stephen shows off the blood on his hand like an apology before disappearing inside.

Without Stephen, driving feels different, the roads as routine as an old network of veins that has pumped the same blood along the same path too long. David yearns for conversation, but there is only the grumble of the engine, the hiss of the tires spinning over the blacktop, the voice of Hank Williams yodeling through the radio.

He swings by Stephen's house once, and then again, looking for a car in the driveway, a light in the window. The third time, when he passes the house at a crawl, he catches sight of his reflection in the living-room window—the Astro van and his dark shape inside it. Without really thinking about it he raises his hand, and it is as if his hand and the hand in the window are trying to reach across those many feet of space to touch.

At the end of the block, he doesn't turn around to drive through the neighborhood again, but instead continues through town until he merges onto Route 20 and drives toward Sisters, then past it, to the plot of land where they went hunting.

He parks the van on a logging road and hikes through the forest to the meadow. His hands are shoved deep in his pockets, the smell of pine drifting all around him. The low rays of sunlight pick out a little red in the soil, the place where they gutted the deer. He kneels there, and though the ground is hard with frost he manages to finger his way into it and pull away a handful of dirt, still the reddish color of blood. He puts it in his pocket, and later in a Ziploc bag, to keep.

Crash

The doctor tells me a car crash at 60 mph threw Karen forward at 120 times her body weight. She remembered to buckle her seat belt so that means 1/10th of a second later she came to a stop. But her internal organs did not. They collided with her bones and broke open. Most people die right off the bat, the doctor says, but not Karen. Karen died minutes later.

I ask how many minutes later.

"Beats me," he says. "No clue."

He says probably she looked okay—probably she even stepped away from the wreck and said, "Thank God,"—but underneath her skin things bled.

The endorphins soon faded, the pain set in, a dull soreness that made her lift up the black blouse I bought her from JCPenney to discover a purplish stain spreading across her distended belly, the scar from her cesarean looking so white against it.

The doctor says there was nothing he could do.

"DOA," he says.

"I'm very sorry," he says, "but these things happen.

This is why I take out my gun sometimes, and look at it.

It is a .357, a revolver, something Dad got me when I turned sixteen. Back then I wanted to be a spy—*not* a dairy farmer—someone who traveled to exotic places and wore tuxedos and drank his martinis shaken. And so the .357 seemed like a step in the right direction, somehow. On my birthday Dad and I went through a whole box of bullets— blasting pop cans, tree knots, the pigeons roosting in the hayloft—so that our hands and ears hurt the next morning.

But that was a long time ago.

Now I take the gun out and look at it and it reminds me how different things were before the crash.

Before the crash we lived in a double-wide trailer twenty steps from the white two-story farmhouse where I grew up. It wasn't the life I wanted. I wanted to go to college—to major in international politics, in political science, *some*thing—but instead stayed on the farm because Dad and Ma asked me to in a collective voice that was more command than question.

This happened at dinner, and I held my knife, but didn't cut with it.

"Don't get stirred up," Ma said. "We need you. Plain and simple."

"I'm going to go," I said. "It's my money."

Dad scooped some mash potatoes and tasted them and studied his plate. "Well then," he said. "I guess you got to do what you got to do."

"I'm going," I said and meant it. I enrolled at UO for the fall, but that summer met a girl named Karen through 4-H. She had long blond hair that was always getting in her way. I liked how she blew it from her face and swept it over her shoulder and chewed on it when watching television. In the bed of my pickup she got pregnant and a month later we were married at the United Methodist. Afterwards there was a reception where people shook our hands and ate cantaloupe wrapped in bacon.

We honeymooned two nights at the Eugene Holiday Inn where she told me to "Take it easy" because I couldn't keep my hands off her. She bit her lower lip a lot and I asked what was her deal? She touched her stomach. It was starting to poke out.

"Oh," I said.

"It's starting to get real," she said.

It was an it—not a baby—like "It moved" or, "It's making me nauseous." We spent no time guessing its gender or cruising the aisles of Wal-Mart for breast pumps or blue or pink jumpers. Maybe *it* would go away if we pretended it didn't exist?

In the hotel Jacuzzi we played a game where we wished for everything under the sun. We wished for yachts, mansions, winters in Tahiti, millions and billions of dollars. What we didn't wish for was a life gone to pot, stuck on the family farm and pregnant at the ripe old age of eighteen.

Then the honeymoon ended, and when we got back home, the brand-new double-wide was waiting for us.

"Now that was a job," Dad said and rubbed his hands as if he hadn't yet cleaned the work off them. "Poured the foundation myself. Townsend's son ran the plumbing and electricity over. Quite a job. Nothing fancy. But she'll do the trick."

Karen liked it. I didn't, but pretended to for her sake. Later on I told Dad, "Even though I'm sticking around, I don't have to like it."

"Might try to," he said.

I stayed angry for a time, but then Hannah was born and I caught myself hugging Dad in the hospital waiting room, partly because I was happy, mostly because I was afraid.

Everything smelled like ammonia when we thumped each other on the back and he said, "I'm glad this happened."

I said, "I'm glad, too." Which sounded right at the time.

The first time Karen got on a plane—she was fifteen and visiting a cousin in Salt Lake—the electricity went out at 30,000 feet. All of sudden, no lights, no engines, no recycled air funneling through the vents. For about ten seconds nobody said a word. She said she had never been more aware how loud quiet could get. Then the screaming started. She thought she was a goner. Bar none, the scariest thing in world history, she said. Then everything kicked back into gear and the pilot got on the intercom and said a prayer of thanksgiving.

It was just one of those things.

The man sitting next to Karen was laughing and crying at the same time. She lent him a tissue, and he said, "Are we in Heaven?" pointing out the window where the clouds were white and puffy. "I bet that's what it looks like."

So whenever we went on vacation, it would be to a place within driving distance: Crater Lake, Yosemite, Newport. She said to hell with the statistics, it was a matter of control. In a plane, who knows if the pilot's been drinking, if the mechanic tightened the five-cent lug nut holding the wing in place, if someone stuck a bomb in their shoe?

"If it's not one thing, it's another," she said. "And I'd rather not tempt fate."

She preferred to be the one in the driver's seat. Here— she said—nothing was out of her control.

The other day Ma was writing out some Christmas cards. On their front was baby Jesus in the manger. Baby Jesus glowed like he had fire under his skin. Everybody—Joseph and Mary and the wise men and donkeys—hung around his cradle and looked worried and amazed and frightened at the same time.

This is how I feel about Hannah.

Right then Hannah—who looks too much like her mother—plopped down on the rug with crayons and a yellow legal pad and Ma asked what are you doing, sweetie?

She said writing a Christmas card. Which I got a kick out of, seeing how she can barely spell her name.

I asked who was she writing to, and she said, "My mommy."

I could feel my mouth unhinge into a big black O. Ma put down her pen and gave me a look. I knew that look. For the past two years I got it everywhere I went. Your eyebrows come together, your cheeks go slack, your lower lip does this tremble thing—it was the Hallmark look.

I'm so sorry, she seemed to be saying. I'm here for you.

Which quite honestly got on my nerves. So I said in a mean voice, "That's just great," looking at Ma, talking to Hannah. "And *how* exactly do you plan on mailing it to her?"

Ma's expression changed to one of disapproval. She clucked her tongue at me and said, "What your daddy means is, do you know which cloud in Heaven your mother lives on? Because we can look it up in the phone book if need be."

Hannah stopped scribbling and stared at me under all that hair. "I'll just send it with you when you go," she said.

The crash happened one mile from the farm, at the intersection of County H and Battlecreek Road, where an asphalt X marks the spot.

Sometimes when I can't sleep I drive to the X and park in its middle and cry in a moaning way. The sound of it embarrasses me so I turn up the oldies station as loud as it goes. The Beach Boys tell me "Don't worry, baby," and I wonder what it feels like to bleed to death without spilling a single drop of blood?

Even at night—if the moon is out—I can see forever, not a stick for miles, just pasture, the silhouettes of Holsteins, silos, barbed-wire fences, and beyond all this, the Townsend farm and then the interstate where headlights turn into taillights, where engines scream as semis downshift their way toward Eugene.

The black pickup—a Dodge—it *must* have seen her zipping home from the mini-mart with bread and orange juice—it must have seen her and thought it could beat her through the intersection? And she must have seen the black truck and figured it would stop like the stop sign told it to?

What a surprise they were in for.

In the morning—after I've milked, after I've scraped clean and hosed down the barn—I drive Hannah through the X and drop her off at kindergarten. There is no snow, but everything looks shiny, laminated by frost, so I take it easy on the roads and imagine our truck turned over in the ditch and flaming while nobody comes to our rescue.

This morning Hannah wears a pink animal sweatshirt. The animal is a teddy bear that has lost its balloon. The teddy bear jumps, paw outstretched, the balloon's string forever out of reach.

I ask is she still my little girl? She doesn't answer, too busy organizing her backpack. I say, "You look real pretty today, Hannah. I like how Grandma did your hair. Is that called a French braid?"

She turns her face from me.

I say, "Hannah?"

"Quiet," she says.

"Quiet?" I say, not angry but amused. "What do I got to be quiet for?"

"I'm talking to Mommy."

For a second I feel afraid, but only for a second. I check the rearview—nothing, nobody—the backseat and highway are empty. And then I feel stupid for feeling afraid. And then I feel angry for feeling stupid. I could spank her, slap her for doing this to me. For looking like a miniature version of her mother. For reminding me—every day—exactly why it is I hurt.

"Damn it," I say. There is nothing else to say.

"Don't swear," she says and I sort of laugh and sort of sob and reach out to touch her cheek with the back of my hand.

All this under a sky as cold and unforgiving as God's good grace.

On the phone—as usual—Ma talks about Hannah.

"Can you believe it, Gertie?" she says. "Have you ever heard of such a thing?" She goes quiet a second, listening. "*Every*day she talks about her. Mommy this, Mommy that." Her voice is serious but excited. "It's funny. It's weird, don't you think? At her age you'd think she'd hardly remember?" She makes a *mm-hmm* noise. "Every single day, Gertie. I think the girl has some sixth sense about her, is what I think."

Hannah lies on the davenport, next to Dad, hopefully asleep but probably faking. I lower my voice to a whisper and say, "Would you stop talking so loud?"

Ma makes a face and bends over her belly, undoes her Keds, peels off her socks.

"Did you hear me?" I say, "You'll just encourage her."

She points at her feet and wiggles her toes and says, "Yes, Gertie, I'm here. Keep going."

I pretend I don't know what she wants. Again she points at her feet, which will smell like warm milk, and I sigh and take them in my hands and feel disgusted for the swollen way her ankles hang over her feet, veins marbling up their paleness.

Dad clears his throat to get my attention. He folds and unfolds the newspaper. It makes a crackling sound like some powerful electricity. He asks did I know Rusty Warner died?

I did not.

He looks at me over his reading glasses. "Got crushed. Tried to loosen up two tons of frozen silage with a sledgehammer." He tightens his lips and shakes his head. "Fool thing to do."

I say, "Just like that?" I run my thumb up and down Ma's arch and she pats my head and says, "Yes, just like that. That's the ticket."

I give my eyes a roll and Dad says, "Yeah. Just like that. And you know, you'd think he'd have known better." He takes off his reading glasses and points them at me. "How they found him was he didn't show up to work. He was always Johnny-on-the-spot when it came to work. Real good work ethic. Good guy. You know I seen him at the gas station just three days ago? Just think, one day you're fine, the next . . ."

I wait for him to maybe flinch, apologize, say, "Oh. Sorry."

But he doesn't. In his mind Karen is ancient history. Every once in a while he'll say something—"She was a real peach," for instance—but in truth he likes how I've moved back into the big house—just like old times—how I go through the motions without complaint.

Ma says, "And what other news do I got? My Joey took me up to Chinook Winds." Her face crumples up when she smiles at me, like: good boy. "So we played the nickel slots, yeah, nothing big, just nickels. Real fun. Nice time." She giggles a little. "And Gertie, you're not going to believe what happened." She puts a hand to her breast and at first I think she might be out of breath. But she's just being dramatic. "I won *twenty* dollars on *one* pull. What was that? Yep. Yes. Oh, can you believe it? Twenty whole dollars." She trades the phone to the other side of her head. "I loved to hear them clinking. Quite a noise." She makes her fingers into falling nickels and goes, "Clink, clink, clink, clink," in a shrill voice that ends in laughter.

Dad says, "For Heaven's sake, can you imagine what that must have been like?" He creases the newspaper. "It must have been like a freight train. Two tons. *Pow!* I bet that won't be no open-coffin funeral. I bet old Rusty is flat as a pancake. Probably never knew what hit him. What a idiot way to go."

In her sleep Hannah whimpers and shakes her head, *no,* and I think about my gun and what will happen next.

Death can be very ordinary. Take for example the half-finished glass of milk Karen left on the counter before she drove off and got killed. For a whole week it stayed there. Part of me hoped she might come back and finish it. First it turned hard on the surface, then gray, then greenish—and before I poured it down the drain I ran my tongue along its rim, knowing her lips had been there, pleasuring in the sour taste. On her sewing table was a piece of paper with her handwriting on it. It read: "Orange juice, bread," and "Dry cleaning," and "Call Norma." I wonder what they would have talked about. To this day the note hasn't moved. Sometimes I see it and feel surprised, like: if she's gone, why don't her things disappear, too?

And death can be very strange. The day after she died,

I went with her parents to pick out a coffin. We were walking around the funeral home, going, "That looks like a good one," when all of a sudden Karen's father's prosthetic hand fell off. He lost the real one years ago. Chopped off by the combine. Anyway, all of a sudden some spring or rubber band or whatever came loose and his prosthetic hand fell off. It made a *thud* sound against the hardwood and we all crowded around and stared at it, lying there, waiting for it to crawl away.

It looked so real I expected blood might start pouring from its stump. But no blood poured. Instead we all started bawling our eyes out.

That hand must have pushed a button in our heads or something.

I take out my gun and look at it.

Two pounds of pressure is all it takes. I put it in my mouth and then to my ear. There it makes noises like a seashell would. I hear a beach—some faraway coconut isle—where gulls screech and waves slap the white sand that would stick to my feet as I chased Karen off her towel and into the ocean, her turquoise bikini lost in the blue of the water.

How beautiful life could be.

Yet here I am in a room crowded with 4-H trophies— golden cows, pigs—and FFA ribbons and toy tractors, little John Deeres, all green and gold and collecting dust, yesterday's treasures. Here is my high school diploma. Here is a pile of *National Geographics* stacked in the corner, high and ready to topple. Here is a photo of Karen. Here are my coveralls, washed and folded and smelling faintly of barn. Here is my life.

Two pounds. When the trigger gives, the hammer will fall and strike one of six .357 caliber bee stings waiting on deck. Right then a tiny spark will combust some 230 grains of gunpowder, pressurizing the chamber to 12,000 lbs/sq inch, sending a conical piece of lead down a 4-inch tunnel and into my ear, obliterating any wax deposits, the drum, some bone, on its way toward the brain—mushrooming— its path growing considerably wider and messier and before long a lot of red will pour out of me.

All this in one terrible second.

I won't have felt a thing.

I will be deaf in one ear. I will have a bullet seeded in my brain. But maybe I will have another heartbeat or two before everything shuts down? If so, then maybe my good ear will finally hear the bullet that killed me? It will have broken the sound barrier, tearing into my head at 800 ft/sec, its sonic boom moving in concert with my smiling lips as I wish my pathetic life good-bye.

Karen floats out of my brain and sits on my lap. I give her a hug and she says, "Listen to me. Okay? If that gun goes off, it will kill you, but it will destroy your family. Think of Hannah."

I think of Hannah sleeping down the hall. In the darkened room her small chest rises and falls. Her eyes, wide open and watching the shadows dance across the ceiling. I feel a mixture of affection and the creeps.

"Fine," I say and put the gun back in its box and kick it under the bed.

Another wish that will never come true.

"Think about it this way," she says. "You really want to trade places with me?" All of a sudden her skin turns gray and then purple and then blacker than a crow before falling off to reveal a skeleton who laughs like that witch from *The Wizard of Oz* and asks do I think life is supposed to be an easy thing?

On Christmas Eve Ma asks me to pick up some things at the Food-4-Less where I nearly crash my cart into another.

"Sorry about that," a guy with a goatee says. And then, "Hey, I know you? Joey! Long time no see."

This is Rick—who was three years ahead of me?—who quarterbacked and dated all the pretty girls and once got suspended for flipping Miss Beasley the bird during gym class.

I put on a smile for him, same as you might for a photographer—not because you're happy, but because you're supposed to look that way. Fact is, seeing him makes me feel ashamed.

I ask what was he up to these days? He says, "I'm in Portland. I'm with Nike. Assistant manager to the chief executive of marketing and research." Which sounds important? Which must be important because he wears nice clothes. The kind you imagine men would wear in high-rise offices when leaning back in a leather chair, their hands behind their heads, talking about dinner reservations or golf handicaps or whatever. His tie is made of a shiny silver material that sucks up light and turns it into every color of the rainbow.

He says, "What about you?"

I say, "Still farming." My smile cramps up.

"That's something else," he says in a full-of-crap voice. "I admire you for it."

"Well," I say, fooling with my belt. "It's not exactly rocket science."

Even his groceries embarrass me. He buys soymilk and these weird brown fruits with hair on them. He buys Frosted Flakes—I buy Frost Bombs—generic crap with a dumb lion on the box.

We talk about Karen and how sorry he is. He says, "When it rains, it pours."

I say, "You can say that again."

On television Jimmy Stewart considers jumping into a cold dark river. And though I've seen *It's a Wonderful Life* a thousand times, I can't help but wonder does he have the balls? Will he do it this Christmas?

The sentimental music rises and Ma says from the kitchen, "Racket. I've had enough of it. Shut that thing off." She bangs around a few pots and everything smells like nutmeg.

I know what comes next. I know that curly haired angel—Clarence? Charlie?—will plop down from the sky and make everything better. But not this year. I kill the TV and the last thing I see is Jimmy watching the river, waiting for it to swallow him up.

Ma says, "It's almost time for supper, Hannah, so maybe you should go get Grandpa from the barn. Tell him to wash up." She spoons some lard into a pan and knobs the burner to high and notices Hannah still staring at the darkened TV screen. "Hannah? Should you go get Grandpa?"

Hannah shrugs, says, "If you want."

"If you want," Ma echoes and throws up her arms. "Pshaw!"

Right then the phone rings and Ma wipes her hands before picking it up. "Yeah? Yeah, Gertie." Her voice gets all cheery and high. "Merry Christmas to you, too."

For a minute Hannah and I watch the dead TV. Then she says, "Something stinks." There is a *woomph* sound followed by a scream, the scream just enough after the *woomph* to seem its echo.

I see fire rising from the pan. I see Ma dropping the phone. It shatters against the floor and a silver-crowned battery rolls into the living room and under the Christmas tree. "Oh no," she says. "Help," she says. "You've got to help." But I don't. I don't even breathe. I watch when she picks the pan off the stove and puts it down on the linoleum to drop a towel over. The towel smokes a second before catching fire and Ma says, "Help me," kicking the whole flaming mess out the door and into the garage. On the floor is a smoking black circle with a brown comet's tail.

Hannah follows the tail to the door and disappears through it. I can hear Ma crying. Between gulping sobs she says, "Should have used soda or salt. Or covered it with a pan."

She comes back inside with Hannah in her arms, Hannah carefully wiping the tears off Ma's cheeks with one tiny white hand.

"Oh no," Ma says, noticing the floor. "Oh for Heaven's sake, what next?"

Right then the smoke alarm goes off and I have this vision.

I see myself in a flaming house. I see myself at the bottom of a river. I see myself shot in the head. I see myself in a totaled car, my liver punctured and leaking a darkish green bile. I see my body in a coffin in the United Methodist. I see Dad taking Ma's hand and pressing it to my chest, making her say good-bye. And I see Hannah wearing a little black dress, sitting in the front pew, her lips moving—in prayer or lullaby—as she colors in her coloring book, looking up now and then when the pastor's voice cracks, her face innocent like you wouldn't believe. I see months pass. I see spring arrive. I see Dad out in the fields—without me—plowing, disking, picking the rocks brought up by winter. I see him seeding and spraying and fertilizing and before long tiny green shoots of soybean and corn would shoot up.

"What next?" Ma says.

I say, "Good question."

When the Bear Came

When the Bear Came

Nothing had happened in a long time. Every now and then someone wrecked a truck or got divorced or shot a six-point elk
or dropped out of college or shipped off for Iraq or bought a
thousand-dollar Lotto scratch ticket at the gas station—and
you know how those kinds of things get around in a small
town like Tumalo—but otherwise, the sand kept blowing,
the bulls kept lowing, and the air kept on smelling like it
always smelled, like juniper and sage. Irrigation pipes got
moved around. Barbed-wire fences got mended. The occasional thunderstorm boiled over the Cascade Mountains and
lit a barn on fire and flattened the alfalfa crop and eventually
rattled apart into a collection of black clouds that made the
sky look full of bears drinking from a big blue bowl. That's
about it.

Really, nothing had happened around here since the train
came off the tracks and five of its cattle-cars rolled through
the mini-mart, leaving behind a twisted snarl of lumber and
metal from which bubbled soda pop and blood. That was
five years ago. The only other thing I can think of is Josh
Henderson, who they found at the dump, dead and apparently

dragged behind a car—back and forth along a strip of county two-lane—his skin unpeeling against the asphalt in a long red trail that drew crows and magpies from all over the county. And that happened eons ago, before I can hardly remember.

There's the train—there's Josh Henderson—there's the Deschutes County Fair and of course the weekend stock-car races and the fat-bellied trout that drift along the shadowy banks of the Metolious River and dozens more diversions, all tiny and meant to distract me from the big spell of nothing that had settled over Tumalo. So when the bear attacks began, things changed and that was just what I needed.

I was on break and finishing off an order of biscuits and gravy, left half-eaten on Table 5 along with a perfectly good strip of bacon, when the door jingled and old Mr. Russell ran in and held up his arms like some kind of prophet. "Everybody!" he said.

This was the Tip Top Diner—9:30ish on a Sunday morning. The Lutheran church hadn't let out yet, so *everybody* consisted of three customers, and Mary, who owns the Tip Top and smells like fryer grease and presently stood behind the counter, leafing through the *Bend Bulletin*. With every turn of the page she licked her forefinger as if it had some sweetness to it.

Mr. Russell, his eyes were so big I thought they might pop out of his skull and roll around on the linoleum. It took him a minute to say what he said next—his chest rising and falling beneath his flannel shirt—but with an out-of-breath gasp interrupting every other word, he eventually got it out: "Girls camping in Dry Canyon got mauled by a bear."

It only took a moment for the diner to empty. Pow, those customers shot out of their chairs like in the cartoons, ghost-gone with a cloud of dust in their wake. They left their plates stacked with pancakes, their mugs steaming with coffee, their checks unpaid. One lady even left her purse. Goes to show how hard up we are for entertainment. A semi tips over on the interstate or a heifer births a two-headed calf and you need only open a window and cup a hand to your ear—in the wind, you'll hear it—phones ringing, hands swiping keys off kitchen counters, garage doors rumbling open, the streets clogged up with trucks and dirt bikes. People want to see.

So in the middle of an empty diner, I'm standing there, gravy on my face, hands in my pockets. And what does Mary do? She folds her newspaper shut and walks to the front door and flips the sign from Open to Closed. "Might as well see what there is to see," she says and off we went.

It was one of those depressing March days, no rain, but cold, the wind tunneling into your ear so you had to cover it with your hand.

Mary drove one of those Jeep Wagoneers with the fake wood paneling on the side. She parked in the parking lot that edged the canyon, the canyon three miles long and about as wide as I can throw a baseball. A file of cars steadily pulled in behind us—the whole town, it looked like. I forgot my jacket, so I hugged my arms to my chest the second I stepped out of the Jeep and into the wind.

A shelf of black lava rock angled downward and then opened up into a trail, a steep series of switchbacks that took us deep into the canyon. The sunlight fell away and a blue shadow took over. The burrs found their way into my socks when I stepped delicately along the trail, making sure, in my sneakers, not to trip over a root or lose traction on a wash of pumice.

After a hundred yards, the trail bottomed out and followed the curve of a dry creek-bed before vanishing into yellow crabgrass. Up ahead, peopled milled about, and soon I was among them. Their feet left craters in the desert dust and stirred up the smell of calcite. They snapped photos with Kodak disposable cameras. They put their hands on their hips and shook their heads as if this was a hell of a thing, a hell of a thing. Two boys raced by, playing tag, the boy in pursuit yelling, "I'm a bear!" in a high joyful voice. Five men stood in a circle and conferred with one another, gesturing with their cigarettes, taking off their seed caps to scratch their scalps. Women, in their Sunday dresses, walked barefoot, carrying their high heels in their hands. A man in a cowboy hat sat on a boulder drinking coffee from a stainless-steel thermos. His eyes were fixed on some far-off point in the landscape. The hat threw a shadow across his face and I peered into its darkness, thinking I recognized—in his broad face and quiet presence—my father. But I was wrong. It was just a man.

I spotted two deputies and a ranger in the near distance and made my way toward them, where a basalt outcropping hung over a flat patch of sand. To the girls this had seemed a safe place, I guess, a place to pitch their little tent and hide from the big black night. The deputies, dressed in their khaki uniforms, stood before the campsite. There was blood all around them, rust-colored ovals and smears that in their ragged designs revealed where the girls had been dragged and thrown and chewed. Near the charcoal remains of their campfire, I noticed what could have been a shard of shale or bone. The tent looked less like a tent and more like an organ excised by blunt scissors. The ranger was busy making a plaster of a paw print. It was the size of a catcher's mitt. The deputies motioned their arms authoritatively, emphatically, as if they were trying to guide, with glowing wands, a plane along the tarmac. They wanted people to back away, and no, they couldn't answer any questions now, damn it.

The voices all around me fell away as the wind picked up, its invisible hand passing through the sagebrush and making it tremble. In the air something lingered. If I flared my nostrils and breathed deeply, I could smell it. It smelled a little like my Labrador, McKenzie, when she comes in out of the rain. Musky. *Hairy.*

I turned around to look for the man in the cowboy hat and he's gone—there's only an empty hole on the boulder where he sat.

We always watched the news while eating supper—me and my mother and my little brother Graham—and on the news that night the KOIN 6 reporter stood at the bottom of Dry Canyon.

"Hey!" Graham said. "That's here! That's *our* canyon!" He wore this look on his face. It was the look my mother used to wear when back in high school I now and then appeared in the sports section for pitching a no-hitter, making the ball blur at speeds close to eighty. But anyway.

You know how on-site reporters are always trying to make things dramatic? Like, if there's a flood, they'll stand hip-deep in water, or if there's a hike in gas prices, they'll hold the microphone with one hand and with the other hang up the pump as if they just topped off their tank. That's what was going on here, as this reporter—who wore a fleece jacket that couldn't hide how nice her boobs were—walked along the dry creek-bed until she reached the campsite, mimicking the passage of the bear.

In the background people waved like people do when in front of a camera. "There's Joe Simpson," I said, and if my father had been there, if my father had been sitting at the head of the table, forking through his hamburger casserole, he would have paused in his chewing and narrowed his eyes at the television and grunted his amusement, Joe being a hunting buddy of his.

There are essentially two types of cowboys. There is the drugstore cowboy, who wears Tony Lama boots and irons his jeans and keeps his cheeks smooth and sweet-smelling with aftershave. He loves the idea of lassoes and spurs and bandanas and galloping toward a blaze orange sunset and the whole rigmarole of Wild West bullshit, but aside from a few guided horseback tours, this guy doesn't know his ass from a bridle. And then there are men like my father. Before he left us, he was a ranch hand at the Lazy H outfit, responsible for breeding and grooming horses, breaking the occasional stallion shipped in from Montana. He wore Carhartt and Wrangler. His breath smelled like coffee and cigarettes. Every few months he collected enough proofs-of-purchase to send off for a new shirt or windbreaker from Marlboro. He liked the pulp novels of Zane Grey and Louis L'Amour. When he took off his hat he revealed a white band of skin along his forehead, as white as the skin of his legs. The parts of him that saw the sun, his arms, his face, were cracked and brown, like beef jerky. He didn't talk much, but when he did, his voice rolled out of his mouth in a measured baritone you paid attention to. I felt about him as you feel about a bear, fearful and full of awe, wanting at once to reach out a hand and back away with your head bowed.

On the TV, the reportress explained what had happened. Sometime in the early morning, when only a red vein of sunlight brightened the horizon, a bear happened upon the campsite. The girls, two teenage girls from Prineville, had left their food and cooking supplies out, rather than washing it and bagging it and hanging it from the highest branch of a juniper tree. Springtime bears possess a terrible hunger, having slept through the long winter, and this one was no exception. One slash of its claws parted the nylon like a zipper. Their screams didn't scare it away, only encouraged it, as it fit its jaws around the head of one girl, chewing her, her scalp finally sliding off her skull. The other, in trying to save her friend, was hurled against the canyon wall, then mauled. They played dead or fainted in their pain and after so many minutes the bear abandoned them. Now both were in critical condition at St. Charles Memorial in Bend.

The reportress interviewed a Forest Service official with a salty beard—just like the one my father grew in the winter—who enjoyed long pauses between words and moved his hands when he talked, pointing in all different directions, making complicated hand-chopping motions that in their effect, I think, meant that it was only a matter of time, the bear would be found.

When she asked him, "What then?" he looked at her boobs and made his hands into a rifle and said, "Bam!"

People went a little crazy. At the tavern, over bottles of Budweiser, they spoke of how nice a bear fur would look hanging from their wall, among their pool cues and trophy fish and beer-stein collections. They wondered if it was a kind of cannibalism, tasting the meat of an animal that had tasted human flesh. They stalked the woods and sat in tree stands, their rifles oiled, ready to fire. They baited traps with raw hamburger. On the hood of his F10, Joe Simpson laid down a square of carpet and screwed in an eyebolt. There he chained his dog, an old hound dog named Cooter, the two of them driving up and down county roads, hoping for the scent that would make Cooter throw back his head in a howl.

And maybe I went a little crazy, too, when I came home and saw what the bear had done.

We live in a single-story cabin surrounded by a half-acre of pasture and three acres of woods. Next to the cabin there is a stable and next to the stable is a corral enclosed by a split-log fence. Here my father's horse, Black Answer, lazily grazed his days away.

This was a Saturday. My mother and Graham were gone, visiting the grandparents in La Pine, while I went fishing along the upper Metolious. It was late afternoon—that time of day when the shadows start to thicken—when I came home. From my fist dangled a stringer of rainbow trout. Soon I would lop off their heads and tear out their bones and guts and bury the whole mess beneath a slab of concrete behind the tool shed so McKenzie wouldn't get into the bones and needle open her intestines.

Black Answer was an old gelding. Many years ago my father rode him deep into the Ochoco and Mount Hood wilderness, through snow-cloaked forests, in search of elk. But now his back was bowed, his hooves splintery. There was some grayness along his snout. He was good only for petting and feeding carrots, and even then, he snapped at you with his long yellow teeth. At this time he circled the corral at a quick trot, as if trying to find a way out. "What's gotten into you, you son-of-a-bitch horse?" I yelled and when he heard me, he threw back his head and whinnied.

I approached our front porch—its roof drooped from the weight of so many winters' worth of so much snow—and saw the dog there. She looked over her shoulder at me and pawed at the front door where she always pawed at the front door, where the paint had worn away in a tan oval. "Hey,

McKenzie," I said and scratched her in her favorite spot, her breast, and she yelped and jumped away from me.

I examined my fingers, warmly tacky with blood. "What happened, girl?"

She huddled a safe distance from me, panting heavily. She is a black dog, making it hard to tell where she was hurt. When I moved toward her she whined, not wanting me to touch her again. So I talked to her in a soft voice, saying, "I'm just looking." Her snout appeared a little chewed-up and the fur along her hind legs could have been bloody or could have been muddy. "What got you?"

As if she understood, she looked away from me, looking into the nearby woods, and I followed her gaze there, seeing nothing except the shadows among the pines growing blacker every second.

Inside, I headed to the kitchen, to dump the fish in the sink and cover them with ice cubes. A naked 60-watt bulb cast an anemic glow that revealed a house different than the one I left that morning.

The lower cupboards yawned open, many of their doors ripped off entirely. A paw had scooped the cans of Mountain Dew and tomato soup and SpaghettiOs, the boxes of Lucky Charms and Ortega taco shells, onto the linoleum, where they lay crumpled and chewed-up, mixed up with the contents of the garbage can, tipped over and rifled through, its coffee grounds and banana peels and chicken bones and candy wrappers. The bear had somehow managed to get into the fridge. Its door hung open, its glass shelves shattered. Among the shards an unopened gallon of milk lay on its side. I could hear the motor working overtime, trying to keep the whole cabin cold, but I didn't bother closing the door, just as I hadn't bothered setting down my fish, too shocked to do anything but look.

A mug of coffee sat on the counter, half full, as if the intruder had been interrupted while drinking it. World's Best Dad, it read.

"Shit," I said. There was nothing else to say. And only then, hearing my voice flutter through the cabin and die, did I realize I was alone. McKenzie still sat on the porch, peering in at me, her head cocked with uncertainty. "Come on," I said to her and she whined in response. I finally laid down my fish and clapped my hands and she lowered her head and stepped hesitantly into the front hall and released a stream of piss onto the hardwood.

It was the smell that scared her. It hung in the air like a dark shambling presence, overpowering the odor of garbage. I remembered it from the canyon.

In Tumalo no one locks their doors. When my mother left that morning, she left the back door open, the screen door closed, to allow for a breeze. The bear had pushed through the screen and in doing so bent the metal frame in half and ripped it from its hinges. I could see this from the living room, just as I could see that the bear had been interested in more than food alone.

Clothes, my mother's clothes, were strewn throughout the living room and back hallway. Skirts and shirts and jeans. At my feet I found a pair of panties. The old lady kind that go way up your waist and corral the belly fat. I picked them up. They were damp with saliva and ripped along the butt. I imagined my mother inside them, the same teeth that gnawed on a skull gnawing on her.

I think that was what bothered me most, the sight of her panties. The bear had done more than trespass in the name of hunger. As I saw it, he had deliberately violated her, and in doing so, violated all of us.

I went to the back door with the intention of closing it. When I laid my hand on the doorknob, its coldness crept up my arm, along with the feeling I was being watched. I scanned the nearby forest for any movement. A chipmunk worried at a pinecone. A camp-robber bird flitted among the trees. Black Answer continued to nervously trot the circumference of his corral.

I closed the door and the feeling didn't go away.

My father taught me how to kill things. How to break apart a rifle and run a brush through its cavities. How to fire a bullet uphill and down. How to rub bitterbrush all over my clothes to camouflage my scent. All sorts of hairy information I tucked away in my mind like socks in a drawer.

I drove to Bend, to the Carmichael Candy factory. Everyday the janitors swept from its floors enough cookie crumbs to fill a fifty-gallon drum. For twenty bucks, they let me take all of it, along with a compromised batch of caramel.

At home, in an industrial bucket, I mashed up a few pounds of cookie crumbs and caramel, then added some fish filets from the freezer, dousing the mixture with a can of Mountain Dew. The smell and the sweetness, I knew, would draw the bear. Two hundred yards behind our cabin, way out in the woods, I found a clearing of cheatgrass and there dug a shallow hole to fit the bucket into, so that it couldn't be overturned by coyotes. On top of the bucket I placed the metal screen of an old rabbit cage, and on top of the screen a small boulder. Only a bear could get into this.

Some hunters, around their bait troughs, douse the dirt with cooking oil. The idea is, the bear gets the oil on the pads of its paws, then tracks the smell around the forest, drawing other bears. But I wasn't interested in other bears. I wanted only one and I knew he lurked nearby.

My father, in the months leading up to deer season, would drive into the mountains, along logging roads, and park next to clear-cuts. He would set up a lawn chair in the bed of his pickup, and through a pair of binoculars he would peer out over the stumps and huckleberries. He kept meticulous notes about the deer he spotted—where and when they appeared, how long they lingered, their herd size, its doe-to-buck ratio—so that when October rolled around, he was ready.

I, too, wanted to be ready. So I went to Gander Mountain and bought a Moultrie camera. I'm not sure how many dinner shifts at the Tip Top this added up to. A lot of them, I can tell you that. But really, after seven years of collecting two-dollar tips from truckers and blue-haired grannies, what had I spent my money on so far? Soda pop and beer. New tires for my truck. Bullets. The occasional blowjob from a Mexican hooker named Juanita. What else did I need? To go off to college, my mother said, but that seemed like something other people did.

"I've got everything under control," I would tell her, when she got on my back, asking about my plans, my life.

"Of course you do," she would say.

The Moultrie is a weatherproof digital camera. You bolt it to a tree along a game trail or a bait station. An infrared beam shoots from it. When triggered, the camera snaps a photo, recording the date and time, so that over the course of several days you can begin to understand the patterns of your prey.

I attached the camera to a ponderosa and trained its beam on the nearby bucket. When the bear came, I would see it, frozen in a flash. I would know what I was dealing with.

My family watches a lot of TV, mainly game shows and *Law & Order* reruns, but I'll tune in to the occasional nature program so long as a snake is trying to swallow a rat. So here we were, planted on the couch, me and Graham and my mother, my mother smoking one Marlboro after the other so that a gray cloud hung over us.

Since my father left, I've been in charge of the remote. I punched its buttons now, flipping through the channels, finally settling on an hour-long special called *I, Bear.*

"Hey," Graham said. "Can you believe it?"

My mother didn't say anything, her eyes unfocused, her mind someplace faraway, but I was right there with him, nodding and smiling. A bear show—he kept saying—a goddamned bear show. It seemed a miracle, as though God had shot a lightning bolt into the satellite dish to make it just so.

We learned that bears have shaggy fur and rudimentary tails and plantigrade feet. Though their eyesight is poor, their noses can decipher dead meat at a distance of at least seven miles. We learned that their ears don't grow with their bodies—remaining the same size, from cub to silverback—so you can measure the age of a bear like so: the smaller the ears appear in relation to its head, the older the animal. We learned that they are among the most behaviorally complex of animals. "Practically as smart as humans," Graham said, as if proud, as if the bear had brought something special to our cabin that reflected on us.

Outside, in the stable, Black Answer whinnied. I went to the window and saw the motion-detector light had clicked on, making a pale yellow cone surrounded by so much darkness.

I wondered what had drawn our bear down from the

mountains—the smell of bacon frying in a pan—the endless supply of garbage cans and Dumpsters—the trout-filled rivers? Hunger had to be the reason. It was always the reason.

The Tip Top Diner is a square brick building that seats thirty. The booths are mustard vinyl and the floor is checkered linoleum. The menu never changes. The building is over a hundred years old. It's lasted through a depression, recessions, wars, so many ice storms and sun-soaked summers.

Two bay windows flank its front door, giving me a view of the Three Sisters. They loom over Tumalo, as silent as stone, dormant for several hundred years, but inside of them a hidden life burns redly. In this way they remind me of my father.

The last time I saw him he came to the Tip Top with his girlfriend, Mona. For supper, if you can believe it. They had been at the Drywood Tavern—where she worked—drinking Budweiser and smoking Marlboros. I knew this because of the smells floating off them, the way they moved loosely and spoke at that level of too loud that drunks prefer.

He waved me over to their table, even though it wasn't my section. I walked there slowly. The clatter of forks and knives, the country music playing over the sound system, all of it fell away. His beard opened up into a smile, as if we were the best of pals. "I want to introduce you to someone," he said, or something. I wasn't really listening, my ears thrumming with blood. When she held out her hand, her fingernails painted every color of the rainbow, I let it float there so long and lonely that my father lost his smile.

"Manners," he said, as if I was the one with lipstick on my teeth.

Over their heads I caught sight of Mary. She stood by the coffee machines, watching me, so I didn't do what I felt like doing—which was spit or turn over the table or take a steak knife and go slit slit slit across their necks and faces. Instead I looked, only looked, staring deep into my father's leathery eyes, seeing in them something made of equal parts shame and fury. His beard moved a little, but he said nothing.

That was the last time I saw him, two years ago. Immediately after he left, he called a lot, but then the time between conversations grew from a week to two weeks to five months now. Maybe he got tired of listening to the silence on the other end of the line. He sent me a graduation card. In it he wrote, "Son, I'm proud of you. You're going places. Love, Dad." The card was marked up with dirty fingerprints, their swirling prints like the patterned dust off a moth's wing.

I still have trouble wrapping my brain around it. My father, who never danced, not even at weddings. Who smelled of horses. Who always left the house with a Leatherman multitool attached to his belt. Who ate everything with ketchup. Who on Christmas gave my mother a framed photograph of him and George W. Bush shaking hands, the photo taken after a stump speech the president gave in Redmond. Who, when I was a boy, helped me up into Black Answer's saddle and laughed when the horse swung his head around and bit me as I dug my heels too sharply into his ribs. Who taught me how to tie a lariat—the running noose with a jammed knot to prevent it from pulling out—and who directed me to sink it over the head of Black Answer and who laughed again when the horse tore off across the pasture, dragging my body behind him.

This same man, my father—who quietly lived in this quiet pine-forested hamlet his entire life—was not only fucking another woman, but had moved with her to Pendleton, where he now worked on a ranch owned by some formerly Californian surfboard developer.

I had heard the rumors, and ignored them, like the faint grumbling of a thunderstorm you hope the wind takes elsewhere. I had seen his pickup parked along the Deschutes River with two shadows inside it. I had listened to him stumble home from the tavern, the noise of the Hideabed unfolding, as he prepared to spend another night in the living room. But still. I hadn't anticipated his sudden departure. That he could just leave us, like a bunch of old shirts that didn't fit him anymore, seemed impossible. Even though he must have been planning it all along—just as he planned every hunting season—taking careful notes in a notebook and envisioning the kill long before he actually pulled the trigger.

Like a mountain, there was such stillness to him—you never would have suspected that deep beneath the layers of his skin, as beneath the deepest layers of the earth, existed a channel for fire.

The bear came. Every morning I trekked into the woods and found the bucket empty and on its side, buzzing with flies, like a hollowed-out carcass. The cheatgrass was flattened and there were tracks and seed-filled droppings everywhere. I unbolted the camera and removed its memory chip and took it to the Tip Top Diner. Mary kept a computer in the backroom and I viewed the photos there.

Some of them were washed out. Others revealed a raccoon or a possum or a coyote struggling to claw through the plastic, to push the boulder off the bucket. But many showed the bear.

The sight of him made my stomach feel weighted down with heavy black stones. If I clicked through the photos quickly enough, they made a sort of movie. The bear would untangle himself from the underbrush and move in an unhurried shamble toward the bucket. Every time the flash went off, its light would redden his eyes, making them appear lit with lamps of blood. One swipe of his claw knocked the boulder from the bucket. He ate with great smacking bites I could almost hear—their noise like feet moving through mud—each bite revealing jagged white teeth nested in blue gums.

One time Mary peered over my shoulder and said, "My."

"Yeah."

"You've got him, don't you?"

"Yeah. I've got him."

"You should let the news reporters know about this. They'd be interested in this."

"No. I want to kill him. That's all."

I heard her breath stop and a moment later start again. She laid a hand on my shoulder and I stiffened under its weight. "Daniel?"

"What?"

"You know you've got a lot of anger hidden in you." It wasn't a question.

I shrugged and she took this as a cue to remove her hand.

"You hold onto it like it's worth something," she said. "But it's not worth shit."

Again, I shrugged, but she was already gone, off to restock napkins or refill ketchup containers or something, the same old motions.

I stared at the screen. Because the camera was stationed at such a low angle, it was difficult to judge the size of the bear. I remembered the nature show and studied his ears. They were horribly small.

I always pick up Graham after school. We have two hours together—before I return to the Tip Top for the dinner shift—and I try to make those two hours count. Sometimes we go fishing. Sometimes we go to the Dairy Queen for a Dilly Bar. And sometimes we drop a Frisbee in the back-yard and call it home plate. He stands next to it with a base-ball bat cocked and ready to swing. I teach him to hold tight in the batter's box, while I whip fastball after fastball at him, trying to make him tougher.

"Hey," he said. "Remember that time, that game against Crook County, when you nailed that guy in the head? And he was like, 'I'm going to kick your ass if you do that again,' and then you did it again."

"What about it?"

"I don't know." He had a smile on his face and it wavered a little. "I'm just remembering."

"Well, quit it."

"Why?"

"None of that matters now. It was a long time ago."

"Not that long ago."

Today we went to Dry Canyon. According to some of the other fifth-grade kids, the riverbed was no longer dry. A stream of blood now ran down it, its currents growing stronger and scabbier every day. Graham wanted to see for himself.

At the Dry Canyon trailhead, I spotted a pair of dirt bikes pitched against a gnarled juniper tree. We soon saw who they belonged to—when we started down the trail, the canyon spread out beneath us like a gaping mouth—two boys with baseball bats.

There, in the dry riverbed, they stood over a large black shape. It was a bear and it was dead. The boys took turns beating it. Every few seconds one of them would steadily lift the bat over his head, as if it were a weighty ax, and then bring it down in a blue flash of metal. It impacted the bear with a meaty thud I could hear from a distance of fifty yards.

They laughed. They pumped their fists, smiling, as if they had won something or conquered something. I knew the feeling. I experienced it every time I brought a rifle to my shoulder, when the safety clicked off and my finger tested the trigger. It felt good, the absolute power that goes along with exercising death. But seeing it secondhand—watching as one of the boys took a home-run swing at the belly of the bear, the bat disappearing into the belly, having torn open a dark gash—I felt something shift inside me.

I went to them. I started down the canyon at a clumsy run, my sneakers sliding in the grit. I put my hands in the air and unhinged my mouth as far as it would go and started screaming. I didn't scream anything in particular—I just made noise, like a siren.

Those two boys, one look at me and *pow*, they were gone.

At the bottom of the canyon, I breathed heavily, my hands on my knees. The smell of decay raced in and out of me. Bluebottle flies rose off the carcass and tasted my sweat and I brushed them away in a hurry.

The bear had a two-gallon jug over its head. Some idiot, I guessed, had used it for a bait barrel. Maybe a foot high with an eight-inch opening, the jug fit tightly around the neck, keeping the bear from drinking or eating or even breathing a fresh breath of air. Scratches and holes decorated the plastic—claw marks from the bear trying to remove it.

The bear was small and thin, no more than a hundred and fifty pounds. Its fur was like a hairy sack draped over a collection of bones. I wondered how long it had wandered around blindly, stumbling over stumps and knocking into trees, eventually collapsing from starvation here.

Right then Graham came up next to me and took my

hand. "Are you okay?" he said and I said, "Of course I'm okay." Then I did like the fathers do on TV and ruffled his hair. "Sorry if I scared you," I said.

He looked at me out of the corner of his eye and shrugged, like: *no harm done, I guess.*

"Is that the bear that got the girls?" he said.

"No."

"How do you know?"

"I know."

"But—"

"It's not the bear, Graham. Okay? Poor fucker just got caught in the crossfire."

He swatted at a fly. "You said fuck."

One of the boys had left behind his bat. It was plastered with blood and hair, like a bone recently cut out of a body. My hands curled around its grip and my shoulders rolled with its familiar weight as I took a few practice swings.

"Good bat," I said and held it out to Graham. "Keep it."

He wrinkled his nose. "I don't think I want it."

"Fine."

I leaned on it like a cane and for several minutes we stood there in silence, looking at the bear, breathing in the smell of death. Then Graham ran off to hunt for arrowheads, to see if he could find any rattlesnakes curled up beneath the stones of the riverbed. I stayed with the bear. Inside of the jug, flies banged their black bodies against the plastic, drunk off blood. I closed my eyes and listened to them buzz and tap and imagined they were trapped inside my head, trying to get out.

When Graham disappeared behind a thick patch of bitter-brush, in a flash of muscle, I turned the cane back into a bat and brought it down on the bear, once, twice, three times, striking the jug until it cracked open. I got down on my knees and grabbed hold of it and pulled—dragging the bear, then bracing my feet against its shoulders—until with a moist sucking sound the jug came off.

I fell back on my butt—the jug in my lap and still buzzing with flies, like some kind of hive. The bear had its mouth open. A long blue tongue hung from it. I had struck its eye with the bat and this blackberry jelly goop slid out of the socket like tears, dripping down and beading the dust.

I turned around and looked to the top of the canyon. But no one was there to howl at me like a siren, to tell me to stop. There was only the wind rushing fast-moving clouds through the sky. I imagined what my father would have done—had he been there—squatting in the shade of a juniper tree with a cigarette fitted along the corner of his mouth. "Why don't you come down and see the bear?" Graham would have asked him. "And be by us?"

And he would have said, "Rather not."

By the end of the day someone had dragged the bear from the canyon and run a rope through its hind leg and hung it from a tree next to the mini-mart. The rope creaked as the carcass turned, blown about by the wind. People came from all around to get their picture taken next to it, some of them holding up their hands like claws, others crossing their arms and frowning, as if bothered by the smell.

On the news, the Forest Service official—the guy with the salty beard—stood behind a many microphoned podium, surrounded by a crowd of reporters from Z-21 and KOIN 6 and all the other affiliates. "Rest easy," he said and gave the thumbs-up. "We've got our man."

But then the paw prints didn't match up. And when they laid out the bear on a stainless-steel table and ran a scalpel along its belly, they found in it a red spermy pudding—the mashed-up remains of huckleberries, grubs and worms, a tennis ball—but no livestock, no bits and pieces of girls.

With this knowledge I could sense—all throughout Tumalo—people glancing over their shoulders, as if bothered by some shadow they couldn't shake. I could relate.

I knew what I needed to do. After Graham went to school and my mother went to work, I took Black Answer by the reins and led him into the woods. In a manzanita thicket he resisted, trying to tug me back, so I withdrew from my pocket a handful of sugar cubes and urged him forward. When we walked I could see, intermittently between the trees, the mountaintops of the Three Sisters, three glacier-covered volcanoes whose white fangs appeared, then disappeared, then reappeared, like something threatening me, or beckoning me on.

We arrived at the clearing and I loosely harnessed the reigns to a pine tree along its periphery. Yesterday, after seeing what had happened to the bear in the canyon, I had removed the bait bucket. Where it once sat, a patch of strawberries had sprung up overnight, their white flowers forming a rectangle, as if something had been buried and remembered here.

Around my shoulder coiled a lariat. I also carried a shotgun, a sixteen-gauge Winchester that had belonged to my father, and before him, to his father. It hung from my shoulder by a leather strap. I removed it now and broke it open along the stock and slid two slugs in and closed the breech with a snap and brought it to my shoulder, taking aim at Black Answer. "I never liked you," I said and pulled the trigger.

The horse recoiled a few steps, then his legs gave out and he collapsed heavily with the still-lingering echo of the shotgun blast bouncing around the forest.

It was noon and it was hot, one of the first hot days of the year. Soon the horse would bloat up and the flies and yellow jackets would find it. A stiff wind raked the woods. It would do a good job spreading the smell.

I rubbed myself all over with bitterbrush and climbed into the low branches of a nearby pine and munched some M&M'S and waited. The sun made its perfect path across the sky. When it at last dipped behind the Cascades, dusk gathered quickly. A thunderstorm had rolled through the other day and now the rain it left behind rose from the ground, gray tendrils of fog that curled around Black Answer like a hand.

Then the bear came gliding in from out of the trees. It was massive and it was so close. Its giant triangular head. Its muscles surging beneath its spiked black fur. Its claws like knife blades. Right there. It swung its head around in a circle and grumbled in its throaty language.

Black Answer lay on his side with his legs sticking out straight. The bear snapped its jaws around one of them, testing the flavor. I could hear the grinding noise of teeth against bone. Then, apparently satisfied, the bear released the leg and let out a huff and approached the underbelly of the horse.

I allowed it to feed. I wanted it relaxed. Around my shoulders I carried a lariat. I removed it now, taking care not to make a noise. I then descended from my perch. My boot scudded against a root or a rock when I dropped from the tree and hid behind it. At the sound the bear rose up on its haunches and swung its head left and right, its ears perked. I knew from the television program it couldn't see any better than your average nearsighted grandpa, so I stayed stock-still. It barked once, a warning. The sound was so heavy with bass it would have taken two large men to pick up and carry.

I felt suddenly small and alone. My hand moved from

the lariat to the shotgun and back to the lariat. I could hear the bear smacking its chops. A moment later it returned to its feeding.

The rope was twenty feet long. I tied its loose end around the tree and then positioned myself as if on the pitcher's mound, eyeing up my target. I could not bobble this throw and make up for it on the next pitch. This moment was decisive. The rope could not fall off course, could not touch the ground, or I would become hamburger. I judged the distance, some dozen feet. I licked my fingers. I tested the weight of the rope in my hands. And then, in one fluid motion that ended with a snap, I swung and let go.

I wanted to catch the bear around the neck, but no sooner had the lariat fallen around it did the animal come alive with such suddenness that the noose slipped to its waist. I pulled, to jam the knot tight, and the bear pulled back. I fell forward, sprawled on the ground, then immediately flipped over, scrambling backwards in a crab-walk. When the shaggy tremendous shape began its charge, I flipped over and righted myself and ran like hell.

I kept my eyes on the ground before me—my feet dodging stumps and clumps of rabbit brush—while the bear swiftly closed the ground between us. I could hear the locomotive breaths huffing from its throat, the flat-footed stomp of its paws. I guessed it had passed the tree by now, which meant the rope would go taut and anchor its charge soon.

A shaft of heat caressed my neck—a breath, I knew—that sent me reeling around in time to see its mouth open hungrily, almost lovingly, for me. I screamed and the bear bellowed and then the rope went tight and the bear stumbled into a praying position before righting itself again, coming up paws swinging.

I was just out of its reach, but not so far that I couldn't

feel the air move, displaced by its claws. It wrestled with the rope a moment, like a dog bothered by a leash, then returned its attention to me. A low growl rumbled from deep in its throat. I could feel its eyes, like two heavy weights, on me. It was hungry. And I imagined what its jaws would feel like working around my skull, or through my belly, my flesh sinking into the dark oblivion of its stomach.

We stayed like this for a time, looking at each other, each afraid and hateful. Minutes passed and the stars wheeled above us and I slowly brought my shotgun down from my shoulder and held it before me. "I should kill you," I said, a gentle sort of loathing in my voice. "You son of a bitch, I should kill you dead."

I could feel the blood pounding through my heart and I could hear the air filling and emptying its lungs. I tried to breathe with the bear and soon our breathing fell into a rhythm where our lungs worked in perfect time with the wind, with the shifting of the branches and shadows. It was as if a rhythm had been beating all along, the rhythm of the land, and finally I had found it, here in the peace of the dark woods, with only one slug and twenty feet of rope between me and absolution.

The text of *Refresh, Refresh* is set in Janson, a typeface based on late-seventeenth-century type designed by the Hungarian printer Miklós Kis. This book was designed by Ann Sudmeier. Composition at Prism Publishing Center. Manufactured by Versa Press on acid-free paper.